THAT BLACK PIG

Ben Colley

Copyright © 2023 Ben Colley
All rights reserved.

An earlier, unfinished version of this novel was serialised on Substack.

ISBN-13: 9798884619425

Cover design by Simon Magill
typegraft.co.uk

THAT BLACK PIG

Ben Colley was born on the south coast of England and grew up in the Yorkshire Dales. He studied Graphic Design & Advertising at Bucks University, before he received an MA in Creative Writing from the University of Manchester. Over the years, he has worked as a bartender, bookseller, actor, teacher, Victorian policeman, copywriter, editor, designer, illustrator, stage manager and comedian. He lives in London.

That Black Pig is his first novel.

For mum and dad.

Sorry for all the rude stuff.
And the violence.
And everything else that happens over the next 300+ pages.

Author's note

I first tried to get *That Black Pig* published in 2013. I got quite close, too. Ultimately, it didn't happen, and for 10 years the manuscript sat untouched on my hard drive. Then, a decade after I finished the thing, I decided I owed it to myself to do something with all the hard work I'd put into it.

I started serialising the novel on Substack, editing as I went. I was buoyed by the feedback sent to me by my readers. But then I hit a snag. The ending had always bothered me. Somehow, when I'd first written the novel, the characters had led me to a place I wasn't comfortable with, even though it seemed to me to be the only logical conclusion.

I decided to rewrite the ending, which took more time than a weekly post would allow. So the Substack posts stopped. Eventually, after a long winter stewing on it, I arrived at something that made more sense to me – the ending of the book you now hold in your hands.

Unfortunately for me (and maybe you), it makes me even more uncomfortable than the original ending. What can you do, ey?

A couple of things to bear in mind

I: This novel is written in the first person but that doesn't mean I share the same views as the protagonist. It's an unfortunate coincidence that Jim's age now matches my own at the date of publication. He was 14 years older than me when I started writing this – which seemed ancient at the time.

II: I didn't update the story to a contemporary setting, so you'll just have to imagine everything takes place around 2010-2011. No Brexit. No Trump. No COVID. What a time to be alive.

That Black Pig

What did it matter where you lay once you were dead? In a dirty sump or in a marble tower? You were dead, you were sleeping the big sleep, you were not bothered by things like that. Oil and water were the same as wind and air to you. You just slept the big sleep, not caring about the nastiness of how you died or where you fell.
Me, I was part of the nastiness now.

Raymond Chandler, The Big Sleep

Nothing that makes one hard is wicked and the only crime in the world is to refuse oneself that pleasure.

Marquis de Sade, The 120 Days of Sodom

Monday

In the waiting room: Magazines are stacked on a low table in the middle of the room, months old, pages curled, covers creased and torn. Mountain climbing magazines. Motoring magazines. Celebrity gossip. Cookery. I search through them for something less depressing than the 'Dealing with AIDS' pamphlets and the 'A to Z of the Big C' pamphlets and the 'Aargh! Meningitis!' pamphlets cluttering the counter by the receptionist's window. There's an issue of *Gotcha*, defaced with biro, the celebrities on the cover now sporting glasses and moustaches, with penises firing dotted jizz-lines from their foreheads. Flicking through the pages it's clear that the artist has done a thorough job, marking every photograph, but their lack of imagination is evident in the recurring motif of glasses, moustache and shooting cock. Beneath *Gotcha* a bright, bubble-fonted magazine called *Fantastic Horses*, something to keep the little girls amused while they wait for their booster injections. Then, right at the bottom of the pile, a copy of *World and Nature*, a photograph of a child's face in subdued shades of grey and brown set in contrast against the bold orange frame of the cover. 'Children in Chernobyl.' I don't need to read the date on the spine to know that the magazine is three years old. I took the photograph on the front.

It takes a lot for me to visit the doctor. Every so often, I get these odd tingles in my left foot and in the fingers of my left hand. An occasional numbness all down that side of my body. There's sometimes a tightness in my chest too. *The lad's got a problem with his ticker*, you might think. Well, you and me both. My old man carked it from a heart attack three weeks before his fiftieth birthday. That sort of thing plays on your mind. But then, the fact that I know it plays on my mind, makes me think my *mind* might be playing *me*. And as soon as I start to think *right, this time I really should go and see the quack*, the pins and needles disappear.

It takes something immediate for me to act, some kind of visual cue. Last time I came here I'd just got back from photographing pounder monkeys in Guatemala. A seemingly harmless scratch from a rainforest vine and my bicep had swollen to the size of my thigh, with yellow skin stretched tight over knots of green veins. Varnell-Spengler's disease, as it turned out. The doctor said if I'd left it any longer, I'd have been looking at an amputation.

This time I've got blood coming out of my arsehole.

You can't ignore that.

Not so much blood that I feel dizzy, but enough to turn my toilet into a crime scene this morning. Something didn't feel *right* when I was doing my business – I couldn't stop, for one thing – but I wasn't expecting to confront a sight quite so *red* when I turned round for a look. I stemmed the flow with a plug of cotton wool balls and a scrunched wad of toilet paper. It's all soaking and growing heavy inside my pants. There's no pain, just a cold throb in my sphincter that lets me know I'm very slowly losing blood.

Across the room a teen mum waggles a pink teddy bear in front of her baby's face. He groans and reaches with podgy digits, struggling against the harness that fixes him to his pram. The mum laughs. I've been watching her since she shunted the front door open and wheeled the kid into the reception area. I tell myself I shouldn't look (at least I shouldn't look the *way* that I'm looking) but the view is irresistible. Soft white flesh. Pushed-up tits. Honest dimples of cellulite around her exposed midriff. Yes, she's young, but she has a child. She's already been corrupted.

I think about impressing her with my article but her tracksuit pants and greasy tied-back hair tell me she isn't your typical *World and Nature* reader. She'd probably be more impressed if I told her it was me that sketched the massive dong on George Clooney's forehead. How would I show her my work anyway? Throw the magazine on the floor? Cough loudly, say 'oh sorry, I just dropped the magazine containing the article for which I won the *Amerstyn Journalism Award*,' and ask her to pass it back to me? Besides, the subject matter isn't particularly sexy. Those Chernobyl kids could recite the 'A to Z of the Big C' with their eyes closed.

Plus there's the blood coming out of my arsehole. Sometimes you have to prioritise.

The door to Dr Parting's office opens and a young man wearing a fedora with his arm in a sling steps out. Moustache, of course. Bowling shirt. Skinny jeans and brothel creepers. He leaves the door open and a minute later Dr Parting appears, gurning in my direction, eyebrows raised.

"Ah, Jim!" he says.

I squelch a little as I stand up. A thin line of blood trickles down the inside of my leg. I don't check the seat to see if it's marked but I can't resist touching the crotch of my trousers. Damp. I try not to move awkwardly as I walk past the teen mum, but it's hard when each step is accompanied by the pain of my arse-hairs being ripped out by tacky clots of tissue paper.

Dr Parting has me bent over the bed, resting my elbows on a polythene sheet. I stand on another sheet, hurriedly spread over the floor for my benefit. As I drop my pants the bundle of tissue falls out with a wet thud. I reach back to remove the cotton wool bung but a gloved-up Parting does it for me, saying, "It's okay, I'll get this," and then, "Oh," and, "Hmmm." A trickle follows the release of pressure.

My most urgent concern: "Is it cancer?"

"Hmmm."

"Is it cancer?"

"Cancer?" he says, hearing the question for the first time.

A finger goes in. He could've warned me.

"Please, try not to clench, Jim."

Two fingers.

I feel them wriggling around before they turn rigid and he presses on something up there with enough force to blur my vision. He maintains the pressure for a few seconds, then his fingers relax.

"Black stools," he says eventually.

"I'm sorry?"

"If you're worried about cancer then you should keep an eye out for black stools. When the blood in your faeces has time to dry and darken, that indicates it's coming from somewhere deep inside. Internal bleeding, Jim. Bowel cancer."

"Right," I nod.

"A bit of fresh blood in your turds, while an understandably alarming sight, is less of a concern. Usually it suggests a tiny tear in the anus or, as in your case, a ruptured haemorrhoid."

"Haemorrhoid? Christ, I've got *haemorrhoids?*"

"Only a mild case. Nothing to get too worked up about. Some people come in here, it looks like Treebeard's poking his head out of their backside. Your haemorrhoids are quite tiny by comparison, even if they have created a substantial mess today."

"Haemorrhoids can't be normal for a man my age."

"Not normal, no, but certainly not uncommon either. You're, what, mid-forties?"

"Thirty-eight."

"Right. It could be a lot worse, believe me."

I wait for a moment, directing all my thoughts away from the lower part of my body, focusing my attention on a tiny crack in the paintwork in front of me. Nothing seems to be happening. Parting isn't saying anything or writing anything down. Eventually I have to ask.

"Um, do your fingers still need to be up there?"

"Oh," he says, extracting himself. "Sorry. Sometimes I forget what I'm doing."

Dr Parting dresses my hole – which involves the careful insertion of a tampon – then he asks me to lie down on the bed.

"You haven't been in here for a while, Jim. Might as well give you a quick once-over while I've got the chance."

He measures my blood pressure, which he says is a little high, then asks me to take off my shirt. He runs his hands over my abdomen and round to my back, grabs a handful of flesh, gives it a squeeze. Then he presses his fingers into my stomach and flexes them as he pushes against my hips with his palms. It feels like he's rearranging my organs. I try not to wince or give any indication that I'm in pain.

"How much would you say you drink, Jim? I notice you have a touch of the old hangover-breath today. Do you often have a hangover on a Monday?"

"I had a couple of pints with a pal last night. Nothing excessive."

Parting smiles. "Your idea of excessive might be a tad different to mine."

He spreads his fingers out over my belly, raising a wave of flab.

"I ask because your liver feels quite firm."

"And that's bad, I suppose?"

"It's probably nothing, but I'd like to get you booked into the hospital for a biopsy all the same."

"That definitely doesn't sound good."

"The procedure can be a smidge uncomfortable but if there is something amiss we'd be better off knowing about it so we can sort it out."

"Should I be worried?"

"Oh, it's just a precaution. Young chap like you, I'm sure you'll be fine. I'm not supposed to say this, but at your age you'd have to be drinking an incredible amount of booze to do yourself any serious damage."

Tuesday

Breakfast News: The next day I'm sitting in my lounge when a report comes on the Breakfast News that makes me put down my whisky. Alan Girth is dead, his body discovered in his flat by his estranged wife. According to the newsreader the police aren't treating the death as suspicious.

I slump back into the sofa, light a cigarette and squint at the TV through a growing headache. Alan Girth. I worked with him a number of times back when I was starting out and he was still an adult film star, shooting sweaty magazine spreads in a grim East End basement. Years later, when he'd reinvented himself as a celebrity chef, I took his picture for a feature in a Sunday paper. He didn't remember me, but I remembered him. You see something like that up close, you don't forget it. People used to tell me about eating in his restaurants. The culinary magic he was capable of conjuring. I'm surprised they could bring themselves to eat what he was plating up – surely they knew where his hands had been.

The report turns into a biographical montage, photos of Alan as a child, then a teenager. I flick ash off my thigh, finish my whisky, pour myself another. There's a home video of him playing football, a clip of Man Food with Girth, Alan's weekly celebration of meat, knives and fire that made him a household name in the nineties. Next, a snippet of music, Alan singing with a chorus of well-known cooks on the cover of Salt N Pepa's *Let's Talk About Sex* (the lyrics changed to *Let's Talk About Chefs*) released for Comic Relief. The montage ends without mention of his porn career. I find that disrespectful. He was a record-breaker, after all.

I check my watch. I've got a meeting scheduled with Mallory Haines in a couple of hours. I decide to call him to say I won't be able to make it. My tormented arse could probably do with the rest and Alan's death gives me a decent excuse. Mal's secretary asks me to hold the line. He answers a minute later.

"Jim, I hope you aren't calling to cancel on me."

"Sorry, Mal. Just found out an old colleague of mine has passed away."

"You aren't talking about Al Girth, are you?"

"As a matter of fact."

"Only just found out myself. Poor bugger. Didn't know he was a friend of yours."

"Friend might be a bit strong. We used to work together, me and Al."

"Is that right? You never told me you were in that business!" Mal laughs, then, guttering the laugh with a cough, says, "No, it's a fucking tragedy. Nice bloke. He was going to do a campaign for us. Suppose we'll have to pull it now… Listen, why don't we keep our meeting but push it back an hour and move it to the pub instead? You know, so we can raise a glass to Al's memory."

"I could do that."

"Excellent. How about *The Black Knight?* Eleven o'clock alright?"

Mal hangs up before I can answer, and I watch a bit more of the news. It's a slow day. Stalled talks in the Middle East. Protesters destroying GM crops in Oxfordshire. Cuts to the police force. Looks like Alan's story will dominate the headlines for a few hours at least.

I have a shower and stuff a fresh tampon up my arse, giving the rusty old one a curious sniff before flushing it. The bleeding has stopped but I'm not taking any chances, no matter how much it itches – and Christ does it ever itch. After Dr Parting booked me in for my biopsy, he suggested I invest in some haemorrhoid cream. That's starting to sound like excellent advice.

Getting dressed, I opt for something appropriately subdued – a charcoal suit, cream shirt and lilac tie – then I dose myself with another whisky before leaving the flat.

As I head for the Tube a kid swaggers along the street towards me, sporting a sidewards baseball cap, a jumbo-sized hoodie, and a sloped sneer of contempt. I'd find his peacocking comical – the way he rolls his shoulders and throws out his elbows – but his movements are so exaggerated I start to doubt that they're intentional; perhaps he suffers from some neurological affliction that distorts his face and makes him drag his feet. As he draws level I check for drool around his mouth. He fixes me with a South London glare, questioning me with an aggressive jerk of the head. Or a spasm – I'm still not sure. I keep my head down and walk on.

At the Tube station the commuter tide is high, even at this time. I have to wait two trains before the crowd on the platform is thin enough for me to fight my way onto the third. The journey takes forty minutes and I stand for most of it, resisting the terrible urge to scratch my ring piece.

A toast to Girth: "My money is on auto-erotic asphyxiation," Mallory says. "Celebrity found dead. Alone. The police say it's not suspicious but they won't give us a cause of death – it reeks of asphyxi-wank gone wrong."

Mal turns and beckons a waitress with a couple of fingers. Two more, he mouths, then points at the empty whisky glasses on our table.

"Alan wasn't the type," I say, my voice strained as I hold in a burp.

"Wasn't the type?" Mal slaps the table. "He was *exactly* the type. The guy worked in porn, for God's sake. He had so much sex, a standard shag couldn't do it for him anymore. Anal had become run-of-the-mill. Then somewhere down the line, a bird he's porking puts him in a chokehold and... *bang!"* another table slap, "Sex is back on the menu."

He's speaking loud enough for everyone else to hear, which, in *The Black Knight,* is anything louder than a whisper. It's less a pub, more a gentleman's club without the membership fee. The high price of the booze keeps out the vagrants and the hounds.

"Everyone's doing it at the moment. What have there been? Three? Four? Five deaths in the last year because of it? The minor-celebs are mad for it. It's a fucking craze."

"But Alan wasn't some sex-maniac. He was a normal bloke."

"A normal bloke? I'll say it again for you, Jim. He was a fucking *porn star.* Anyway, look at that interior design fellow, Jeremy Carter-Bainbridge. He might have been a bit of a fruit, but you wouldn't think they'd find him hanging from a coat-hook with his pants round his ankles. And that martial arts guy, the actor, whatsisface, they found him in a Las Vegas hotel room dangling from a loop of extension cord.

Don't tell me you saw that coming. Normal people don't exist, not when sex is involved. And sex is *always* involved."

Listening to him talk, I know I'll eventually agree. It's what you do with Mallory. It's what people have been doing with him for over sixty years. I imagine him as a little boy, arguing with his mother, dodging her compromises, berating her until vegetables stop appearing on the dinner plate. It's no surprise he can argue a point. He's the 'H' in ADHD, after all. His fortune is built on persuasion.

ADHD: I've always thought it was at odds with the creative nature of the industry that so many ad agencies are named, like law firms or accountancy firms, with an acronym that combines the surnames of the agency's founding partners. When John Aldridge, John Doors, John Dawes and Mallory Haines first formed their agency in the early eighties they succumbed to vanity like everyone else and Aldridge Doors Haines Dawes was born. Their only concession to the creative impulse was to place the 'H' between the two 'Ds'. It was simple coincidence that the ordering of those letters would become associated with a psychological condition, allowing them to stand out from the crowded advertising marketplace. The agency's personality became that of a restless child, never willing to settle into a niche, never happy unless it was already ahead of the latest trend. They sold themselves as forward-thinkers, pushing boundaries, stamping on the box rather than just thinking outside of it. Perhaps all this would have happened anyway. Perhaps ADHD was destined to become a global advertising phenomenon regardless of the name. But it certainly didn't do them any harm.

As the agency moved into the 21st century it maintained this restless spirit, embracing new technologies while the old advertising giants floundered. Well before the internet took over from television as the number one advertising media, ADHD was investing in it, realising that lower costs and a rapidly increasing audience would quickly become attractive to their clients. Right from its inception, the agency garnered awards and accolades within the industry. In over two decades, that's the only thing that hasn't changed.

A lot of this success is down to Mal, now global creative director and chief stakeholder in the company. He was the influence behind all of the agency's original award winners; the 'Cider... Cider? Cider!' television ads for *Buttwick's Cider;* the controversial *Hoare's Cheese* 'Cheesier Than Thou' campaign; the ground-breaking billboards for *Henderson's Multivitamins,* initially banned for their graphic sexual imagery but recently ranked in an industry poll among the ten greatest ad campaigns ever produced.

His defining achievement came in the early nineties when he orchestrated the 'Damn, there goes the fourth engine!' campaign for *Yalta Airways,* showing the kind of creative ingenuity that could spin an airline disaster into a massive sales upturn. No-one, before or since, has come close to pulling off anything similar.

It isn't just in his own creative executions that Mal excels. Over the years, he's nurtured students fresh from college, giving them jobs and gradually turning them into creative heavyweights. I met him back in 1991, after he gave a talk at my college, where I was studying for my foundation diploma in art. After the lecture, the head of the course took Mal on a tour around our exhibition space, where we were all mounting our work in preparation for the end of year show. Mal showed particular interest in a series of photos I'd taken of London Zoo's recently acquired giant panda, Zuì Zuì. He became strangely emotional, saying I'd done an incredible job capturing the animal's dignity and quiet sadness. Before he left he gave me his card and told me to get in touch when I graduated.

Satnav: By the time we get round to business we've had more than a bottle between us. The bar is filling up with creatives – the ones that aren't working through the night on pitches or production deadlines. They keep their distance but throw sidelong glances our way. At Mal. A thick fog of yearning settles in the room. They sense the opportunity to make an impression with one of the titans of Adland.

Our table stinks of whisky where I've spilled my glass. Or where Mal has spilled his glass. My sleeve is resting in it but I don't move my arm. I can't. I'm hunched over, leaning on it with my face, speaking into the table.

"What's the job, Mal?"

"Simple. We're going to stick you in a helicopter, get you to take aerial shots all over London." He claps his hands, "That's it."

"What's it paying?"

"Sixty grand, Jim. Sixty grand. Big client… some Finnish satnav outfit. Sixty grand. Couple of weeks work. Simple."

"Sixty grand?"

"Sixty grand."

"Any wiggle on the fee?"

"Are you taking the piss?"

"Sixty grand then. Sounds do-able."

"Yes. Very fucking *do-able*, Jim."

"Who's the creative team?"

"Raul and Birgitta."

"And they don't mind you putting me on their job?"

"They know you're my go-to guy."

"Well then!"

Without lifting my head, I hold up the arm I'm not leaning on and extend my hand across the table. Mal takes it and gives it a vigorous shake.

"Marvellous," he says. "Now that we've taken care of that, shall we move on somewhere else for a proper drink?"

Stretching my back, I lift my head up so that I'm looking at Mal down the length of my nose, then I tip my head forwards, sending my chin into my chest, before throwing my head back again. A hard-worked nod.

"Where to?" he asks.

"Titty bar?"

"Titty bar!"

I slide off the leather chair, feeling a thrum in the seat of my pants. When I stand up, Mal puts an arm over my shoulders and walks me to the door. We both wave goodbye to the waitress. I think she smiles.

"Mal," I say as we step out into the grey dusk, "I've got haemorrhoids."

"Oh, haven't we all, Jim." He looks at me and smiles. "Haven't we all."

Eddie Gitt's: When Mal hears me tell the taxi driver where we're going, he Roger-Moores an eyebrow at me.

"I thought we were going to a strip club?"

"Burlesque. Same thing."

"I have to disagree, Jim. Burlesque clubs have the smut, but they don't have the filth. And it's the filth I'm after. Burlesque is all about artfully hiding the nipple with tassels or cute little love hearts. I want to see the *whole nork*. I want the nips. I want neon G-strings and the graceless slap of thighs against a greasy silver pole."

"I'm more focused on the drink tonight and Eddie has got a nice top shelf."

"I suppose I can't disagree with you there."

"And there's something else."

"Oh?"

"A while ago I heard that somebody I used to work with dances for Eddie. She might not be there anymore but–"

"Oh ho ho! *Now* you're talking!"

"I wouldn't mind having a chat with her."

"Say no more! On to Eddie's we go."

I lean my cheek against the cold window and stare at the blur of passing streets, a rush of amber shadows broken by strobes of red neon and strip-lit 24-hour convenience. My body is seduced by the motion, by the turns of the cab, succumbing to the pull of the corners.

"Don't fall asleep," Mal says.

I open my eyes and see that his are closed. He's talking to himself, trying to keep himself awake.

"Mal," I say, sternly.

His brow creases, his eyelids snap wide and his eyeballs roll about the cab hunting for a point of reference before settling on the direction of my voice.

"Do you want to go home?" I say.

Mal has crumpled into himself, his shirt suddenly creased, his tie askew, his collar open wide, revealing an object hanging among the thick curls of his chest hair, something black and white, a pendant the shape of a bear. He plants his hands firmly onto the seat and straightens his back.

"You can go home if you want. I'm not going to bed until I've laid my eyes on a nice set of milkers."

We pull up outside Eddie Gitt's Revue Bar and I take my time paying the fare. We've sobered up during the journey, but we haven't sobered up nearly enough. One slurred word to either of the gentlemen guarding the door, one footstep out of place, and our night's over.

"Don't say anything to the bouncers," I tell Mal. "Walk straight past them and sit down at the first empty table you find."

The bouncers nod a welcome as we approach, we nod back, continue on through the entrance, down a long corridor draped with purple curtains. At the end there's a heavy fire door, as well as a desk, a till and a great big unsmiling heft of a woman with the bowl-cut hair of a ten-year-old boy. Again, we don't say a word. We hand over our money, take our tickets and pull open the door. It's like breaking the seal on an airlock, sound rushing at us, equalising a sudden disparity in air pressure. A band. The competition of trumpets. Drums. Machinegun bursts of alto sax.

"Jesus," Mal says, stepping back.

The air is fumed with laughter and whisky. Smoke. Up around the ceiling, there it is, huge looped wisps of it caught in the stage lights. People are smoking.

"People are smoking."

My voice is lost in the noise. On stage the trumpeter flares his instrument in the direction of the guy with the sax, who holds a note, squeezes it, fills his cheeks, rocks back and forth on his heels with his hands twisting in front of him as he wrestles the brass serpent.

"Where are the poles?" Mal shouts, "Where are the *women?*"

The tables are crowded with men in suits. Men like Mal. Palm greasers and tree shakers. Deck chair shufflers and cat herders and brass tacks get-down-toers. Crooks and clowns and everything in between.

Over by the wall there's an empty booth, which I point out. We move through the crowd, edging between the seats, placing our hands on shoulders, patting our thanks as people shuffle chairs to let us by, working our way across the room. The music dies and the colour of the lights begins to shift, white to red, as we reach our table and slide into the seats. Onstage the set is being rearranged, the musicians merging with the shadows around a wide disc of light.

"Here come the women."

The music starts, rumbling slow, a heartbeat from the drums, a sigh from a clarinet. A waitress with a red feather in her hair, wearing a crimson corset and black stockings, spins through the crowd with a tray held high in her hand, passing down drinks and collecting tips. She sees our cleared table and comes over.

"What are you boys drinking?"

Her voice is high and nasal with an accent that makes me think of knife crime, probably the reason she's working the floor rather than on stage.

"We can smoke in here?"

"Yeah."

"How come?"

The waitress shrugs.

"Do you do a Sazerac?" I ask, placing a cigarette in my mouth, then lighting it.

"Just rye, or fifty-fifty?"

"Just rye." I look at Mal for a signal but he's concentrating on the stage. "He'll have the same."

She scribbles on her pad and winks as she turns to leave but I raise my finger.

"Is Blue working tonight?"

"Blue?"

"She's an old friend. Heard she was working here."

"Don't know anyone called Blue. But I only started recently. I haven't met all the girls yet. I'll ask the bar manager. Blue, right?"

"Yeah, Blue."

"And two Sazeracs."

"Thanks."

The curtain rises slowly and about ten women march forwards in a line, carrying huge fans. A wall of silver half-moons. They all turn to the side, whipping the fans around quickly, maintaining their cover. The music rises.

"This is exactly what I was talking about," Mal says angrily. "Choreography. You don't have any of this bollocks in a strip club. It gets in the way of the tits."

The line breaks into two, the new lines shuffling back to either side of the stage, still shielded with the fans. Then each girl twists, lifts her arms and opens herself to the audience, only for an instant. Flesh, bare and perfect. Except for the nipple tassels, of course. Mal shakes his head.

Again they cover themselves, run back into the middle, hold out the fans. This time when they break a rolling wave of drums breaks too, with a crash of cymbals, and a woman is revealed, alone in a circle of light that seems suddenly brighter.

The waitress is back. She places a couple of napkins on the table, then a Nick & Nora glass on top of each.

"I asked about your friend."

"You did?"

"She's in the chorus line."

I scan the stage but the girls have disappeared into darkness, except for the lead, who strokes a gloved hand slowly from her thigh to her shoulder.

"It's just Marianne on stage now. The other girls will be back in the dressing room. I can try and get a message to her for you?"

"I'd appreciate it. Tell her Jim Stakes is here."

"Is that everything?"

"For now, but we'll be done with these soon enough."

I take a big sip of the cocktail and she smiles.

Blue comes out to see me halfway through the act, by which point Mal has forgotten about his need for luminescent panties and greasy thigh slaps. Marianne, with her gradual nudity and her long graceful arms, has all of his attention as she stalks the corners of the stage and peels herself from her clothes.

I see Blue opening a door on the other side of the room and wave her over. She grins and waves back, hurries through the tables, causing men to duck her outstretched arms. The short dress she wears sparkles like smashed glass as she runs.

"Oh my God, *Jimmy!*"

I stand up and she puts her arms around my neck, kissing my cheek, then my mouth. She smells just as I remember, like a day on the beach, coconut oil and salt. She tightens the hug before pulling back.

"Must be, what, twenty years?" she says.

"Not far off."

"You look—"

"Terrible?"

She smiles and punches my shoulder, then notices Mal sitting behind me.

"Don't worry about him," I point at the stage. "He's concentrating."

We sit down and for a moment do nothing but smile at each other. She's hardly changed. The thick stage make-up she's wearing has cracked, exaggerating wrinkles she didn't have before, around her eyes and the corners of her mouth, but apart from that she's the same. Same body, same voice. Same smell. I think about how I must look to her now, the weight I've gained, and I shift uncomfortably in my seat as the tampon wedged up my hole reminds me just how much my body has been corrupted by time.

"Suppose you heard about Al. Is that why you're here?"

I nod. "I felt like I needed to see someone who knew him back then. Do you know what I mean?"

"I didn't realise you were close."

"We weren't. I don't know, I just feel peculiar about it."

Her hand slides onto my knee, squeezes it, and I remember sitting like this with her before.

"Me too," she says.

"Well, yeah, it must be weird for you. I mean, you two–"

"*Worked* together."

"Yeah."

I take a sip from my drink and ask her if she'd like one.

"Not while I'm on the clock."

"You're going back on stage?"

"I've got about ten minutes."

"Cigarette, then?"

"Thanks."

"How come we can smoke in here? Do you know?"

She shrugs.

As I light her cigarette she says, "Did you hear about Keith?"

"Keith?"

"Keith Rumbold?"

I throw open my hands and shake my head.

"He was a sound engineer. Maybe you didn't work with him. Passed away a few weeks ago too."

"Wait, a sound engineer? A *porn* sound engineer? Did he work with Al?"

She nods and blows smoke away from her hair.

"Plenty of times," she says.

"And he's dead? How?"

"Misadventure, whatever that means."

"Drinking? Drugs?"

She shakes her head.

"There's a rumour going round that he might've been doing that thing, oh what do you call it… that thing that Tory MPs are always doing?"

I know exactly the thing she's talking about. And so does Mal, who has suddenly become interested in our conversation.

"Auto-erotic asphyxiation," he says, slapping the table.

The Golden Hole: Mal lives North and I live South, so our night ends at the taxi rank. He hugs me before I get into my cab but it feels more like the clinch of a worn-out boxer than anything affectionate.

"The one that got away, eh?" he says, breathing heavily.

"Sorry?"

"Oh come on, Jim. You can't hide it from old... from old Mallory."

"We were friendly once."

"Hm. Well, I will say... I will say this. That... in there... was a Jim I've not seen before. More open... somehow... and more guarded... at the same time. I don't know."

"You're drunk, Mal."

"Something about her intimidates you," he rocks back and holds my face between his hands, "and it's not just because she's got a tremendous pair of tits. This... is the first time I've seen you try to hide your attraction to a woman. Which only makes it more... more obvious."

He smiles, pats my cheek and shambles over to the next cab, shouting, "You should call her," over his shoulder as he opens the door.

The journey home is tense, the cabbie occasionally flicking a silent glare at me in the mirror while he shanks the taxi into a curve, throwing out the vehicle's big black ass as he pulls it round. Every turn lurches and I lurch with it, my skin growing cold, my forehead spotted with sweat. Perhaps this guy is angling for a soiling charge. We hit Putney

Bridge and I tell the driver that once we're across the river, that's it. I'm out. I can't take any more.

He stops outside a twenty-four-hour *O'Donnell's* and I realise that my sudden sickness must be down to the food I haven't eaten, so I charge through the double doors, throw a few notes in the direction of the cashier and tell him to get me an extra-large Don Daddy meal, with a caramel shake and an extra cheeseburger.

And then I tear into it. The burger, the layers, it all starts to fall apart as soon as I pick it up, spilling salad, spilling cheese, spilling crumbs of meat and bread. The bun disintegrates and my fingers shine with grease and ketchup and mayonnaise and something uncompromisingly orange that the adverts call Captain O'Donnell's Surprise Sauce. And I paw at the fries, scooping up piles of them, mashing them into my face because I don't have the patience to deal with this meal one chip at a time. And then I'm onto my second burger and I'm starting to get signals from my gut that I should maybe slow down but I keep going. And this time there's no salad, just burger and cheese and ketchup and mustard and a limp slice of gherkin, and the sandwich stays together, neat until the very end. And then onto the caramel shake, which is a meal in itself, embolism-inducingly thick. I discard the straw and tip the contents of the cup straight down my throat.

I leave the place with a vulgar weight in my belly, and I curse the great bronze 'O' — the *Golden Hole* — and I curse that smug bastard Captain O'Donnell and I curse myself for the crime I've just perpetrated against my own digestive system.

The walk home from this point on becomes a battle. Every step is laden with a doomful swilling in my stomach. The only upside, if it can be called an upside, is that fighting the inclination to throw up focuses my attention away from the twinges in my serrated arsehole.

There are some people who take the easy way out with nausea, jabbing at their tonsils with their fingers to purge themselves. As much as I like the idea of getting things over quickly, I'm too much of a coward for an action so swift and brutal. It's the same with suicide. If I had the balls I'd have topped myself a long time ago. I don't want to give the impression that I'm the depressed type. It isn't sadness that drives these feelings, it's a kind of nihilistic *laziness*. I mean, really, who can be bothered with living? Is it really worth all the effort? There are some truly amazing things to be seen in this world but the trouble is you usually have to go through the pain of hauling your arse up a mountain before you can see them. The best part of my day is when I'm asleep. When nothing is happening. When I'm totally, blissfully unaware of my own existence. Honestly, I cannot wait to be dead. But suicide, all that pain and mess... No, I don't have the stones. So I endure. With life. With nausea.

My gut swells with chemical reactions and gaseous developments, and the milk churns inside me, and my mouth fills with saliva, and I lick the grease and the salt from my lips, and I lean against a wall, resting my forehead on the back of my hand, and I spit at the floor and those cold spots of sweat are back, and everything, all that crap inside me, starts to expand, pushing against my lungs, rising in my throat. I lean against the wall, lean hard against it, spitting and gasping, with my eyes closed, with my greasy lips drawn tight, and eventually it passes. And I know it'll be back but for now I can breathe. I can rest.

Then what happens? A hand grabs my mouth, jerks my head back and another hand comes up to my throat. I hear the click of a switchblade and feel a cold edge of metal pressed against my Adam's apple. I can smell a woman on the fingers clamped beneath my nose. I don't mean the fingers belong to a woman, I mean they've been *inside* a woman. Recently. And why not? Which rulebook is it that tells a mugger he can't take care of pleasure before he takes care of business?

"Your wallet." he says.

Those fingers. I try to breathe through my mouth but the hand covering it is fused in place, giving no air. And, taking a breath, I get another gust of that smell, a smell I would take satisfaction from if only it was on *my* fingers, and I gag. A plume of vomit pushes itself up into my chest and there's nothing I can do now to hold it back. My shoulders jump and a geyser of pale yellow bursts through my assailant's fingers. He makes a disgusted noise, a retch of his own. There's a clatter, the switchblade dropping to the pavement. Still heaving, I turn to face him, landing a brackish fast-food projectile in his lap.

He looks at me, stunned, tears in his eyes, and I throw up again, hurling every last cloying piece of my half-digested meal into his face. I cough and burp, spitting out bitter lumps from behind my teeth as I crouch down for the knife. The back of my throat burns from the acid but all I can really taste is Captain O'Donnell's Surprise Sauce.

Rising shakily, I jab the knife out in front of me.

"Still want my wallet?"

He turns, flees, and it's only when I see the retreating silhouette of his sidewards baseball cap that I realise who he is; the puffed up youth with the spastic pimp-walk.

I unlock the knife, the blade snapping back safely into the handle, and I put it in my jacket pocket. The matted puke on the front of my shirt is starting to cool. The material sticks to my chest. I take a moment to appreciate what just took place, the satisfaction of being purged and the satisfaction of victory. Then I throw up on my shoes.

Wednesday

Rätsel: You might think that would be enough to sober a man up – that getting rid of all that poison would sort me out. But you'd be underestimating the spectacular volume of booze I've consumed.

I call the police when I've finally dodged my way home. I do my best to explain the situation but my words are poorly formed, syllables stumbling into each other as they fall out of my mouth. The operator says she'll send someone round.

I fight my way out of my vomit-spattered clothing, popping buttons and tearing zips, before unplugging the rancid tampon from my arse and attempting to dress myself again. A shirt proves impossible – I can't deal with buttons – and trousers present a challenge that is nothing short of Rubikian. So I answer the heavy police-knock at my door wearing a bright yellow T-shirt and a pair of Bermuda swimming shorts.

A plainclothes Detective shows me his badge. Tall and thick, with a firm stance and a load-bearing moustache, he's clearly a military man. Five years at least. Falklands probably, from his age. I read the name. *Rätsel*.

"Detective Inspector Razzle?" I say, suppressing a belch. "Where's DI Dazzle?"

He ignores my excellent joke, stepping past me, muttering something about something rhyming with 'pretzel'. Pretzel? What kind of bastardized tangent is this?

He walks through to the lounge and when I offer him a seat he opts for a nimble-framed wooden chair with a back as hard and straight as his own.

"Want a drink? Tea? Coffee?" I see him glance at the open bottle of 21-year-old Hyland on the coffee table, "Hey, that's right! You're not in uniform, are you? Fancy a little nip?"

He coughs.

"No, I'm fine for a drink, thank you."

I sit down and tap a cigarette out of its packet.

"Do you mind?"

He shakes his head.

"Perhaps we should start with the attack," he says.

So I light up my fag and lay it all out for him. I tell him everything, give him all the gore. The bile and the chyme. The Surprise Sauce. And he takes it all in without a smirk, without so much as a twitch of that ungainly facial hair. I tell him about the slow-walking kid with the sidewards baseball cap. He makes notes in a little black flip-pad.

"When you spoke with my colleague on the telephone you said you thought this attack was somehow related to the death of a friend of yours, a Mr Alan Girth, is that right?"

"Did I say that? I don't remember saying that. Suppose I must've said something, otherwise you wouldn't have asked…"

"Mr Stakes?"

"Right. Well… how do I put this? Something about Al's death doesn't seem… right… to me. I don't think he's the sort of bloke that'd go out like that, you know? And then there's this other bloke… this other bloke he used to work with died in similar circumstances."

DI Rätsel stops making notes.

"And what circumstances would those be?"

"You know," I grab at my throat with one hand, mock-strangling myself, while I pump at my crotch with the other. "Keith Rumbold – that's the name of the other bloke – they reckon he died the same way."

"Keith Rumbold?"

"He worked in porn. With Al. And maybe me."

"Maybe you?"

"I'm not sure. Keith was a sound technician, apparently. They didn't use sound guys too much for the shoots I worked on. Too low budget."

Rätsel leans forward, elbows on his knees.

"I'm sorry, Mr Stakes, I'm struggling to see what you're saying. You think that what? Mr Girth and Mr Rumbold died, er–"

"–strangle-wanking."

"Right. And then you think that, in actual fact, somebody murdered them, doing so in such a way as to make it *look* like they were, er–"

"–strangle-wanking."

"Yes. And this all somehow links to the assault on you this evening?"

I take a long draw from the fag and blow smoke out through my nose.

"All I'm saying is, doesn't it seem a little bit… um… whatsit… a bit…"

"Coincidental?"

"That's it, yeah. A bit *coincidental* that two people who knew each other died doing… that… to themselves within a short space of time? And, you know, these are guys I worked with, or might've worked with, and suddenly I'm attacked too. You must admit there's at least a possibility that this is all, um, you know…"

"Connected."

"Right. *Connected.*"

Rätsel stares at me then without blinking, like I'm one of those Magic Eye puzzles and he's read the description beneath it – *boxing kangaroos* – but no matter how hard he looks he can't see them. He can't see the kangaroos.

Eventually he speaks.

"Let's put Mr Girth and Mr…"

"Rumbold."

"Rumbold. Let's put Mr Girth and Mr Rumbold to one side for a moment. What happened tonight seems quite obvious. You're clearly wealthy, you're alone and you're drunk. Disgustingly drunk, if I may be frank."

"Oh, by all means."

"The smell alone..."

"Oh trust me, *I know.*"

"Look, you're an easy target. Someone sees you, and they see an opportunity they can take advantage of. Typical mugging. Sad fact is it happens all over London every night of the week. The only thing that should concern you is that you put yourself in that kind of danger in the first place." He raises a couple of condescending eyebrows. "I don't think you should be worried that someone is trying to kill you. The mugger asked for your wallet, didn't he? If murder was his intention, he wouldn't have said anything, just," Rätsel conjures a dagger, slits his own throat with it. "I'm sure when you've slept on it and sobered up you'll see the logic."

I rest my chin in my palms, staring at the detective through a gateway of fingers.

"You're right," I say. "I suppose this thing with Al... hearing about it this morning... it's been on my mind all day."

Rätsel nods. Then he narrows his stare. His voice hardens.

"Now, let me ask *you* a question. How is it that you know how Alan Girth died?"

"Come again?"

"You've just described the exact manner of his death, despite the fact that those details are yet to be made public."

"That was only... um... speculation-"

"Pretty accurate speculation."

"It wasn't even me speculating."

"Oh. Who was speculating?"

"Mal."

"Who's Mal?"

"Mal's a... friend of mine. We were talking about it earlier today and he said, you know, something about erotic choking or whatever."

"Mal said this?"

"Yeah."

"And Mal is?"

"My—"

"—Friend, right. But who is he?"

"Mallory Haines."

Rätsel makes a new note in his black book, reading out the spelling, checking with me that he's got it right.

"We were just talking. It was a theory. I don't know anything. *Mal* doesn't know anything."

"Yes? Keith Rumbold, was that just a *theory* too?"

"Rumbold? Yes. Of course. A theory. I didn't even know his name until tonight."

I realise I'm jigging my knee nervously and I stop and Rätsel sees me stop. He looks at the knee, smiling for the first time. It's the kind of smile that makes you wonder if he's got more than one row of teeth.

"Am I being accused of something?" I ask.

Rätsel stands.

"Accused? No. Accused of what?"

Cultural Epitaph: Dawn breaks through the window like a wrecking ball, exploding into the room, daubing its obnoxious glare across all four walls. I wake with the expected hangover, still slumped on the sofa, muscles strained down one side of my neck because of the way my head has keeled during the night. My arse is thrumming. Throwing up last night clearly did me a huge favour, and I don't just mean it saved my wallet. Imagine how I'd be feeling this morning if my machinery was still clogged up with all that toxic bilge.

According to the mantelpiece clock it's 7am, which doesn't give me much time for anything. I've got to be over the other side of London in two hours for a shoot. There may be a spate of ex-pornographers choking to death, but I've still got to pay my mortgage. I quickly fix myself a Bloody Mary for the nausea, follow it with a whisky for the headache, then I lope upstairs to the bathroom and enter into careful negotiations with a turd. I'm up against the clock, but I'd rather take my time playing chess with my bowels than risk the fast, bloody alternative. After that, with so much of my morning already spent, the rest becomes a desperate rush of foaming gels, shave-enhancing lubricants and tobacco-resistant ultra-white toothpaste. I put on the same suit I was wearing last night, even though there's a light speckling of vomit around the lapels, because it's the closest thing to hand. I always keep a spare suit in the wardrobe at my studio. I'll change when I get there.

Talk to my agent and she'll tell you I'm an alcoholic, but I don't think she's qualified to pass judgement, considering she doesn't drink herself. She's right that I drink and I can't deny that I get drunk, but her argument falls apart when she tries to diagnose this *disease* called alcoholism. Look at the symptoms. Alcoholics allow booze to get in the way of their lives. It infects them, changes their appearance. They lose the shine from their skin. The creases fall out of their trousers. And their noses – God, have you seen what happens to their noses?

Now look at me with my Dapper Dan hair. First thing in the morning my edges might be softened, but I do what's necessary to deal with it. I mop up the puke. I wash away the sweat. I spray on the spice. See me now as I leave the house in my crisp suit, with my jib cut the way anyone will like, without a single carbuncular protrusion to upset the straight line of my snout. I'm still peering through thick banks of morning fog, but you wouldn't know it to look at me because I can cope. As far as anyone else is concerned the skies are clear. An alcoholic wouldn't be able to hold down my job, wouldn't live in my million-pound pad. The days of scraping the last notes from the floor of my bank account were left behind when I stopped working with people like Blue Darling and Alan Girth. When you forgo food so you can afford to drink – that's when you have a problem. I don't forgo anything.

She calls me, my agent, to remind me about the shoot booked in my studio. She asks me if I've been drinking. It's the question she asks me every time I speak to her. I tell her I'm already on my way, that she should have more faith. I ask her if I've ever let her down.

The studio takes up the top floor of an old arms factory, squatting over a canal in a corner of the Docklands that's still waiting to be regenerated, surrounded by derelict factories, red brick terraced houses, tracts of mossy tarmac and a racial blur of knife-fights and hate crime. Door-to-door, it takes me almost an hour and a half to get here, but the rent is half what I'd be paying anywhere closer to home and I'm never in the studio more than once a week.

George, my assistant, has already started setting up when I arrive. He's a lank, narrow-nosed hipster, with a penchant for granddad shirts, slip-on shoes and wooden jewellery. When he speaks, he struggles to conceal a West Midlands accent, repressing it with slow speech and considered vowels.

"Morning, G," I call out as I kick open the door.

"Morning Mr S."

I stand with a couple of coffees, watching him unfurl huge white screens at the far end of the room. Peals of thunder fill the empty space each time he fixes a stand and lets the paper drop.

"There's a coffee for you here," I say.

George is a good worker, with a handsome personality yet I barely pay him enough money to survive. Competition for jobs is so fierce in the creative industries that you can find people willing to work for practically nothing. George has been working with me for six months. Soon he'll decide he needs more money. He'll tell me how hard he's worked, that he loves the job, but he can't live off a diet of Bombay Mix and Lucozade forever. He'll tell me that vegetables are a distant memory, that fruit is nothing but a myth. And I'll say I'm sorry. I'll say he deserves better but I can't afford to pay him more, and I'll send him on his way with a spanking reference and a pat on the back. Then I'll post a new job ad.

There's an oak liquor cabinet next to the front door, which I open with designs on making my coffee Irish, only to find it's been cleared out.

"Which bugger drank all the whisky?"

"You did, last time you were in."

"Could've sworn there were a couple of full bottles in here."

"There were."

"Bastard! Is there champagne in the fridge for the girls, at least?"

"Yes."

"Okay, good."

"Want me to go out and get some more whisky?"

"Yes."

I check my watch.

"Shit! No. We'd better get all this stuff sorted before the models turn up. Have the props been delivered?"

"I unloaded them first thing. They're in the dressing room."

I head through. There's a stack of boxes filled with fake furs, fake rubbery entrails and bottles of fake blood. Lying on its side in the corner of the room is a model of what looks like a savaged horse.

"G, this thing looks like a horse?"

"There's a pair of antlers in one of the boxes."

"Right you are."

The shoot is an arty commission for *Cultural Epitaph*, a thick, high-priced quarterly aimed at people just like George. They offered me a blank canvass, ten pages to fill with whatever I want, so I'm going to shoot a trio of naked models draped in wolf furs, standing around a deer carcass, playing with its blood. A humans-as-animals sort of deal – but sexy. The concept is pretty loose, but I know I can get some good contrasts out of the colours. The magical combo of sex and violence always works for the camera. I'll leave it for someone else to figure out what I'm trying to say.

After changing out of my soiled grey suit into a dry-cleaned blue pinstripe, I drag the carcass out and lay it down by the screens. I'm crouched stuffing six feet of intestines into a cavity on the deer's belly when the three models arrive. Over my shoulder I hear George letting them in, then anxious silence. He doesn't quite know how to handle himself around the models yet. I've seen him holding court with a couple of nice birds down the pub before, but there's a big difference between chatting up a bit of skirt on a Friday night and talking to a woman whose face could be insured for a few million quid. There's a sharp twitch in the pit of my arse as I rise to greet them. I fail to suppress a grimace.

"Now then ladies. I hope make-up wasn't too stressful for you this morning?"

One of the models, a Norwegian called Kjersti, smiles, "Do we look stressed?"

"You look gorgeous. As always. It's just that Jennifer can be a bit of a prickly bitch if you catch her in the wrong mood."

"You always talk about Jennifer like this. She is very nice woman."

"Not to me, she isn't. I think it's because she knows I'd rather photograph roadkill than take a picture of her bulbous face. Weird thing about make-up artists – the best ones are always terrible to look at."

Kjersti flexes her pencilled brow.

"Don't be mean, Jimmy."

"True though, isn't it? Suppose it's because they get so much practice trying to cover up their own shortcomings."

What a girl, Kjersti. A proper egg timer. Only in a comic book can you find tits like those, with an arse like that, either side of a waist so small. The way she moves, that arrogant sway of her hips as her feet pound into the hard floor – you just *know* she's a master between the sheets. It hurts to look at her. Knowing you can never have her – it makes you want to die.

And then there's Mette, another Scandinavian with a burdensome chest, and an arse like a couple of wind-worn boulders. Her suggestive, skewed smile is worth her fee alone. There's something vigorous about her. Something brutal. Prehistoric. Definitely an on-top-slapping-you-round-the-face kind of girl.

And the third girl... the third girl, I realise, I don't know.

"Who are you? Where's Titania?"

The new girl smiles nervously.

"I'm Louisa. Titania couldn't make it today so the agency sent me in her place."

"This is the first I've heard of it."

"Unfortunately Titania has been afflicted with a facial anomaly."

The words 'zit', 'spot' or 'blemish' are as unutterable for a model as the word 'Macbeth' is for a stage actor. If it's not a 'facial anomaly' it's a 'skin malfunction' or a 'dermatological glitch'.

"A spot?" I say just to hear them gasp. "They send a different girl without calling me first because of a *fucking pimple?*"

"It's on the tip of her nose," Kjersti says. "It's *big.*"

"The agency said I'd be fine for this shoot," Louisa says.

"The agency said that? Quite a presumption for them to make. Do they even know what Titania looks like? How could they possibly consider you an adequate replacement?"

Louisa's grin slackens and disappears.

"I'm not saying you aren't pretty," I add, "but I only use realistic girls on my shoots. You – you're far too thin. Whenever I see one of you Size Zeroes, I'm amazed the human mechanism can function with so little flesh to support it. The agency should know by now I don't want this in my pictures."

I take out my phone. While I'm dialling, I tell the girls to go back into the dressing room and crack open the champagne. I tell George to get them some glasses. Meanwhile my call goes straight through to Bob Walloon, the fat-voiced New Yorker who heads the modelling agency.

"Bob, it's Jim Stakes."

"Yeah, I got caller ID, Jim. How can I help?"

"Your people sent the wrong girl to my shoot this morning."

"My people sent the wrong girl?"

"I booked Titania, but your people pulled her because she's got a spot on her nose or something. I didn't know anything about it until the replacement showed up."

"Hey, what do you want me to do? The girl can't do the job, so we send somebody else. Standard procedure."

"But nobody told *me* it was happening. You didn't give me any options, Bob. The girl you sent doesn't have anything close to the right look. No tits. No arse. My *wrists* are thicker than her *thighs*. The least you could've done is take a bit of time to pick out someone appropriate."

"Jim, I know the kind of girls you like – hey, they're the kind of girls *I* like – but, truth is, I don't have many girls with curves on my books. I got fashion models here, Jim. Girls that look good on a runway. Girls that know how to wear a Giorgio Barbuto. You want glamour models, we aren't the kind of agency to book 'em."

"Glamour models? I get work on the cover of *Phizog* every season and you're talking about *glamour models?* What do you think I'm doing here? Snapping shots for some jazz-rag?"

"I meant no disrespect."

"Maybe you're right. Maybe it's time I started booking my women through someone else."

"Jim, I'm just telling you to be more open-minded. It *is* possible to take pictures of girls you don't want to fuck."

"Now what would be the point in that? I'm sending her back."

"*Sending her back?* I got nobody else I can give you. Anybody that isn't at Stuttgart Fashion Week is already booked on another job."

The phone starts to beep. An incoming call. I check the display. It's Mal.

"Sorry, Bob, I'm going to have to go. Got another call on the line."

"But who you gonna find at this kind of notice?"

"Hopefully someone with a great big pair of tits."

"Jim, listen—"

"Sorry Bob, got to go."

I pick up the call from Mal and I'm surprised that it's Mal I'm actually talking to – usually he gets his secretary to call me first. Something's wrong. His voice lacks its usual verve.

"I had a visit from the filth this morning, Jim."

"The filth?"

"A detective. German-sounding name. He was asking me questions about Al Girth."

"Oh."

"Yes. We need to talk. Can you come over to my place this evening? We'll have dinner and a few drinks."

"Sounds very civilised."
"Eight o'clock. Don't be late."
Forget civilised, this sounds *serious*.

Substitute: When I tell Louisa she has to leave that same false, triangled smile splits her cheeks. From the looks of her, she's one lip-quiver away from tears so I get George to accompany her downstairs to wait with her for a cab. I slip seventy quid in his pocket so he can pick up a few bottles of Glenbergen from the off-licence afterwards.

Kjersti and Mette head for the dressing room, re-emerging minutes later, naked except for a few discrete scraps of wolf fur. We try to set up a scene, the two of them striking poses over the deer carcass, but the composition feels empty without a third woman. It fails to fulfil the sexual drama of what I'd envisioned. I pour a couple of glasses of champagne and tell them to take a break.

When George returns with my whisky, I give him a list of modelling agencies to call through, which he does without any success.

"You don't know any girls that'd like to model for me do you, G?"

"Yeah. But none of them come anywhere close to those two."

"There aren't many that do," I sigh. "Whisky?"

He hesitates so I pour him one before he can answer. I top up the girls' glasses with champagne and light a cigarette.

"Are we finish for today?" Kjersti asks.

"Unless you have any modelling friends that can come down here in the next couple of hours?"

Kjersti shakes her head, "You don't know anybody?"

"Everyone I know," I say. "I know through agencies, and all the agencies say they're booked up because of Stuttgart Fashion Week."

"Stuttgart," She repeats mournfully. "There is not a beautiful woman in your life?"

"No. Hasn't been for a long time."

She places a hand on top of mine and says, "Oh poor Jimmy," frowning sympathetically, a gesture that would be easy to misinterpret. I've spent enough time around models to know they only act like they want you to fuck them right up to the point when you actually *try* to fuck them. That's one good thing that could be said about pornstars – they were never devious when it came to sex. They'd already shown you everything they had to hide, so what was the point in messing about?

"Actually, Kjersti, now that I think about it there is someone. I bumped into her last night, hadn't seen her in years."

"A model?"

"Yeah… she was a kind of model. She's a dancer now."

"And you have her number?"

I nod, exhaling smoke.

"Then call her."

"You don't think it'll seem strange?"

"Is perfect! Very flattering for her because you think she looks like model."

I slug back the whisky, pour myself another, walk with it to the other end of the studio and make the call.

"Hi Blue."

"Jimmy! Didn't think I'd hear from you again for at least another decade. God, you must be feeling it today."

"Feeling what?"

"Last night! You were *hilarious*. You and your friend were completely trashed."

"Oh. Right. Last night. Was I? No, I don't feel too bad."

"I'm im*pressed*. Thought you'd be in bed all day."

"Actually, I'm working. I'm in the studio right now. Which is why I'm calling you, as it happens."

"Oh?"

"Um, I was wondering if you could do me a favour."

"Anything."

"I'm a model short for a shoot that I really need to wrap today."

"And you think I might know someone?"

"Actually... um, Blue, I was thinking of... you. I mean, I was wondering if you'd... you know, model for me. Well, for this shoot, I mean."

"*Me?* Oh, Jimmy, I'm no model."

"You used to be."

"Different *kind* of model. You know that. You think I'd have worked in *that* business if I had a chance at being a fashion model? You think I'd be doing what I'm doing *now?* Anyway, I'm too old."

"You looked the same last night as the last time I saw you."

"Last night *was* the last time you saw me."

"You know what I mean. Honestly, I wouldn't ask you to do this if I didn't think you fit the bill."

"Not even if you were desperate because all the other models are in Stuttgart?"

I sigh.

"Okay, I'm desperate. But I know you can do this, and I've got the *eye* for knowing. It's why I'm so good at my job."

"Who's it for?"

"*Cultural Epitaph.*"

"Never heard of them."

"Doesn't surprise me. They call it the Shoreditch bible. Full of pointless, meandering hipster-bollocks. Things that are cool because no-one else knows about them yet."

"Doesn't sound like your kind of thing."

"It's not, believe me. I even tried pricing myself out of the job but they were willing to pay my ridiculous fee. I could hardly say no after that!"

"I'm flattered Jimmy, but..."

"How about you come over and I pay you for an hour? If you aren't happy, you can leave. No hard feelings. And you'll still be four hundred quid better off."

"You're paying four hundred *pounds* an *hour*?"

"Perhaps I should've opened with that."

Blue was the youngest starlet I ever worked with – seventeen the first time we met – and she was also the most confident. She didn't enjoy the job, she told me that, but nerves were never a problem. She'd arrive on set, throw off her robe and get straight down to it. If the guy was having trouble getting ready, she didn't bother to hide her frustration.

Some girls thought all they had to do was lie back and honk like a clown's trumpet each time the guy thrusted. Others would start moaning before they'd even hitched aside their knickers, and then they wouldn't stop, stretching out one long, undulating wail that would last until the final pop-shot. But not Blue. She knew how to act. She drew you in, built things up slowly. And when she hit those high notes you really believed she was feeling it. When you saw her biting her lip, saw her muscles flutter and her limbs twitch, you knew it was real.

As soon as there was a break in the scene she'd come and stand by me to cadge a fag. She didn't bother to cover up, felt no shame, just stood there chatting and smoking with her crotch oiled and her nipples chewed and her arse paddle-smacked raw. Her voice was soft and as sweet as a Mackinaw peach. That whore's mouth you heard during a take was just another part of her act. Off camera she never said 'cunt' or 'fuck', hardly ever swore at all.

I was still physically inexperienced, despite everything I'd seen, and Blue ripped my mind apart. At a time in my life when the hormonal fury was telling me to fuck anything and everything, in every conceivable way, here was a girl – the most *amazing* girl – doing just that inches from my eyes. I was in a perpetual state of arousal that caused me actual physical discomfort. Stabs in my scrotum. Hot flashes of nausea. And my daily wank-quotient, which had already been quite substantial, rocketed. I started using margarine as a masturbation aid just to stave off cock-burn. And for all that, I would've cut off my bollocks just to be able to hold Blue's hand.

Nearly twenty years later my body has changed in mostly horrific ways, but its responses to Blue are almost identical. Since I last saw her naked body, I've become dependant on various pills and powders to attain the vigour of youth… Christ, *the vigour of youth?* Why don't I just call it what it is – a properly workable erection. And I can't remember having a *spontaneous* erection any time in the last decade. But when Blue comes out of the dressing room, stripped down, bare-breasted, nothing but a slender scrap of wolf fur around her waist, and strides the length of the studio to join Kjersti and Mette by the carcass, I feel a familiar electric jolt zap into my bellend.

Here and now, with the close juxtaposition of bodies, I can see Blue was right – there is a difference between her and these catwalk models. But it's nothing to do with Blue being any less attractive. No, the difference comes from a quality she shares with all good starlets, a way of looking at a man that makes him think, however small, there is still a *chance*. Kjersti and Mette, six-feet tall and iron postured, arouse no such idle belief.

The girls start to pose, and I hand out bottles of fake blood for them to daub themselves with, telling them they can use it however they want. The words are only half out of my mouth when Mette gives Kjersti a surreptitious squirt. Kjersti retaliates by wiping a bloody hand on Mette's back. Any concerns I have about Blue being excluded are dispelled when Kjersti slaps Blue's breast, leaving a vibrant handprint over her nipple, and I feel another electric surge in my crotch. They giggle, flinging increasing amounts of blood at each other, giving me exactly the sort of unfiltered facial expressions I'd hoped for. Kjersti steps out of the fray, approaches me like a mischievous toddler with outstretched hands, smeared and sticky, laughing crazily when I flinch away from her advances while also trying to hide the burgeoning tent pole between my thighs. As soon as I tell them the blood is edible Mette guzzles some from a bottle, rolls it around her mouth, dribbles it down her chin and neck.

"Minty taste!" she says, giving the camera a horror-film grin.

I tell them to attack the deer and they jump on it, ripping its insides out, play-fighting over glistening shanks and cutlets, wrestling for the antlers in a pool of deep crimson. Blue plucks out the beast's heart, screams, holds the prized organ aloft. I take the shot from a low angle, catch the light through her wild blood-streaked hair.

"Mette, I want you to lick the blood off Blue's body," I say.

"And Kjersti, I want you to put your arms around Mette's waist. Yeah, smear some of that blood down her thighs. Good. Okay, now move in and kiss Blue. Trust me, this'll work. Blue, kiss her back. With your tongue. Show me some *passion*. Kjersti, take hold of Blue's tits. Good. This is really good stuff girls. Really good. Grab her arse, Blue. Perfect. Hold onto it. *Squeeze* it. Kjersti, you need to get into it more. Really get *into* it. There it is! *Beautiful.* Mette, you come round the back. Hold her shoulder's, Blue. Pin her down like you're going to fuck her right on top of that carcass. Force her down. She wants it but she doesn't know it, so *show* her. Show her what she wants. That's right. And Mette, you *do* want it. Make me believe you want it. You haven't eaten in a long time and you're hungry. Good. Great. And–"

And Blue stops. She pulls back, jerks her head round to me, fixes me with a hard stare.

"What is this? What the hell am I *doing?*"

Afterwards we all sit on the floor, another bottle of champagne opened, another couple of whiskies poured. Kjersti lies with her head in Mette's lap, eyes closed, while Mette stares away into nothing, sucking on a slick red finger. George watches them shamelessly, ignoring his whisky. I put a cigarette in my mouth and toss the pack onto the floor in front of Blue. She looks at the pack then at me and holds up her bloody hands, fingers splayed.

"Of course. Sorry." I take a cigarette out of the pack for her, place it in her mouth, light it. "No, really. I am sorry. I got carried away."

"That gave me... flashbacks."

"I know. I didn't mean for that to happen. But the three of you, half naked, wrestling each other... it might be the sexiest thing I've ever seen."

"Three women covered in blood, fighting each other on top of a dead animal, *that* might be the sexiest thing you've ever seen?"

All I can do is shrug. Blue laughs.

"I have to admit, I was enjoying myself," she says. "Up until you started barking orders, anyway."

She flicks my glass, leaves a greasy red streak on its surface.

"Do you drink like this every day?"

I take a sip.

"I might have the odd one now and then."

"You'd had more than just the odd one last night."

I consider this for a moment.

"It's this industry. Everyone drinks..."

Blue doesn't blink, parts her lips like she's about to say something but takes a drag from her cigarette instead.

"Listen, I've been thinking about that Keith Rumbold guy," I say. "Whether or not I worked with him."

"Can't help you there. I don't even know which films *I* worked with him on. I only remember him because he was a sweet guy and sweet guys were pretty thin on the ground back then."

"Thing is, I think I might've landed myself in a bit of trouble... I don't know... But it'd definitely help me if I could say whether or not I knew Keith."

"What sort of trouble?"

I tell her about my visit from Detective Rätsel.

"He told you that's how they died? He *told* you that?"

"Yes."

"Doesn't seem very professional. If they aren't releasing that information to the public, why would he tell you?"

"He was an arrogant prick. It felt like he suspected me of something. I don't know what he thinks I'm involved in, but maybe he thought he could scare me into talking."

She finishes her champagne. I pick up the bottle to pour her another glass, but she declines.

"Is there a shower around here?"

"Through the dressing room. Door on the left. Towels are on the radiator and there should be shampoo and other stuff in the cabinet. You'll see it."

She stands and crosses the room. Just as she reaches the door she turns.

"You know there's one person who could definitely tell you if you worked with Keith."

"Yes, I know. I was hoping it wouldn't come to that."

"Dane."

"Yes. Dane."

Dane Biggerman.

Of course he'd know.

Dane knew it all.

Dane Biggerman: The Lord of the Dance.

During the eighties and nineties, he controlled all the smut lines. Every skin-flick and jazz-rag produced in London passed through his organisation, and he had files on everyone who'd ever worked for him, kept a record just in case they ever broke out and made it big in the real world. You can't blackmail a starlet – the evidence is already out there for everybody to see – but having a background in porn can be surprisingly damaging for anyone working on the other side of the camera. Dane had even threatened me when I made my first move outside the business. Up until then I'd considered him, if not a friend, then at least somebody I could trust to look out for my best interests.

"I heard he works out of Dagenham now," she says. "Much smaller operation. I don't think he expected the internet to affect things as much as it did."

"No. He wasn't much of a forward thinker. Just a thug who got lucky. If I can avoid ever being in the same room with him again, I will."

Starting to pong: I arrive at Mal's ten minutes early with an unvintaged supermarket red under my arm. It's an ironic gesture. No point bringing a proper bottle, not when Mal's got a cellar filled with plonk that includes magnums of pinot noir recovered from a galleon shipwrecked in the 18th century. It looks like Mal's having some landscaping done in his garden, although I can't imagine the sort of water feature that would necessitate the enormous crater carved out of the earth in front of his mansion. A bulldozer and an excavator are parked idly alongside, marked off with tape and cones and flashing orange lights. Just as I hammer the door with my fist, I feel the ghost of an itch circling my own crater. Mal answers a minute later, denying me the opportunity for a quick scratch, and takes the offered bottle. I was expecting a cooler reception after that arsey phone call this morning but the smile he gives me seems genuine enough, tweaking the corners of his eyes.

"Ah! French Red! I don't believe I've tried this one," he laughs. "Come in, come in."

"What's going on here then?" I ask, hooking a thumb over my shoulder in the direction of the pit.

"Oh, that. Just having a bit of work done in the garden."

The hot buttery smell of fried onions fills the house – no mean feat considering this particular house's size. The entrance hall is large enough to accommodate a life-sized marble statue of a giant panda, rising up three stories around it to a domed ceiling and an enormous art deco chandelier. Those must be some serious onions.

"Smells good, Mal."

He waves away the compliment, directs me past the panda into the lounge, tells me he just needs to check up on the food and that I should help myself to anything from the bar. Normally when people talk about having a bar in their home, they mean a high table with perhaps a couple of optics screwed into the wall behind it. Not Mal. His is ten feet of solid oak, with a brass foot rail, brass taps, polished pumps, drip trays – the whole deal. In fact the optics are the only things he doesn't have. I asked him about that once – he told me he didn't think it showed the correct level of respect to hang a bottle of booze by its ankles.

I take time choosing my tipple – you don't often get a chance to choose from a spread like this – eventually settling on the 36-year-old *Fòghnaidh*, a barrel strength single malt from the western isles of Scotland with a honking nose and a finish like a bogman's punch to the back of the throat. Before Mal returns, I spend a good five minutes rearranging the inside of my trousers, detaching my boxer shorts from the crack of my arse, giving my hole a vigorous rub with the pad of my index finger, careful not to catch it with the nail. I've never been much of an arse-scratcher, never been much of an anything-scratcher, but I don't have a choice in the matter anymore. I must remember to buy some of that 'roid cream.

Out of the panoramic windows I get a better view of the temporary wasteland that Mal's garden has become. What used to be a neatly striped lawn has been turned into a mud-flung battlefield, an eruption of loose earth and ragged turf, the ditches and gullies cast in deep shadow by the bright external guard light. Looking down into the nearest hole I can see some sort of half-completed concrete foundation, a basement floor perhaps, with steel-wired support columns rising around it. *Just having a bit of work done in the garden?*

I turn back to the room when Mal enters. He grins expectantly at the glass in my hand.

"The *Fòghnaidh*," I say. "36-year-old."

He claps his hands together.

"Bloody good choice. Very sexy dram, that. Vaguest hint of minge to it, although they won't tell you that in any of the tasting notes, of course."

I dip my nose in the glass, take a deep breath as I sip. The alcohol burns the tender skin of my nostrils.

"Not getting any minge, Mal, vague or otherwise."

"It's there. Give it time. Cigar?"

He opens up what I once assumed was a reading table to reveal a humidor the size of a hotel mini bar, cigar boxes stacked on the shelves, each one labeled with region and age.

"Any preference?" he says.

"I know nothing about cigars. Whatever you're having."

"Try this." He puts a cigar in my hand that's not much thicker than a cigarette but almost double the length. Its outer skin is the colour of charcoal. "Rhodesian," he says. "A white tobacco farmer put some of his last crop into vacuum storage. Didn't want his legacy to die along with his country. That there is one of the finest cigars ever made by a man."

We sit at the bar on leather-cushioned stools and acknowledge each other's reflections in the huge mirror behind it. Mal pulls a rabbi from his pocket and cuts the cigars. I notice he hasn't poured himself a drink yet.

"Where's your wife tonight?" I ask.

"Maria? She's at the theatre with some friends. It's the opening night of that French musical *Toulouse le Balls*, or whatever it's called."

"I don't think it's called *that*."

"No? Well, anyway, you know how she is. Always out and about."

"Yes. She is, isn't she? Never around. I still haven't met her, you know. In all these years. Haven't even seen a picture of her."

"Really? Ha! How strange," Mal says, making no effort to remedy the situation by finding a photograph to show me. His whole marriage is very odd. Secretive. The wedding took place about five years ago, in Antigua. He ran off with a woman supposedly half his age and did it all behind closed doors. No friends, no family. The butler and the maid from his serviced beach house acted as witnesses. Where he met this woman... how they fell in love... I have no idea. Rumours abound that she was a high-class prostitute. I'm sure Mal's told me the truth, but there are so many gaps in my memory where Mal is concerned...

"I'm starting to think you're embarrassed to introduce me to her," I say.

"Nonsense, old bean. I'm sure you'll meet her soon enough."

He uses a little flambé torch to light the cigars, turning them slowly, creating an even glow across the tip, then he signals that mine is ready and watches me take three puffs. The smoke is heavy but very smooth, almost buttery to taste.

"Velvety," I say.

"Velvety! *Exactly*. Smooth as a... as a whatsit. And full bodied too. You don't often get the two together, usually have to compromise on the depth if you want a smooth cigar. You know what that cigar is worth?"

This is a bad habit of Mal's. It makes his generosity feel disingenuous, as if the only reason he shares his riches with you is because it allows him to brag.

"No idea, Mal."

"Have a guess. Go on, what do you reckon?"

"Fifty quid."

"Try more like *two hundred* and fifty."

"Fuck off. For a cigar? That's ridiculous."

"Worth it though, for that *flavour*."

"Is it?" I say. "Is it really worth it?"

"Oh I think so. Yes. Absolutely."

"Have you ever been to *Gleeson*, Mal?"

"Of course! Their ostrich risotto is *the biz*. Best restaurant on the South Bank."

"There's no denying that. But there's no denying that their menu prices out ninety percent of the people in this city, either."

"It is a touch costly, yes."

"How about *Good Cod Almighty?* Been there?"

Mal shakes his head.

"It's a couple of streets back from the river, a five-minute walk from *Gleeson*. No contest, they do the finest fish and chips in London. Perhaps that isn't saying much, given the state of the fish and chips in this city. Regardless, I go there pretty much every Friday for lunch. A couple of lads from Scarborough came down and set it up ten years ago. They fry everything in beef dripping."

"No good if you're a pescatarian, then."

"A what?"

"A pescatarian. Someone who eats fish but doesn't eat meat."

"Did you just make that up?"

"It's a thing, Jimbo."

"Sounds made up to me."

Mal shrugs.

"Anyway, there's a bench that faces *Gleeson*, and I like to sit there eating my fish and chips under the scrutiny of the lunchtime crowd. Because that's what everybody does when they go to *Gleeson*, they eat and they drink and they watch the world going past those huge river-front windows. And I know that what I'm eating – the paper-thin batter, the fluffy white cod, the greasy, thick-cut chips – is far more satisfying than the micro-portions of hay-baked ox tongue and sautéed beetroot shavings being consumed only fifteen feet away. And I also know that there's at least one side-staring person in there, perhaps on a client lunch, seeing my fish and chips, experiencing the worst kind of food envy possible – the kind that pits a £350 meal up against one that costs a tenner and favours the latter."

"I see…" Mal says, taking the cigar from his mouth, pinching it, staring at the smoking tip. His lips part slightly as if he's about to say something, but he dismisses the thought with a shrug, before he puts the cigar back between his lips. After blowing a couple of lazy smoke rings he says, "So then, Jim. What the bloody hell have you gone and got us mixed up in?"

"Mal, honestly, you've already got as much idea as I do."

I give him a quick rundown of everything that happened after we went our separate ways the previous night.

When I'm finished Mal makes a satisfied grunt and says, "Doesn't sound too serious. A lot of circumstantial nothing. I'd say this Rätsel fellow is just testing the water. See how you react. But really, if you were involved in… in whatever's going on, why on earth would you have called him? Practically a confession. It's ludicrous that he should suspect you of anything."

"I was pretty well soused. I think he could tell."

"The human instinct for self-preservation overrides everything, including a skinful."

I gesture at the empty space on the bar in front of him.

"Speaking of which, aren't you drinking tonight?"

"No," he says, sucking his teeth. "No. Need a clear head."

"What's going on, Mal? You sounded pretty pissed off on the phone this morning."

"Yes. Well. It was just a bit of a shock getting a visit from that copper. Barged right into the office flashing about his warrant card. Thoroughly unpleasant chap."

"Smug bastard, isn't he? Seems to think he's always got one over on you."

"Listen, Jim, I really do wish you hadn't mentioned my name. I can't be getting mixed up in something like this. Involving myself in a police investigation is one thing but this has got the whole pornography angle to it as well. I can't be associated with that kind of sleaze. Ad men have got a bad enough reputation as it is."

"You were already working with Al Girth anyway, so what does it matter?"

"Al had managed to *legitimize* himself. A few more years and people would've been calling him a national treasure. But with this Keith chap getting topped as well, the whole thing is starting to pong. I've got to think about my position at the company. The board won't accept a scandal, Jim."

"Well, I wouldn't worry about it. The only thing connecting you to any of this is an off-hand remark about autoerotic asphyxiation."

Mal blows a slow stream of smoke out of his nose.

"That *is* the only thing connecting you to this, isn't it Mal?"

"Yes," he says. "*Yes*. But what about you? Is there a connection between you and this Keith Rumbold chap?"

"It's unlikely but it's not impossible."

"Is there a way of finding out?"

"There is someone I could talk to. But he's a real villain, a relic of the old East End. *A right horrible bastard.*"

"Doesn't matter. Talk to him. You need to know where you stand. If Rätsel starts asking you any more questions you want to be able to give him the right answers."

I finish my whisky and move round the bar to pour myself another.

"Are you sure you're not going to have a drink, Mal?"

"See, the thing is, is this. The thing is, is that hot water, you see, it's something to do with the molecules, but hot water… *hot* water actually freezes *faster* than cold water."

"That's bollocks, Mal… *Bollocks*. I'm telling you, that's…it's bollocks."

"It is! It is! I swear on my… I swear on my… I swear on that!"

Mal flaps a hand towards a brash zigzag of colours on the other side of the dining room, a canvas that's probably worth a few hundred grand, yet has been thoughtlessly hung away from any decent light.

"It's science, Jim! The hotter something is then the faster… it cools, so if you get something really hot then it's going to get cold before something that's just a bit warm. Isn't it?"

Someone has told him this. Some old hound dealing out cod-science from the dark end of a bar somewhere has told him this. And Mal's fallen for it. He has. He's fallen for it. It's a good one, I have to admit. Sounds strange-but-true enough to be strange but true. But it doesn't add up. No. Something doesn't make sense here.

"No. But that doesn't make *sense*."

"Why not?"

"I don't... know. I can't think about it. It just doesn't."

"Aha! You see! You can't prove I'm wrong, so..."

"But I know it's... bollocks, Mal. *Bollocks*. I know it is."

I take a knife to the Suffolk Stinker on the board between us, spread the soft white cheese onto an oat biscuit and have a bite. The biscuit starts to break up in my hand so I stuff the remainder into my mouth before it collapses completely.

"This Stinker's bloody marvellous," I say between chews, spraying buttered crumbs over the surface of the table and the meaty slab of wood with its settlements of cheese.

"Isn't it! Know how much that cheese costs?"

I shake my head, which wreaks havoc with the colours of the room.

"Fucking... fucking *shitloads*," Mal says. "Have you tried the Banbury Blue yet? That stuff'll knock your bloody... block off."

"Which one's... that?"

"The blue one."

"Right. Yeah, I had a go... on that one. Needed a full glass of... of port... afterwards. Bloody salty."

"Don't I know it!"

Mal reaches for the bottle of port.

"Shit," he says.

"What?"

"No more port."

He grins with a mouth packed full of maroon teeth and tries to stand. He misjudges his rise from the table, overcompensates by staggering too hard in the wrong direction, bangs his knee, compensates for the overcompensation – but compensates too much. He staggers left to right, right to left, forward and back like someone struggling to carry a stack of watermelons.

"Mal, sit down. *Sit down*. We'll have whisky... instead."

"Whisky with cheese? We can't have... whisky... with cheese."

"Yes we can, now sit... sit down."

He pulls his chair from the table, although it was already some way out from under it to begin with, and successfully lands half of one buttock on the edge. He sidles with great effort until the rest of his arse is on the chair.

"Shit," I say, as I start to lift the bottle of barrel strength McCulkin's.

"What?"

"Whisky's empty too."

Mal starts to rise again but I wave him down.

"S'alright," I say. "I'll get it."

And now it's my turn to struggle. I push myself up from the table, rattling the bloodied plates and knives. The gravity – oh it's all wrong in here. One step I'm being pulled down through the floor, through my own *body*, like I'm standing on the surface of a neutron star, and the next step I'm on a small moon fighting to keep myself anchored, my arms rising at my sides in slow motion. The room starts to complicate things, rolling hard from port to starboard and I have to slam myself into a shuddering bookcase to keep steady.

"Use the walls, lad!" Mal shouts. "Use the walls!"

I use the walls. I lean my face up against the smooth plaster, press my chest against it, take the weight off my legs, which I start to pedal, propelling myself forwards. My lips drag against the cool surface, slide open, and I can feel the trailed saliva on my nose and on my cheek and on my ear. I make it to the end of the hall, back into the lounge. The bar is way over the other side of the room, thirty-five feet away, the space in between vast and bewildering. Behind me I can hear Mal's mobile phone ringing, then a thud, and finally Mal's voice, which is oddly muffled as he answers the call.

I traverse the room cautiously, using the armrests of chairs and the tops of low tables for support, swinging my legs in slow circles when I hit an area of empty carpet, arms straightened out for extra balance. Mal's voice rises, takes on a severe tone, but I can't quite make out what he's saying. Six feet from the bar I throw myself at it, misjudge the distance (turns out it's more like five-and-a-half feet) and chin the countertop. There's a possibility I black out for a microsecond, but I still manage to take hold of a beer pump and haul myself upright.

Behind me Mal shouts, *"I can't deal with it right now!"* into his phone.

I round the perimeter of the bar. Things are easy now that I've only got one obstacle to clear. I pull myself alongside the bottles of spirits and rest for a moment with my back on the burnished oak, staring at the horror of my own face in the mirror, the ghastly, washed-out horror of it all. My yellow eyes are wide with the madness of drink, the swollen pupils drowning in bloody horizons.

Mal shouts, "No chance. This thing is fucking *fragile!* I need more time!"

I lean further into the mirror and draw the loose skin down from my cheek, exposing the vibrant sheen of my stretched eyelid. The shining pink of my lip and my gums. Fine cracks in my grey teeth are pronounced by the stain of the port. Skin so pale. So oily. Stubble so dense and dark. I tilt my head back and stroke a finger along the line of my jaw to my chin, which is tender and red and impatient for the bruise.

"Look, I'll pay you another hundred. You're just going to have to *fucking wait!*"

I take a deep breath, scan the blurred labels in front of me, grasp a bottle of *Nobrotte Port* tightly in one trembling hand, grasp a bottle of *Creasey's Single Malt* tightly in the other. There's pain in my left armpit, like the pressure of a rigid finger pointing towards my lungs. My lower back feels cramped and beaten. The throb continues in my arse with a persistence that's becoming admirable.

There's a small explosion in the dining room, followed by a sprinkling of debris. Mal's phone striking the wall.

The weight of the bottles helps with my balance. I hold them by their necks, stride with them in front of me, planting them downwards like alpine sticks, covering the distance back to the dining room in half the time. Mal is lying on the floor with his face pressed into the ample weft of the Persian rug, his chair toppled beside him.

"Mal."

He turns his face to look at me, blinks one eye slowly, the other buried in the soft oriental weave.

"I've figured it all out," I say. "I know what's going on, you bugger."

He shakes his head and purses his lips.

"The water..." I say. "It might be hotter... to begin with but at some point as it cools it's going to get to the same temperature as the cold water. Do you see what I mean? The rate at which it... cools... will then be the... same. As the cold water was. The same as what the cold water... it'll be the same. But the cold water is... it's been cooling too... so it's *already* colder. So the cold water freezes first."

He closes his eyes and blows a long raspberry, speckling the carpet with foamy saliva. Scattered around the room are the fragments of his broken phone.

"Also, Mal? What the fuck was *that* all about?"

Thursday

The Satsuma: What *was* that all about? Mal wouldn't say. Not much later he fell asleep, still on the floor with his face in the carpet. Or at least I thought he was asleep, but just as I was leaving he mumbled, "Sort yourself out, Jim. Go and see that bloke."

I knew who Mal meant, even if he didn't. He meant Dane Biggerman.

I took the cab all the way home this time. No getting off after Putney Bridge. No fast food. No grief. No nausea. The cheese board had prepared me for the worst. The poison couldn't infiltrate such a fatty line of defence protecting my gut. Hardly anything for the hangover to get hold of – although I still needed a straightener this morning, a swift vodka and Tabasco sauce to see me right. But after that I was away.

Away to see Dane.

In my opinion the drinking ban on public transport was a fine idea. Tube journeys in the late hours have certainly improved without those stooped wretches who would lurch along the carriage with a cradled can of high-strength lager, biting at the air as they went. Much better now that they're gone. When people drink now, they do it with discretion. There's nothing objectionable about a man in a fine suit sliding a hip flask from his inside pocket to take a quick swig, because people know he'll keep to himself – they even *like* to see it. It's the quiet statement of a distinguished rogue.

If two trips to the East End in two days isn't a reason for a drink then I don't know what is, especially when you consider the particular hell I'll be visiting on myself today. My little studio might be in a rough part of town but it's only a pocket of resistance, a stubborn little stain that'll soon be rubbed out by the wealth of the surrounding boroughs. Head out further, out where the long shadows of Canary Wharf can't reach, and you find the real villains. The real hate. Dagenham is a different world, an extremity of London in every sense of the word.

The journey from West Putney station to Dagenham Playfields is long. It requires half the flask, and since the flask was only half full when I started, a top-up will be needed before the return leg. After forty minutes shrieking through darkness the train emerges, squinting into the hard light of the East End. I only have to walk a short distance from the station, and for that I should be thankful. There's a pervading sense of hostility to the outsider around here. These streets know I don't belong. These streets have *potential*. I'm menaced by the glare of every person I pass, by the derelict gazes of the children and the hateful, corner-eyed glances of ragged pensioners.

The office is above a kebab shop, on a street of steel-shuttered shop fronts. That should probably tell you all you need to know about the kind of operation we're dealing with. I see a sweaty wheel of meat revolving behind a window and I think I must've taken a wrong turn – in this part of London every turn is a wrong turn – then I notice a doorway, framed in blistered paintwork, standing separate from the Turkish takeaway, with a battered intercom loosely fixed to the wall alongside. One of the buttons has 'Biggerman Productions' scrawled on it in red biro. I push it, let the buzzer ring a couple of times, then wait. No answer. I press it again, hold it down for about half a minute until, "What the fuck do you want?" hisses out of the speaker. Male voice. Native. Glottal stops and dropped aitches.

"I've come to see Dane Biggerman."

"Not 'ere, mate."

"I used to work for him. This will only take a minute."

"Like I said, 'e's not 'ere."

"Can I come inside anyway?"

"Fuck for?"

"You might be able to help."

A sigh speckled with static wheezes from the speaker.

"Fuck's sake."

The electronic catch buzzes. I push the door open onto a narrow stairway, lit by a dusty yellow bulb. Movie posters line the walls, mostly parodies – *Nosferatool*, *Assablanca*, *The Gapes of Wrath*, that sort of thing. There are a few straight-up hardcore titles too. *Ballin' the Babysitter*. *Oily Stepdaughters 3*. I look up, shielding the light from my eyes, and see a man standing at the top of the stairs with his arms folded. A man I recognise.

"Terry?"

Terry 'The Satsuma' Smethurst.

Terry earned the moniker after a public altercation with one of his debtors. He kicked the poor sap to the ground, knelt on his shoulders and pissed in his face. At the time Terry was taking medication for a super-powered strain of gonorrhea and his piss came out a cheap shade of orange. Every illicit organisation seems to have use for a lunk like Terry and, as I said, the kebab shop below says all you need to know about this particular organisation's level of sophistication.

He narrows his eyes, shifts his bulk from one foot to the other.

"Fuck are you?"

"It's Jim." I hold my arms out at my sides and smile. "Jim Stakes."

He cocks his head, frowns.

"Nah. Don't know any Jim Stakes."

"Come on, Terry! I used to work here. Well, not *here*. I used to work with Dane. And you. I took the photos, did some camerawork back in the early nineties."

I slow my voice, enunciate every syllable. If my tone is patronising, Terry doesn't seem offended.

"Look, what do you want?" he says.

"I need to have a quick chat with Dane, that's all."

"Yeah, and I've told you twice already, 'e's not 'ere. 'Asn't been for the last week."

"Where is he?"

"'Oliday."

"Abroad? Or has he just taken some time off?"

"'E's still about, if 'at's what you mean."

"Is there a way I can get in touch with him? A number? Or an address?"

"'E wouldn't want me givin' out 'at sort of inf'mation to a stranger."

"But I'm not a stranger."

"If I was a kid, I wouldn't be gettin' in your van to go and look at fuckin' puppies."

I'm close to giving up, saying I'll come back when Dane's returned to work. Then my eyes drift over to a pair of tanned cheeks flecked with gems of sweat. A poster for *Ass Train: Volume XIII*. I snap my fingers.

"Ass Train!" I say, pointing at Terry. "Volume one. I was there when they first tried to film it. So were you. And the lead actress was sick. She had stomach cramps and started throwing up. Bad shellfish, if I remember rightly. There was no way we could use her for the shoot but we didn't have any other actresses in the studio, which we'd booked out for the whole day. It looked like we were going to lose the deposit for the recording session until Dane asked his secretary if she'd step in. Now this girl, this secretary, I can't remember her name, but she was pretty. A girl-next-door type. And she was enthusiastic too. Overjoyed, even. She attacked it like a pro, didn't even hesitate when they told her there'd be anal involved. But we fucked up, didn't we? We forgot the standard procedure for anal, because we'd been through it already with the original actress. And the secretary didn't know much about porn – certainly not that she was supposed to have an enema."

Terry winces. Oh yes, he remembers this story alright.

"I was the one holding the camera, Terry. I was right in there, up close, when the secretary went from moaning 'Yes, yes, yes,' to shouting 'Oh God no.' She'd had the shellfish too, hadn't she. I realised what was about to happen about half a second before anyone else, whipping away my camera just as the actor pulled out, uncorking her like a bottle of Bolly, and sending a jet of liquid shit across the room," I snap my fingers and point at Terry, "right to where you were standing."

Dane Biggerman: Terry gives me a number and an address and then he tells me to fuck off. I oblige. Outside, I think about calling Dane, but I'm alert to the passers-by and the threat concealed beneath the tired layers of their clothing. As soon as I pull out my phone – which would seem like a relic from an advanced civilisation to the denizens of this post-apocalypse – they'll take it, and my hand with it. Perhaps it would be better to confront Dane face-to-face.

I nip into the licensed newsagents next to the station. The only whisky they have is some blended abomination from a Welsh distillery. *A Welsh distillery.* There's no way I can adjust to such a drop in quality, certainly not after the fine 21-year-old that was in my flask. I have to switch drinks. So for the rest of the day I'll be on the *Ahoy There!* I like rum, but it does tend to take a lot of it to get me properly lubed – though that might not be such a bad thing when I'm running my little investigation.

Dane's house is in Finchley, which means another hour on the Tube. Another journey along London's sliding scale of wealth. Twenty minutes into the trip a little kid hops aboard with his mum. When I say little, I really mean short. This kid's got plenty of volume. He's got the stature of a manatee, this kid. He looks to be about six or seven years old and it's remarkable to think he's got so fat, so fast. He must've popped out of the womb eating ice cream. His face is all puffed up, bloated to the point of monsterism, and he has these tits, fully formed and feminine, that stretch his otherwise baggy T-shirt at the nipples.

This kid is a marvel. I can't stop staring.

His mother sees me looking. She's not so bad – quite pretty, actually – maybe a little bit chubby but not in any grotesque way like her son. She sees me looking and she blushes, unable to meet my gaze. She's ashamed on behalf of her kid and ashamed on her own behalf, because of what she's created – what she's *nurtured*. And I feel shame too. Shame that I've shamed her. I look away, concentrate on an advert for *Hoare's Cheese* over the other side of the carriage. A couple of badly behaved cheese-children are being scolded by the Master Cheesemaker. *Maturity Matters* says the strap line. Christ. Who came up with *that?* I hope Mal's agency doesn't handle the account anymore.

Mother and child stay on the Tube all the way to North Finchley. As I disembark, I afford myself one last glance. This kid's tits really are something. Back in the day we would've based whole scenes around tits like those.

By the time I make it back out into the open air, the tectonic slide of the clouds has finally yielded a break overhead, a sliver of blue sky. In this God-beam it's almost warm, almost pleasant, and I ignore the line of waiting taxis in favour of walking. A bit of outdoor movement is good for my arse, gets the air circulating, works up some friction to subdue any itches that might be developing. I take out my phone and call Dane to give him some advance warning that I'm on my way, but the dial tone rings unanswered. I don't leave a message.

The address leads me to a tree-lined row of detached houses, crude hulks that speak of wealth only because of their enormous size. The architecture is boxy, inter-war, the facades stuccoed with a mixture of cement and smashed rock aggregate, the fragments too large to qualify as pebbledash. It's exactly the sort of place I would've imagined Dane inhabiting. I count my way up the house numbers, following the road round until I see a crowd of vehicles parked in one of the driveways. Flashing blue lights. Two police cars. An ambulance. Characters dressed all in white mingling around the front door. A straight-backed figure in a cheap brown suit steps out from the shadowed porch and takes a bite from an apple. He chews thoughtfully for a moment and then, as if sensing a disturbance in the Force, snaps his head in my direction, smiles disbelievingly and waves. Rätsel.

He walks towards me, head back, shoulders locked. I anticipate a sarcastic 'fancy seeing you here'. Instead he says, "Got any theories about this one?"

I shake my head.

"Go on, have a punt."

"Burglary?"

Rätsel bites into the apple again, gives me a sarcastic grin, then speaks as he chews.

"Dane Biggerman. You know him?"

"I did."

"Past tense. You catch on fast."

"I mean I used to know him. I haven't seen him in years."

Rätsel angles his head to one side but doesn't say anything.

"How long since it happened?" I ask.

"You tell me." Rätsel's eyes darken, "He was found about an hour and a half ago, but by the smell of him I'd say it's been a while. Three days, maybe. Usually, I can judge the time of death pretty well from the stink, but he shat himself so that's upped the ante a bit. Might've affected my estimates."

"Oh Christ."

Rätsel shrugs, "Happens a lot in cases of strangulation, what with all the strain in that last fight for air. Your old buddy, Al, he was the same. Created quite a mess." He turns to look back at the house. "You on your way to visit him, were you?"

"I was going to ask him about Keith Rumbold."

"Ah. Of course. *Keith the sound engineer.*"

"So, what do you think?"

"What do I think?" He inhales theatrically. "I think two of your *strangle-wanks* might be a coincidence. I think *three* is a pattern. I think I see you here, a guy that seems to be connected to everything in this case, and I wonder why. I think me and you, Mr Stakes, we need to have ourselves a proper chat."

"I thought we had a proper chat the other night."

"The other night you were completely goosed. You still look a bit tiddled, I have to say, but hopefully I can get some sense out of you."

"Are you arresting me?"

"Do I need to arrest you?"

He starts walking back to the driveway, expecting me to follow. I hesitate. What else am I going to be able to tell him? He'll ask me about Al, about Keith, and now about Dane, how I'm connected to them, where I was when they died. I'll tell him the truth and he'll assume I'm lying. He'll keep me locked up for as long as he can, until a lack of evidence forces him to set me free. How long will all that take? Hours? Days? Police interrogations must be pretty tedious for the innocent. At least when you're guilty there's a competitive element, a bit of tension, but there'll be no battle of wits for me. When Rätsel tries to trick me with a question I'll avoid the trap simply by answering honestly.

Rätsel reaches his car.

"Can we have our chat later?" I say, "I have plans this evening."

"Oh, I'd hate to think I was coming between you and your next drink. Don't worry, this shouldn't take too long."

"But it might."

A look of mild amusement drains slowly from his face. He opens the rear door.

"Get in the fucking car, Jim."

Leeway: I should've heeded Dr Parting's advice and bought some haemorrhoid cream when I had the chance. A new itch announces itself just below my tailbone as Rätsel pulls us into the police station car park. I almost cry out, it comes on so suddenly. It's the kind of itch that travels to unrelated parts of your body. You feel it in your teeth. It jabs at the balls of your feet. I clench my cheeks, try to get a grip on it, but this itch is skilful. Evasive. I try and snuff it out, shifting from one tensed buttock to the other. No joy. I need that cream.

The car stops. Rätsel comes round and opens my door. My body is rigid. I can barely extract myself from the vehicle. Teeth fastened, toes curled against the soles of my shoes, I rock from one foot to the other and follow Rätsel into the building.

He signs me in and leads me across the chequered linoleum to a door so thickly coated in white emulsion that a faint plastic aroma still hangs in the air. I've been arrested before, but it's always been for everyday stuff – throwing a few punches in a bar fight or pissing against a war memorial – the sort of bang-to-rights incidents where there's been no need for an interview room. Seeing the inside of one for the first time, it's exactly what I've come to expect from countless hours of TV police procedurals; nicotine colours, anaemic lighting, a couple of moulded plastic chairs either side of a steel table and a tape recorder. Rätsel asks if I want a coffee – "Sorry I haven't got any single malt to offer you" – then takes the seat opposite. He switches the tape recorder on, states our names, the date and time.

"We estimate that Alan Girth died on the afternoon of the Twelfth. Would you be able to tell me what you did that day?"

I take a moment, lean forward onto my elbows so that I can drag my arse backwards over the rough surface of the chair, killing the itch for a few precious seconds.

"The Twelfth? What day are we on now?"

"Thursday. The Seventeenth."

"And the Twelfth was?"

"Saturday."

"Saturday... What did I do on Saturday?"

"That is what I'm asking, yes."

"Saturday... When was I mugged?"

"That would be late Tuesday night or very early yesterday morning."

"Right. So, Tuesday was when I went to the burlesque club with Mal. And then Monday... What did I do on Monday?"

"It's Saturday I'm interested in."

"What hope do I have with Saturday if I haven't figured out Monday?"

"Fine. Take your time."

I pause again, rotating my arse slowly in the seat, grinding down the itch until it's almost bearable, incorporating the action by wagging my head from side to side so it looks like part of my thought process.

"I went to see the doctor!" I say with a hint of triumph.

"On Saturday?"

"Monday."

"Of course."

"And I had a hangover, so I must've been drinking on Sunday. I think Sunday I probably just went down *The Oath.*"

Rätsel doesn't say anything. His features have sagged with boredom.

"The Oath and Omen," I say. "My local. They do an all-you-can-eat carvery every Sunday. Four different meats. Pretty spectacular."

"And Saturday?"

"Um… Steak night, I think. Twenty quid for a ribeye and a bottle of—"

"No. What did you *do* on Saturday?"

I drum my fingers on the table. Each finger thuds against the steel with satisfying volume.

"I can't be sure. Probably *The Oath* again. But I couldn't say with any certainty."

"I'm not going to have much luck if I ask you about the Third, am I?"

I smile.

"My agent could tell you better than I can. She keeps track of me, makes sure I show up for jobs on time. I've been on quite a few shoots recently, so you might be able to work things out that way."

"You really have no idea what you were doing on Saturday?"

"It's the weekend, you know? You have a few drinks, see some friends… it's easy to lose track of time."

"So you might have seen some friends? Would they be able to verify your whereabouts?"

"Come on," I say. "Do I really need an alibi? You don't seriously think I'm a murderer. You can't. It's ridiculous. You've got me here for some other reason."

Very slowly, Rätsel lays a lighter and a packet of cigarettes on the table, then leans back.

"Help yourself," he says eventually, spreading his hands in the air.

There's a shift in his composure. He relaxes in his chair, his shoulders dropping a fraction. Somehow that small movement makes me relax too. It's as if he's stopped the clock, stopped being a police officer.

"We can smoke in here?" I say. "How come?"

Rätsel shrugs.

I take a cigarette out of the pack and light it. One long puff and the irritation in my arse has dulled considerably.

"You're right," he says. "I don't suspect you of murder. For one thing you don't strike me as the sort of person that cares enough about anything to want to kill for it."

"Thanks."

"That wasn't a compliment."

"You just said you don't think I would murder someone, so..?"

Rätsel stares at me, incredulous for some reason, then shakes his head.

"Anyway," he says. "You *are* involved in this somehow. Of that I'm in no doubt. Just watching you squirm in that chair tells me you're hiding something."

"But... no. I'm not. The squirming is nothing to do with..."

"Wednesday morning, I got called out to your house because you were mugged. Didn't you think it was a little bit odd that a homicide detective was sent to deal with a mugging?"

"I suppose, now that you mention it..."

"You told the operator you thought somebody was trying to kill you, and that the same person had also murdered Alan Girth and Keith Rumbold."

"Ah."

"Now your story made no sense at all. There was absolutely nothing connecting your attacker to the deaths of your old colleagues. Except, that is, for your reaction. You were mugged by some opportunistic hoodie and your first response was to think that somebody was out to murder you."

"I was pretty well soused."

"No, that doesn't hold up. That's not the kind of leap of logic you make just because you're pissed. If that were the case, we'd be getting a hundred call outs for attempted murder every day. No," he shakes his head and taps the desk. "You know something and it scares you. Whatever you know is important enough to land you in trouble with some very nasty people."

"How do you know how nasty these people are?"

"Whoever is doing this has put a lot of planning into it. A lot of time. They've calculated it beautifully. Killing people with auto-erotic asphyxiation… it's inspired."

"Inspired?"

"As a means to commit murder? Absolutely. The main problem in cases of this kind is that we have to give a certain amount of leeway in terms of crime scene contamination."

"Why?"

"First, it's a violent way to go. This isn't suicide, remember, it's an error of judgement. And as soon as the victim realises their error, they fight with everything they have to try and save themselves, just as if they were fighting off an attacker. That causes all kinds of damage to the forensic evidence."

Rätsel illustrates his point by tipping his head back and scratching his hands around his throat. I find the choking noises he makes a little unnecessary.

"And there's a second problem," he says. "Imagine you come home and find someone you love, your son or your husband, dead, noosed up, with their cock out. What do you do? It's pretty obvious what's happened, that there's no foul play involved, but you don't want this person's memory sullied by an embarrassing mistake."

"I suppose I might try to cover it up a bit."

"Exactly. You pull up their pants, button up their shirt, try and make it look like a conventional suicide. And here's the problem. Even the subtlest movements, little shifts in the weight of the corpse, can affect the stresses exerted on the wound where the ligature has tightened. Capillaries rupture. Tiny new bruises bloom beneath the skin. If there was a struggle prior to the strangling, then it might be hidden by someone innocently trying to preserve a little bit of dignity for their loved one."

"Surely something like that shows up in an autopsy?"

"Not if you aren't specifically looking for it. There was no reason to suspect Keith Rumbold had been murdered. Or Alan Girth. Initially we didn't pick up on any connection between the two men because they hadn't worked together in more than fifteen years. And when we pushed Alan Girth's ex-wife in her interview she broke down and admitted to moving the body after she found it."

"You didn't even bother to look for foul play?"

"Do you have any idea how many people die like that, Jim?"

"I've heard it's something of a craze at the moment."

"We aren't lazy, we just don't have the resources to pursue every death as if it's suspicious. If ninety-nine percent of the evidence points towards an accident, then that's how we treat it. But now we have Mr Biggerman, and as far as we can tell nobody has moved the body. His cleaner found him – she wasn't going to risk incriminating herself for the sake of a porn kingpin's reputation. This time we're going to scrutinise everything, every mark, every blemish, every millimetre of broken skin. Up to now the killer has been lucky because we haven't been *looking* for a killer. Not anymore."

"Great. *Fantastic*. I hope Dane's corpse gives you all the information you need. But, as you've just told me, *I am not a suspect*. So if you aren't going to charge me with anything then I assume I'm free to go?"

"Of course."

I stub the half-smoked fag out on the table, leaving the butt in a mound of ash.

"But?" I say.

"But what?"

"You aren't going to let me walk out of here, not without saying something else. You're going to hit me with some sort of *Columbo* manoeuvre the second I touch that door handle, I can tell. It's written all over your self-satisfied face."

Rätsel gives me his shark-grin but the moustache maintains its shape.

"There is one more thing," he says, raising a finger. "Keith Rumbold. He stopped working in porn about five years after you did. Know what he'd been doing since then?"

"Selling cars? Dealing coke? I have no idea."

"Oh no. He carried on as a sound engineer, but he moved on to a less *sordid* side of the business. Did quite well for himself as it happens. A bit of TV. A couple of independent films. Music videos. But the bulk of his work, his bread and butter…"

"Advertising."

"You *do* catch on fast. *Advertising*. That's right."

That black pig: An hour after I leave the police station, I step through the doors of *The Oath and Omen*, my local piss-hole, riven by thirst, beleaguered by doubts.

The Oath is old school, old man territory. Ale and cracked leather. It's got the look of an old pub because it *is* an old pub. There are no brewery-chain falsehoods here, no decorative beams lacking structural purpose, no penny-farthings anchored to the wall. The tell is in the chips to the paintwork and plaster – the minute revelations of a brighter white beneath, untouched by decades of tobacco. Brass ornaments, kettles and jugs, occupy the windowsills, having done so since the time when it was properly fashionable to decorate your pub with them, before it became unfashionable, and before it become fashionable again, but only in a quasi-ironic way. It's a pub without ambition, happy to please as long as it doesn't have to try too hard.

It could be said that the regulars are lacking in ambition too, but that's an easy misapprehension to make with these down-to-earth types. These salt-of-the-earth types. Very *earthy*, these men. Lots of soil under the fingernails. Men with names like Farmer Gerald, so-called because he'll bore the arse off you about his council allotment given the chance, or Frank the Clap, whose moniker *doesn't* come as a result of any great inclination to applaud, but rather his winter-long solo trips to Southeast Asia. There's Paedo Phil, a man who once made the mistake of being too honest when it came to his thoughts on girls that 'develop' at an early age, and Brian the Antique, who's just really fucking old. Massive earlobes.

And then there's me, Mucky Jim. I don't often bring up my porn career in company, but with old boys like these a sliver of bawdiness commands a great deal of respect.

I enter to polite applause from a TV crowd. The landlord, a northerner called Barry Fettler, is watching cricket.

"Ah, Mucky Jim." he says, without looking away from the screen.

"Afternoon, Barry."

"Pint, is it?"

"That would be lovely."

"Usual?" He asks and, without waiting for my response, moves down the bar, jams a glass under one of the taps and pumps it stiffly, still without taking his eyes off the match.

"Who's playing?" I ask.

"Ireland and, um, Rhodesia."

"Zimbabwe?"

"Aye, that's the one," he says, putting the pint down in front of me, a tongue of white foam sliding down the glass onto the brass drip tray. I hand him a fiver and he looks at me for the first time.

"Christ," he says. "Are you alright, lad?"

"What...? Why?" I say, touching my face.

"You look bloody awful."

"Thanks."

"You know I don't see any point mincing words. You look like shit, lad. That must be a pretty hefty black pig you're carrying."

"A what?"

Barry leans over the bar, scrunching the fiver in his hairy fist.

"You don't know what a black pig is?"

"Literally, yes. Metaphorically, no."

"Must be an expression that hasn't travelled," he says. "You know that feeling you get when you wake up hungover, regretting something you did the night before, but you can't quite remember the actual thing that you did to make you feel this... vague sense of shame?"

"Oh yes. I certainly know *that* one."

"Where I come from, that's called having a black pig on your shoulder. He's a sinister little bastard and he sits there all day, threatening to remind you about your misdeeds. Silent. Accusatory. Impossible to ignore."

I shake my head and gulp down a third of the pint.

"I'm fine," I say with a gasp. "No black pigs on me today."

Barry squints at me, unconvinced, but eventually rings up the sale and gives me my change.

"Is this an important match, then?" I say, rolling my eyes at the telly.

"It's Ireland against Zimbabwe, Jim. In what realm is that ever going to be important?"

"You seem to be enjoying it."

"Aye, well, it's a beautiful game, is cricket."

I pull up one of the barstools, worn smooth by a thousand fat arses.

"I thought that was football," I say.

"Bollocks to that. Load of old shite, football. Bunch of bloody nancy-boys. You'll see more grit thrown on a road in July than you'll see on a football pitch."

"The way the weather's going at the moment, that might not be saying much."

Barry nods a grudging agreement and his eyes move back to the screen.

"Oh, there you go! See what I mean?" he says. "Look at that! *Look. At. That!*"

The camera tracks a red ball until it rolls across a line of white rope. There are shots of a sparsely populated stadium and more quiet applause, then a replay of the red ball rolling across the white rope.

"I'll take your word for it," I say, turning back from the screen. "Nobody else in today?"

"Antique was in first thing to read papers but he's buggered off home now. Been quiet all afternoon."

"Sounds like I'd better do you a favour and put some money in your till," I say, before sinking the rest of my pint. "Same again, Barry. I'll just nip for a piss while you pull it."

The pint is waiting for me on the bar when I return, along with a folded copy of today's *Herald*, a signal that I'll have to keep my own company for a little while. Barry sits on a stool at the end of the bar, talking on the phone, probably to his solicitor. He's been waiting for a big payout ever since he tore a ligament in his hip slipping on a spillage of washing up liquid in the supermarket. It's dominated his life in the subsequent months, not because of the inconvenience of the injury, but the inconvenience of making the claim for it. It's a full-time pursuit.

I raise my pint in Barry's direction to get his attention and I put the money I owe on the bar – he nods and mouths the word 'ta' – then I take the drink and the newspaper over to a table by the window, where there's just enough natural light penetrating the gloom for me to read.

As I'm sitting down, I see Farmer Gerald approaching along the street outside. He nods at me through the window and smiles, pushing through the door into the pub.

"Ay-up, Mucky Jim. How are you keeping?" he says.

"Not bad at all, Gerald. Yourself?"

"Oh, you know… buggering on as usual."

He trudges over to the bar. Barry gets up and serves him with the phone still clamped between his ear and his shoulder.

Gerald's farmer-like attributes don't end at the allotment – he reinforces his nickname with a Yorkshire drawl (much like Barry's accent, unsoftened by years spent in the company of southerners) and his tendency to dress as if he's been strollin' t' moors, with boots, flat cap and dark green wax jacket.

"Barry ont' phone again about 'is claim?" he says, positioning himself on a barstool so he has a view of the cricket.

"That he is," I say.

"Eeee, it's been going on a while now, 'ant it?"

I nod, taking a gulp from my pint.

A conversational void quickly forms between us, a polite tension that's intensified by the quiet enthusiasm of the cricket spectators and the humming of the bottle fridges behind the bar – sounds so unobtrusive that hearing them emphasises our own lack of speech.

Gerald breaks the deadlock, nodding at the paper on my table and saying, "Owt 'appenin' int' world I should know about?"

I look at the front page, which is dominated by a photograph of an American flag, scorched into tatters, held aloft by an indignant mob of brown-skinned people.

"The usual Middle East stuff. An American drone missed its target and hit a hospital in Waziristan," I say. "The locals aren't happy."

"Eeeee bloody 'ell. It's always same story, int it? An' it's same argument too – either America is righting wrongs and these drone strikes are necessary to fight terrorists, or the Americans are a set of bastards and the drone strikes are examples of imperialist war crimes," Gerald says. He takes a gulp from his pint, gasps with pleasure, and continues, "They're both right, though, aren't they? I suppose it's a question of who's *more* right. And who's more wrong. Is a pre-emptive strike killing scores of innocent folk worse than a potential terrorist strike that *could* kill scores of innocent folk?"

"Best not to think about it too much," I say. "There are enough sober-minded people out there to argue the toss on our behalf."

"Aye well, world'd be a much better place if we dint 'ave religion, that's all I'll say. Americans might be exploiting the situation for their own agenda, but if we dint 'ave Islam int' first place there wouldn't be any of this trouble."

I shake my head.

"We'll always find something to fight about, Gerald. It's how we've evolved. We've got millions of years of nature to contend with, against a few thousand years of philosophy and technology. Evolution has armed us to survive, as individuals, with hate and bitterness and greed. The desire for a peaceful global society isn't coded in our DNA.

To achieve something like that we need to fight our natural instincts and there are always going to be people that can't resist their baser urges."

"Aye, well..." Gerald says, letting his thought trail away for a moment while he concentrates on an Irish batsman, who is bowled out to relatively wild applause. "Aye, well, if you're talking about things going against human nature, Islam does that as well. No booze... no bacon butties... no birds in short skirts... How can you say there's something wrong with a nice bit of leg, eh? You used to make dirty pictures, didn't you! I mean, what do you reckon the Taliban would think of *that?*"

Dialling under the influence: When the doorbell rings, I'm sitting on the floor of the lounge, my back resting against the sofa, my shirt unbuttoned all the way, my fly undone so that the flump of my gut can bounce out over the rim of my striped boxers to support a heavy tumbler, half-filled with whisky. I've somehow managed to find a TV channel that still plays white noise after midnight and I haven't felt the need to change it. The doorbell rings again, an electronic double chime, and it occurs to me that I should probably do something about it, but I can't generate the required energy to do anything beyond setting the glass on the floor and rolling onto my right elbow while breathing heavily. A third ring and I turn all the way onto my front, then tuck my knees up under myself, raising my arse in the air, using first my face, then my hands, to push my body up off the carpet.

"Jimmy, it's me!"

Blue's voice, echoing through the letterbox, is enough to tighten the skin around my bollocks with a spasm of arousal.

I totter into the hallway, squeezing my gut back into my trousers, buttoning up the fly, before opening the door.

"Well isn't this a pleasant surprise!" I say as I lean against the doorjamb exuding an air of cool nonchalance – or I would be, except it sounds like a kitten has been playing with my vocal cords. "How the hell did you find my house?"

"You gave me the address. When you called me? About forty minutes ago?"

"Oh, right. Yes. Of course. Um… I called you?"

"Yes! You said you needed to talk to me urgently... something about Dane Biggerman shitting himself to death?"

"No... Right... Yes," I cough, trying to clear the dry grass from my throat. "Of course I did. I'm sorry, it's been a bit... chaotic tonight. Please..."

I gesture into the hallway, towards the lounge, stepping back against the wall to allow Blue passage. She's wearing a white blouse and a black knee-length skirt that wrinkles against the movement of her ample rump. How can something as simple as a curve create such a firestorm of biological reactions? But it isn't just the curve, is it? It's what the curve represents. I mean, you don't get a hard-on looking at a balloon, do you?

"Can I get you a drink?"

"I'm fine," she says, crossing one leg over the other as she sits down. "What's going on, Jimmy? Did that really happen? Did Dane... shit himself to death?"

"Ah... Not quite, no. Sorry. I obviously wasn't very clear."

"So he isn't dead?"

"Dane is definitely dead. But he shat himself *before* he died. Or perhaps... *while* he died. The point is, Dane *did* shit himself, but that wasn't the cause of his death. Strangulation was. The shit was just a... a by-product."

Blue leans forward, elbows on her knees, head in her hands, and her blouse hangs in a ruffled curve to expose her magnificent cleavage. I resist the urge to stare, but resistance is futile. I've seen those things out in all their glory, juddering for a steamy camera lens, and I've seen this girl in enough positions to know exactly what those big, beautiful bangers would look like right now if the clothes were removed. To expect me *not* to picture it would be unreasonable. In a way, it's like being at the same dinner party as an ex, sitting across from her and her new boyfriend, fulfilling all your social obligations, acting with the correct levels of cordiality, while inside your head a voice is screaming

'I'VE SEEN YOUR TITS! I'VE SEEN YOUR TITS! I'VE SEEN YOUR TITS!'

Not that I get invited to many dinner parties.

I shake my head in an attempt to clear it as Blue quietly says, "What does this mean?"

Now my eyes are drawn to her bright red lips. Their slow dance of seduction. The flex and wave and curve of them, her long pink tongue clicking and spinning behind. I've seen those lips do terrible things. Staggering acts of degeneracy. I've seen that tongue probing orifices, tugging at waxed scrotums, rolling up spunk and blowing it out in bubbles. Yet, despite all that, I feel a sudden Tourettic urge to dive across the room and plant my own mouth over hers. To absorb all of her filth. Her history. The compulsion is so strong I can hardly respond to her question. I have to ball up my fists and dig my nails into my palms.

"It means there are three deaths now. All connected," I say, with cracks in my voice. "The police can't ignore it. They aren't treating any of the deaths as accidents anymore."

"Did they give any indication about who they think might be doing it? Or why?"

I cough, but I still can't get rid of the rasp from my voice.

"Are you okay, Jimmy?"

I wave away her concerns with one hand, while coughing into the other.

"It's nothing," I say. "Karaoke night at the pub down the road. Think I might've torn my vocal cords singing *Great Gig in the Sky*."

"Pink Floyd?" Blue says, laughing. "That's not your typical karaoke song."

"No... Instead of any comprehensible lyrics, it was just one long line of vowels at the bottom of the screen."

Blue laughs again, throwing her head back. Her throat – God, look at her throat! The tendons in her neck. The shadows under her collarbone, etched in high definition like something knocked up by

Caravaggio. My line of work, I know all about the effectiveness of chiaroscuro and it's really making the most of the fine bodywork in front of me. It's all there, captured under the spotlights in strong contrasts of light and dark. And let's not even *talk* about what the lighting does to her tits. Her magnificent tits.

"He keeps talking about Mal," I say, seriously, trying to distract my lust.

"Who does? Who's Mal?"

I tell her everything Rätsel said. I break down the interview for her, including that final mention of Rumbold's involvement in advertising. I leave out the itchy arse, of course.

"Do you think your friend is a part of this?"

"That's what Rätsel thinks. I don't even have an opinion."

Blue arches an eyebrow.

"You've got to have an opinion," she says.

"Mal is like a, well... not a *dad*... but a much older brother, you know? I've known him for years. The idea he'd be involved in... in murder is... ridiculous. He's ruthless. No denying that. He'd have to be, to... you know... to achieve what he has in any business, never mind advertising in the eighties, when every cunt was out to trample their competition. But evil? *Psychotic?* No... no, I can't see it. What could possibly be in it for him anyway? He has everything he could ever want. How do three men that used to work in porn present any kind of... um... obstacle... to him?"

"He did seem pretty harmless when I met him."

"That's because he *is* harmless."

I cough again, but this time as an excuse to take a long drink of whisky. My nerves are shattered. Until now I hadn't fully appreciated the size of the torch I've kept burning for Blue. It's fucking *Olympic*. Twenty years of lust, dammed up behind the frustrations of what is essentially the look-but-don't-touch relationship between a stripper and her client. Ten minutes with a good lapdancer under those conditions is enough to turn any man into a twitch-faced lunatic. I've spent the last two decades only knowing this woman by sight, always wondering how she'd feel beneath me… on top of me… And those *tits*…

I'm biting my bottom lip so hard my teeth almost meet.

This can't go on, can it? It's unsustainable. I'm under no illusions about the kind of fat mess I must look like to her. But I've got money, and fame, and *reach*. I'm a real prospect, whichever way you look at me, even if it's from down below with a full view of my numerous chins and the vague fleshy agglomeration that is my neck. And there *is* chemistry between me and Blue – I'm not imagining it. She laughs at almost everything I say. She smiles openly and honestly. She touches me and plays with her hair. Perhaps all it would take is for me to make the first move.

I knock back the rest of the whisky, get up from my chair, and pour myself another, before sitting back down, this time on the couch next to Blue.

"Tomorrow," I say. "I'm going to do some digging."

I don't hide the fact that I'm ogling her chest. I allow my eyes to drag over the contours of her body. Before I make my move, I need to make my intentions clear so she can prepare herself for the onslaught.

"What kind of digging?" Blue says, turning her head towards me and tilting it to one side. She reaches across and strokes my cheek with a hand that's soft and warm, a sure invitation for me to touch her back. I lean my head against her gentle fingers and close my eyes, breathing in her scent.

"I'm going to find out about Keith Rumbold," I say in a low croak. "I'm going to see if he connects to me. I'm going to find out what he was mixed up in."

Friday

The Bunker: I wake up exactly as she left me, with a full whisky glass, miraculously unspilled, clutched between my thighs, alongside an impressively tenacious erection. I don't remember falling asleep but it's pretty obvious I never made my move, and that Blue has been gone for some time. If I was the sort of man to over-think things, I might question what it means that she left me in such a position, without making sure I was comfortable – without even throwing a blanket over me to keep me warm. But there are other more pressing questions to be answered, questions about murder and motive, under which I can bury any Blue-related doubts or insecurities.

Despite what Rätsel might think, I still have no idea whether or not I'm even involved in this plot. As far as I know I'm only directly connected to two of the three dead men. I need more information about Keith Rumbold before I can really start to worry, and with Dane dead that kind of information will be hard to come by.

Hard, but not impossible.

If you want to research something these days your first port of call is usually the internet, especially if the thing you're 'researching' is porn. Modern porn, anyway. Twenty-year-old porn is much harder to investigate online. There's very little interest in it. People log on in search of a quick fix. With a rapid turnover of starlets, and a whole world of studios grinding out films – not to mention all the amateurs getting in on the action – there's enough variety out there, enough new videos being uploaded, to render a back catalogue obsolete. Only the hardcore *hardcore* aficionados care about the old stuff and they don't want to watch a pixellated video. They don't want to wait for it to buffer. They want something tangible. Something with history.

The Bunker is revered by this kind of pornophile. Situated in the basement of a converted theatre on Charing Cross Road, it isn't actually a bunker, and it never was, but that's the aesthetic the owners have aimed for. I'm not entirely sure where the theme came from – some sort of war-torn, sex-starved dystopia perhaps – but they've really run with it, even installing a metre-thick nuclear blast door in the entryway. The walls are lined with breeze blocks and concrete, exposed pipework and ducting. The porn itself is laid out for perusal on the tops of counters in metal ammunition boxes, arranged in alphabetical order by star rather than title. Magazines, sealed in plastic, are stacked underneath the countertops. Old wood-panelled tube televisions hang in the corners, playing vintage skin flicks on a silent loop.

The steps down to the shop are narrow and steep and I have to take them carefully because my vodka hangover-remedy has left me marginally discoordinated. I shimmy, with my back to the wall, sliding my hands along the banister, through the blast door threshold at the bottom, where I'm confronted by an alarmingly life-sized rubber fist, clenched and ready for action behind glass that says *Break In Case Of Emergency*. I stop myself before I imagine the crisis that would call for that kind of assistance. There are other dongs, bungs, plugs and vibrating twizzlers, and a couple of deflated sex dolls, packed in similar emergency boxes and mounted on the walls around the shop.

Customers browsing in *The Bunker* do so with the unspoken rule that there should be no eye contact made *under any circumstances*. Rumours abound about the kind of material available if you get to know the management, everything from Moldovan menstruation parties to Japanese shit sermons, to legit snuff videos shipped straight from the dungeons of Poland.

I angle past a couple of dead-eyed patrons swaddled in anoraks, over to the boxes of DVDs. Porn, famously, is that rare business in which women are paid more than men and, as a result, receive higher billing, but I figure that Al, with his cock the size of a Star Destroyer, was a big enough draw to have his own section in the shop. I'm wrong – the Gs go straight from Greta Gashberg to Lucy Growler, without a showing from Girth in between. Next, I try looking through their selection of Blue's titles, thinking the films he shot with her might be on display but, again, no luck. In the process, I catch a glimpse of Blue, hair dyed ginger, on the cover of interracial gang-bang movie *The Red and the Blacks*, and I'm submerged beneath successive waves of lust and jealousy and nausea.

I wander over to the main sales hub. A large, red-lettered sign hanging above the till says:

At The Bunker we understand that sexual desires are complex, often hard to explain and almost always uncontrollable. We aim to serve all tastes. If you cannot find something you are looking for, please do not hesitate to ask one of our assistants, no matter how dark you think your desires might be. We are experts and we make it our business to know the boundaries of the law, but we don't expect you to have the same level of knowledge. In the unlikely event that your pursuits are too extreme, even for us, we will simply tell you that it will not be possible for us to satisfy your needs. We do not talk. We do not judge.

– The Management

The bearded attendant behind the counter sees me over the top of his *Bitches in Breeches* magazine, but he doesn't look up. He raises a finger, as if telling me to wait while he finishes reading a sentence. Except there's no writing on the page, nothing but a picture of a chubby, bare-breasted woman posing in a powdered wig and 18th century hose. He stares at the image for perhaps half a minute longer, then sighs and closes the magazine.

"Yes?" he says.

"I wonder if you can help me. I've just been having a look through your DVD selection and I'm struggling to locate any of Al Girth's movies."

"Well, yes. That's to be expected, isn't it?" the attendant says.

"It is?"

He nods.

"We're sold out," he says.

"You're sold out?"

"We are *sold* out."

"Of everything?"

"DVDs. Videos. Magazines. Replica dildos. The whole lot."

"Will you be getting any more in stock?"

"Eventually. We had a bit of a rush on his stuff, as I'm sure you can imagine."

"I'm sure I can't."

"You didn't hear? He passed away earlier this week. All our Girth products were sold off within a few hours."

"They were?"

"Of course. The same thing happens every time a big name dies. The erotic currency of an actor increases once they're dead… in certain circles."

"That's a bit morbid."

"Well, we don't *judge*."

"So I've read."

"Is there anything else?" he says, one hand returning to the cover of his magazine.

"You wouldn't happen to have a list of his titles, would you?"

The attendant rolls his eyes, takes a deep breath.

"Hold on," he says as he heaves an enormous ring binder out from beneath the counter. He flips it open to a tab of card with 'Girth' written on it and rifles through a few sheets of ruled A4 to a scrap of photocopied paper, which he places on the counter.

"This is a list of all of Girth's straight titles. I can get you a list of his gay stuff too, if you'd like?"

"I didn't even know he made any gay porn," I say.

"Uncredited, but you can tell it's him. There's no mistaking that cock."

"I'll take your word for it. I'm actually only looking for videos produced by Biggerman Studios."

"Of course you are," the attendant sneers. "His *mainstream* stuff. It's all at the bottom of that list."

I read through and see a couple of titles I recognise.

"Do you have a copy of this list I can take?"

The attendant shakes his head.

"A pen and paper, then?"

He provides me with a piece of tea-stained paper and a chewed biro. I quickly scribble down the list and read through it again. It feels like there's something missing.

"This list is complete?"

"Except for the gay titles, yes."

There's a faint quiver in his voice and a twitch at the corner of his mouth that make me question his honesty.

"So those are *all* the Biggerman films on there?"

"*Yes*," he says, his voice hardened by impatience.

"You don't happen to have cast and crew listings for these films, do you?"

"No. I'm afraid you'll have to watch the videos yourself to get that information. It's doubtful you'll be able to find it online."

I pause for a moment, holding the attendant's gaze. He blinks lazily, one eye after the other.

"Look," I lower my voice. "You don't have a few of those videos held back to one side, do you? For the shop's *private* collection? I really need to get my hands on them and I'd be willing to pay well above the odds."

He leans forward, close enough for me to catch his greasy scent. It's as if his clothes have been laundered in a deep fat fryer.

"Would you be willing to beg me for them?" he asks with a yellow smile.

"I don't think so, no."

"Well," he sucks his teeth. "We don't put anything *to one side* anyway. I'm afraid you're out of luck."

"Do you have a business card, then? I might call back later to place an order."

He takes a plastic card from his shirt pocket and hands it over. *Brendan Hardy*, it says. *Deviant Services.*

Malarkey: I know that if *The Bunker* doesn't have what I need I've little chance finding it elsewhere. Still, I try all the other vice houses and jerk rooms in the vicinity. They're out of stock, as expected. Each time I ask for a complete list of Girth titles I'm shown the same inventory and each time I get the same feeling that there's a piece of the puzzle missing.

With a rising thirst I reach Leicester Square and I angle off Charing Cross Road, cutting through towards Covent Garden. There's a boozer I'm rather fond of hidden up one of the alleyways in this area, but I can never quite remember where it is. Or what it's called. Or what it looks like. I shamble through the cobbled maze, searching in vain for a place that, now that I think about it, might not even be in this part of London, until my back is aching from the useless burden of my own weight, and I'm forced to take refuge in a dingy little alleyway scrotehole called *The Open Arms*. It's a low-ceilinged Tudor building, one of those uncommon wooden structures that managed to see out the great fire.

On entry I'm hit by a powerful reek. It smells like a nightmare in here – like a sweat-soaked bad dream. The air has texture. Substance. I can feel it sliding down my throat and into my lungs. It's more than just a physical smell – there's a sinister, emotional quality to it as well. It's the smell of despair, of toileted ambition, and it gets thicker and darker all the way to the bar. I breathe with my mouth and order a pint of *Warstarter* from the plump barmaid, who's huffing and puffing her way through a lunchtime rush of three customers. She's sweating enough to arouse my olfactory suspicions but otherwise seems clean.

The other customers look more capable; an elderly businessman at the end of the bar, surrounded by empty glasses, holding his head in his hands, staring at a ketchup-smeared plate, dressed in a harrowed suit with a shirt stained like an old tooth; behind him, in the corner, another lost soul in layers of dead clothing, with his cheek on the table, nursing a centimetre of ale in the bottom of a scum-streaked pint glass.

I see my first drink away at the bar and take the next one over to a cramped booth that's furthest from the stench, along with a wooden spoon that has a '7' painted on it to signify that I'm waiting for an order of onion rings. I dump myself onto the carpeted bench with a groan and try to make my drink last until the food arrives.

"Another Warstarter, please love," I call over to the barmaid a few minutes later.

"You'll have to come over here and get it."

"Of course, my dear. Wouldn't want you overstretching yourself, would we?"

My onion rings are brought out of the kitchen while I'm at the bar. The boss-eyed gloit carrying them scans the tables with a look of confusion that borders on disillusionment, as if my food order has provoked some kind of existential crisis within him.

"Onion rings?" he calls out desperately.

"Those are mine," I say.

"Number seven?"

I nod.

"That's me."

"But where's your spoon?" he asks.

"On that table over there," I point.

He sees the spoon, turns back to me, looks back at the spoon, turns to me again, stares at me like a feckless trout, his slack jaw dawdling. His pupils are huge, dilated like twin eclipses, with only thin coronas of blue surrounding them.

"Are you okay?" I say.

"Where do you want your onion rings?"

"On the table is fine."

He throws them onto the table and hurries out of the room.

"Is he alright?" I ask the barmaid.

"Andy?" she says. "He's fine, just a bit slow. Sometimes he suffers from flashbacks."

"Oh, I see. What happened to him?"

"The nineties rave scene," she says.

I take my beer back to my seat and pick up one of the onion rings, attracting the attention of the slumped groaker in the corner. His head lifts a couple of inches off the table and he peers at me with a snakeish glimmer. Then he grins and I know I'm about to have company.

"Hey... *Hey* those look *tasty*," he says in Glaswegian, rising from his chair. "Mind if I have one?"

"Actually, yes. I do mind."

He recoils dramatically, hands lifting towards his face as if to protect it.

"Did ye just say *no?*"

"Well, I said I minded if you had one of my onion rings. That's a *no* of sorts."

I bite down purposefully into the hot batter and he laughs.

"Ah, come on, pal. Jest the one! Ye won't miss it."

I shake my head, chewing.

"Ah, don't be tight," he says, coming closer.

"I'm not being *tight*. It just irks me when somebody asks me if they can have some of my food."

"Oh, aye," he laughs again. "Irks ye, does it?"

"It does. When somebody asks if they can have a bit of your food, a chip or a crisp or an *onion ring*, it's socially unacceptable to say 'no'. Saying 'no' makes you, as you said, *tight.*"

"Aye."

"So when *you* ask *me* for some of my food, what you're really saying is 'your food looks nice, I'm going to take some of it,' because you expect me to play along. To be polite. You're basically threatening me with the prospect of creating an uncomfortable situation. Well I'm an uncomfortable *person* and these are *my* fucking onion rings."

The Scotsman roars.

"Ahahaha! *Ha!* God, I love you English!"

He tips back his head, swallows the dregs from his glass, gasps, puts the empty on the bar.

"For that, ye can keep your onion rings!" he says, still laughing. "And I'll even buy ye a pint."

Bonce is his name. Bonce Malarkey. A wanderer, he tells me. A poet. Almost certainly destitute, though he pulls enough copper and bronze from his pockets to pay for a couple of rounds before I start footing the bill. He has all his teeth, most of his hair, a deep tan of dirt on his skin to go with the filth on his coat. Thankfully, though, Bonce isn't the source of the stink. It stayed away when he drew closer, suggesting it belongs to the abject businessman propping up the bar, whose lifetime of failure seems to have manifested itself into a honking great gas cloud of woes.

We get to doing some serious drinking, me and Bonce. We go at it hard and old fashioned, beer first, then whisky, working our way through a surprisingly decent array of single malts. We do all the isles. We hammer the bens, the glens and the lochs. We get that stumpy little barmaid climbing on chairs, pulling bottles from hidden shelves, dusty, with faded labels – whiskies so old and forgotten they don't even have a price or a key on the cash register.

We drink it all, and we drink more, and I decide that this Bonce chap really is a good sort. He's had it hard and, somehow, he's missed all the breaks.

"I'm going... to help you, Bonce," I say.

"Help me what?"

"Get... on your feet."

"I'm on my feet!" he shouts. "Do I no look like a man on his feet?"

"I know... people... Bonce. People with jobs..."

"Aye, I know plenty of people wi' jobs too, Jimmy. See 'em walkin' past me every day."

"No, Bonce... jobs for you. People that can get... *you*... a job."

"What do I want wi' a job?"

"Money?"

"An' what do I want wi' *money?*"

"You can... buy things."

"Aye, I can buy *things*. I can buy lots of *things*. But what am I sellin'?"

"Selling...? You aren't selling... anything."

"Oh yes I am, Jimmy. People with *jobs*, they're sellin' the most precious thing they have. They're sellin' their *time*. But time... *time* is invaluable. It's a finite resource. The vast majority get less than a hundred years of it, and they sell almost all o' that for *money* so they can buy *things*. Ye can keep yer flat-panel TVs an' yer fancy cars. Ye can keep yer *money*. I've got my time an' I won't sell it fer all the tit-wanks in Thailand."

"Bonce, my good fellow... I think that deserves a drink."

We clatter our glasses, spill half the contents on the carpet.

"What about you, Jimmy. Who're you selling your time to?"

"Self employed... I suppose. Well... freelance. I only do as much work... as I want to."

"I suppose if you're gonnae do it then that's the way *to* do it."

"...Yup."

"Why ye in here, then, in this fucken... *purgatory?* Why ye lookin' so full of sorrows?"

"There's this woman–"

"Ah! O' course there is! O' course there's a woman!"

"To be quite frank, I've wanted to fuck her for twenty years, Bonce. It's been there, this raging... desire – no, not *desire*... it's more than that now... it's a need..."

"Oh, aye, I know that feeling, pal!"

"This *need*, it's been there, occupying a space at the back of my mind all this time. And I've seen her *naked*... God, I couldn't even tell you how many times... And that only makes it worse."

"Ye've seen her in the scuddie? But you've no actually done the deed? That sounds like a mightily fucked up situation to me!" He says, sipping his drink. "Aye, a *mightily* fucked up situation, and no mistake."

I nod.

"Enough to turn a man to drink, in fact!" Bonce shouts, smiling, raising his glass.

"It's not just her that I'm worried about," I say. "There are bigger things going on in my life right now. More *immediate* things. And there's somebody trying to convince me that my best friend might be involved in some very bad business. *Murder*, Bonce."

"Jesus. That's a hell of an accusation for someone to be makin' 'boot yer pal."

"It is... indeed. But the more I think about it... the more I can't rid myself of the feeling that... maybe... maybe my friend *is* involved."

"Well, what does this friend have to say in their defence?"

"I don't know. We haven't really... discussed it."

"Don't ye think ye should give them the chance to argue their case before you convince yersen that they're a fucken killer? Maybe instead o' sittin' here gettin' gashed with me ye should be havin' a conversation wi' them. Not that I don't appreciate the company, y'understand."

"You're right, aren't you? Bonce, you're absolutely... you're fucking *right*."

"Course I am! Give me enough time an' I'm always right, one way or the other. Get yersen out o' this shite-hole. Go an' show that bastard friend o' yours what's *what!*"

I jump up, rocking the table, grasping the top of the wooden partition that encloses the booth.

"Bonce, my man, you're an inspiration. I'm doing it, I'm fucking going!"

"Aye, go on, Jim! An' maybe afterwards ye can bump fuzzies wi' yer ladyfriend!"

I duck out of the pub into the clean air and the solid light, Bonce shouting behind me, feeding my momentum. I take one last look at the beams and the white panels and the friendly sign swinging above the doorway, *The Open Arms* creaking in the wind, and it wasn't such a bad place after all, was it?

No, you don't find many alehouses like that anymore.

I'll make sure I remember that one.

For everything bad, mezcal: I step out of the Tube, reeling. I can feel that beer working me over, kicking me in the guts. I already cleared out half a carriage with a couple of seismic prumps. Now come the sweats, patching through the collar of my shirt, making the razor-burn on my neck itch.

I know the route from the platform to Mal's office, but I'm spinning like a dinghy in a tempest. The ambling crowd divides when it sees me cannoning forward, and I use those amblers, I grope and fondle my way up the stairs, along the pavement, out into the traffic. Taxis yelp and stutter at my heels as I stride across the writhing street.

ADHD resides inside a big, pinched dome of glass they call the crystal peanut. It doesn't look much like a peanut to me, but all the big architecture needs cute names these days. Shapes you can cuddle. It stifles the menace. That financial institution, the one that's stuffing your assets down its pants, the one that took away your house, your job, your wife and your kids, *that* financial institution is housed inside a giant dodecahedron they call *the pineapple*. Its sister, the insurance conglomerate, the one that wouldn't pay out life insurance when your uncle died of cancer, does its filthy business out of a concrete *turnip*. So – you think – these swindlers and rapists can't be *all* bad. At least they have a sense of humour. If they were really evil, if they *really* wanted to fuck up the planet, then we wouldn't even know about the secret volcano lairs they're operating from.

With the late afternoon sun behind it, casting the girders and support lines in silhouette, curving the light and colouring it through prisms of glass, the crystal peanut is a bright, modern pimple amidst the grey stonework and pillared entryways of Knightsbridge. This is helpful to me in my current state – it gives me a big shiny blur to home in on.

Dennis the Ugandan doorman grins at me from beneath the wide peak of his cap as I pile through the revolving doors. The security company forces the poor fucker to wear a uniform that wouldn't look out of place in a North Korean military band.

"Hello, Mr Stakes!" he says.

Even if I didn't have a security card, he'd let me through the gates. Dennis is a fan. The half-gallon of spiced rum I give him at Christmas sees to that.

"Lovely day for it, Dennis, old chap!" I holler. "Just paying a quick visit to the big man."

He unlocks the turnstile, waves me through, into the atrium, which is filled with an installation by Danish artist Slag Jensen, whose signature is recreating real-world objects in inflatable form. Here, he's created a jungle of blow-up plants. Vines and creepers curl around lilo-cushioned mahogany trees that rise thirty feet to the ceiling, where their branches stretch into a lush plastic canopy just below the spotlights and halos. The electric hum of cicadas and howling of monkeys plays from speakers hidden within the synthetic vegetation, activated by motion sensors as you pass through. It's a firm sign that you're entering adland, that beyond this point creativity and pretension exist in abundance. A client used to working in a utilitarian, cost driven environment is supposed to encounter this vibrant display and realise that they couldn't possibly conceptualise an ad campaign as effectively as the mind-bending leftfield specialists that occupy such a workplace.

I tumble through the plastic copse, through an overwhelming smell of new car, batting aside saplings and ferns, tripping over exposed rubber roots until I find myself falling into, then wrestling, then hugging an incongruous giant panda.

"Sorry about that, big fella," I tell him as I push myself away.

Out of the rainforest I'm confronted by a couple of receptionists seated behind a desk that could comfortably accommodate twenty. They're both dressed in a sort of porn-parody of office attire, their skirts a little bit too short and tight, their tops a little too low.

"Just paying a quick visit to the big man," I tell them.

"Very nice, Mr Stakes," they say as I stagger past and punch the button for the lift. A couple of suits walk by while I wait, accompanied by a guy bouncing along in a Hawaiian shirt, Thai fishing pants, flip-flops and Buddy Holly glasses. He'll be the one in charge – that's how things work around here.

I take the lift all the way up to the top floor, which is reserved for Mal's office. When the lift doors release me, I'm faced with an empty desk, normally occupied by Mal's delightful secretary Pats, another woman well practiced in the art of suggestion. I check my watch. It's nearly five. Perhaps she finished early for the weekend.

Bypassing the desk, I follow a short corridor lined with sticks of bamboo, through a huge oak door, into a room that resembles a cathedral cloister, clad in stone, with vaulted ceilings and wrought iron chandeliers. The sudden shift from modern to medieval is like a kick in the bollocks if you aren't expecting it – a very impressive theatrical display for any clients important enough to actually get an audience with Mal.

Across the other side of the room, beyond giant embroidered prayer cushions that serve as sofas and an altar draped in silk that doubles as a bar, the door to Mal's inner sanctum lies open. I can't see him, but I can see through to his view of southwest London, and I can hear his articulate drawl echoing off the stone. It's a sound I've always welcomed, the arched, swaying, exuberant, mad-as-a-badger voice of a true English aristocrat. But right now, here in this rooftop temple, amplified, echoing, his voice has taken on a much harder edge. He's on the phone. Unusually for Mal, it seems that the person on the other end of the line is doing most of the talking. He makes the occasional statement, the odd murmur of assent, but these are broken by long silences as he pauses to listen. Then he starts shouting.

"Money isn't an issue," he yells. "Money is *not* an issue. I have all the money you need and you know that."

A long pause, then, "Look—"

Another pause.

"But—"

Another pause.

"Look, I know things haven't gone according to script, but I can't deal with him myself. *I can't.* There's too much of a spotlight on me. The police are asking questions."

Pause.

"It doesn't matter, they're still asking questions."

Pause.

"For fuck's sake, they're all over me. I can't do it. You're just going to have to keep doing things as you've been doing them and take care of him yourself."

I make the decision to announce my presence, knocking on the open door, poking my head into the room. Mal spins round to face me, clearly startled. His expression is the same as the expression I imagine was on my face the time that my mum caught me wanking. My reaction now isn't much different from hers then, as I back out of the room, silently mouthing the words 'I'll leave you to it.' Mal waves back frantically, mouthing 'no, no, not at all,' then, holding up a finger. 'One minute,' he mouths.

"Look… I'm going to have to call you back, darling," Mal says into the phone. "A very important client just walked into the office. A *very* important client."

Pause.

"Yes. I know. I will."

Pause.

"Yes. I understand. Um… love you."

Mal drops the receiver into its cradle and bounces up from his seat.

"Jim!" he shouts. "Bloody good to see you, as always!"

"I hope I didn't interrupt anything serious..."

"That? Nothing at all. Just the... um... just the wife overreacting. You know how it is."

Mal puts a hand on my shoulder and guides me back out of his office, over to the altar-bar.

"I still haven't had any contracts drawn up, I'm afraid," he says, indicating for me to sit down on one of those giant, purple prayer cushions while he walks behind the bar.

"Contracts?" I say.

"Yes. For the sixty-grand Satnav job. I assume that's why you dropped by?"

Mal ducks down behind the bar and I hear the creak of a cabinet door opening, then the scrape of glass against wood, then the chimes of booze bottles striking against each other.

"Actually," I say. "There was something I wanted to talk to you about..."

"Yes?" Mal raises his head above the bar for an instant, but only an instant, before he ducks back down again to move around more bottles.

"Where the fuck has she put it?" he grunts, mostly to himself, then, "Sorry, Jim. I *am* listening. It's just I asked Pats to keep a special bottle of booze safe for me, so you could try some the next time you came for a visit, and now I can't find the bloody thi– hold on... *hold on*... Aha!"

Mal emerges again, triumphant, holding a bottle of light brown liquid to his chest.

"What's that?" I ask.

"You know how you point blank *refuse* to drink tequila?"

I nod hesitantly.

"Well this," Mal pours a couple of fingers of the liquid into a glass, "is *mezcal.*"

"As far as I know, that's basically the same thing," I say.

"No, Jim. *No*. They are *not* the same. And *this* mezcal is something else *entirely*."

He hands me the glass and holds out the bottle by its neck so I can read the label.

"*Los Suicidas?*" I say. "Not exactly a name that inspires confidence."

"Taste it, Jim. Trust me. This stuff is like Aphrodite's tit-milk compared to the piss you've tried before."

I dip my nose into the glass and sniff the contents.

"Smells like tequila to me. Maybe a little smokier, but it's still got that horrible reek of petrol."

"It isn't tequila. Please, just try it once. That's all I ask. You have *no idea* how much that bottle cost me!"

"Oh for fuck's sake, alright," I say, raising the glass in a mini toast.

I open up my throat before I've even put the glass to my lips, and I throw back the shot, trying to clear my tongue. Mal watches with a curious squint and an expectant smile.

"And?" he says.

"It tastes…" I hold the glass against my eye to examine the remaining film of alcohol coating it and say, "Surprisingly good."

Mal claps his hands together, then points at me.

"I knew you'd like it!" he says, taking my glass to pour another for me. This time he pours himself one too.

"Now try sipping it. You should drink good mezcal the way you'd drink good single malt. With respect. They don't make this stuff anymore."

"It can't be that good if they stopped making it."

"You just tasted it, didn't you?"

I concede the point with a shrug and take a long sip.

"That really is… an extraordinary drink."

We finished off the bottle, all the way down to the tumescent grey worm residing at the bottom, which I was tasked with eating because I'd never eaten a tequila – or *mezcal* – worm before. I chewed through it without complaint but an hour later I can still feel a phantom of the bastard wriggling in my stomach.

Bum Hero: After a short cab ride to Soho, we set ourselves up in a basement bar, bribing our way to a table through the throng of creative types celebrating the end of another working week. Except for most of them this won't really be the end; there'll be directors to chase, clients to appease, pitches to finalise... messages will keep pinging back and forth right up until it all kicks off again, 8am, Monday. Looking around the room at all the tired eyes and tired smiles, listening to the self-deluding volume of their laughter, I wonder if maybe that mad Scottish tramp had the right idea. Time is too precious to be wasted in the pursuit of wealth.

Me and Mal, we're both completely twisted at this point, although I've got the tolerance advantage that comes from starting early – you can only get so drunk before you plateau, and my plateau is fucking Tibetan. Once you reach your peak you learn to control yourself, to account for the room spin and the five-second delays, like a sniper adjusting his shots in a strong wind. Mal is still on his way up, still coming to terms with the foot-drag and the visual slurring, which means that even though *technically* I'm more intoxicated, he's the one that's showing it.

I marvel at our waiter's braided beard as he takes our food order, which is large enough for six people. A platter of cured meat from Tuscany, hot coarse-ground sausages and pickled cabbage from the Black Forest, and a great wedge of Spanish tortilla with manchego and cactus fruit jam. Sizzling kebab skewers. Deep-fried aubergines. English cheeses, served at room temperature, all ripe and unpasteurised and entirely indecent. An enormous basket of warm bread with a brick of artisanal Danish butter. It's brought out to us on wooden planks, the way it always is, everywhere, these days. Plates have had their day. Plates are *done*. From now on the human race doesn't want its food served on anything but slabs of two-by-four!

I hollow out a torpedo of French bread, seal the inside with butter and start stuffing it with meat and cheese. Mal asks the waiter for tomatoes and stuffed olives. I ask for pâté and then change my mind and ask for a lobster instead. We wash our feast down with buckets of thick, dark wine. Just as our appetites are getting close to being sated a tall brunette in a leather jacket and killer heels trots over to our table from the bar area.

"Mal?" she says.

Mal turns his head and grins up at her with one eye closed.

"Oh Christ," he says. "Rebecca!"

"Becky, please."

"Yes, of course, my dear! How lovely... to see you! Jim! Jim, this is Rebecca. She's a producer at a... um... post-production agency... we use. Um... *Fat Lad...* is it?"

Becky nods.

"Haha! *Fat Lad!*" Mal shouts. "Tremendous name."

"I saw you sitting over here. Just thought I'd say hi."

"Oh, of course. *Of course*. And... ah... Rebecca... this is Jim. He's a good friend of mine, and a bloody good photographer to boot."

I smile and make a hand signal somewhere between a wave and a salute.

"Yes, hello, Jim," Becky says. "We've met before, actually. A few times."

I nod and smile back at her but decide not to risk saying anything for fear of slurring and giving away that I haven't got a fucking clue who she is.

"Why don't you join us?" Mal says. "We've got a bit of food left over if you're hungry... and there's plenty of wine."

"Oh no. I don't want to interrupt. Besides I'm out with a few friends…"

"Female friends..?" Mal asks, squinting.

Becky nods.

"Well bring them over too! The more the merrier!"

So she did. She brought them over. Four more girls, all of them high sixes or sevens, Becky herself being a very solid eight-out-of-ten. And we bought them food and drinks, as they knew we would, and eventually they managed to convince us that it'd be a good idea to go to a club with them, where we would continue to pick up the tab.

Which is how I end up in the middle of a dance floor, a glass of whisky in my hand, multi-coloured tiles lighting up under my feet, shuffling to some seventies funk, thrusting my hips in the direction of a twenty-something runner from the same post-production house as Becky. And speaking of Becky, she's now sitting at a table in a dark corner with Mal, touching his shoulder playfully and throwing back her head in a surge of laughter every time he opens his mouth. The other girls are on the dance floor with me, and we've basically got the place to ourselves because it's still very early for a Friday night, the roving strobes of light casting long glances across the empty club.

The runner, the one I'm thrusting towards, is encouragingly drunk, swatting the air with her blonde ponytail as she snaps her chin from side to side, her eyes barely open, and I'm starting to think that if I play this right, if I can get her alone, away from the protection of the pack, then I might be in with a sniff. She might not cause the same kind of supernatural resurgences in me as Blue – I'm feeling pretty dead below the waist, to be honest – but her schoolgirl stockings and porno make-up are worth popping a couple of blue pills for. I move in closer, rest a hand against her hip, then slide it up to her stomach, which is firm and gives very little when I gently squeeze. Her eyes open wide and she snaps her head round to look at me, biting her bottom lip seductively, smiling. *Still got it, Jimbo.*

And then, with one hip gyration too many, I aggravate an ants' nest in my pants. Those pulsating haemorrhoids, almost forgotten, seize their moment with a clarity of pain that cuts through the alcoholic blur and almost kicks my legs out from underneath me. I shiver and shimmy and lurch from one foot to the other, twisting my arms, tensing them against the irritation, and as I flail I notice the girls forming a circle around me, laughing and toasting with their champagne glasses, and then they all start to twitch too, throwing their arms in jagged shapes, rocking their shoulders, kicking their heels, and I realise that they're copying me – they think I'm aping some kind of retro dance manoeuvre and they're trying to mirror my spasms with their own spastic thrashing.

I back away with feet arched high and toes curled tight at the tips of my shoes, taking reverse cowboy strides over to Mal's dim-lit table.

"Mal," I grunt. "I have... to go."

"But we only just got here, Jimbo," he says quietly, without looking away from the brunette, whose score has risen markedly now that we're in the shadows.

"It's... it's the haemorrhoids, Mal. Christ. Oh Christ... I can't... I can't bear it."

"Haemorrhoids, you say?" Now he turns to me.

"Fuck, Mal... I've got to... I've got to go."

"What about that pretty little blonde piece you were dancing with over there? You aren't just going to leave her, are you? You aren't going to let some other bugger swoop in and take the credit for all the hard work you've been putting in?"

"Pfffff... I don't care, Mal. Fuck ... I'm out of here."

As I'm turning away Mal leans out of the darkness.

"Now, Jim," he says. "Wasn't there something you wanted to talk to me about? Earlier? Wasn't there a reason you came to see me in my office? I'm sure you said something..."

"Oh God... yes... yes there was... but, Mal... fuck it... I can't... remember... It doesn't... oooh fuck... it doesn't... yaaahaha... it doesn't... fucking... matter... whatever it is."

The bouncers think I'm on something, that I'm raging somehow, but I tell them the situation, no time for embarrassment, and they point me in the direction of a chemist only a couple of streets over.

"Haemorrhoid cream?" I ask the checkout girl. She hears the strain in my voice, sees the wince in my eye and makes a sympathetic grimace as she points to the relevant aisle. The product display is baffling. I can't focus with the terrible itch screaming inside my head. What am I looking for? Antiseptic? Antifungal? Do I want an oil, an ointment or a balm? What the hell is the difference anyway?

And then, there it is, jagged purple letters exploding off the packet. ***Bum Hero!***

I crush the box, pop out the tube, break the seal and squeeze a golf ball of cream into the palm of my hand. Discarding the instructions, I reach into my pants and smear the greasy substance between my cheeks. The effect is immediate and very cold, like receiving a rim job from Jack Frost. I suck air, close my eyes and clench my fists until the cold burn eases to a soothing chill. It's almost worth the preceding agony to experience such intense, euphoric relief. I slump against the shelf, groaning with pleasure until I notice a goat-faced old lady staring at me, her rigid claw suspended in the air between her basket and a row of shampoo bottles. I extract my hand from my trousers, nod 'good day' to her, grab another couple of boxes of *Bum Hero!* and take them to the checkout.

Out on the street I hail a taxi. Cream squeezes along the crack of my arse when I sit in the back, spreads behind my balls, bursts out of my underwear. Spots of grease soak through the material of the trousers around my crotch. I promise myself that someday I'll make it through a week without ruining a suit.

The cab driver preaches to me through the busted partition – something about a change in the constitution of the EU and an impending tsunami of Eastern European immigrants. I nod and *mm-hm* my way through the cockney white noise but he chooses not to notice that my attention's diverted.

Haemorrhoids placated, my mind falls back on that other itch. There *was* something I wanted to talk to Mal about, wasn't there? I wanted to put him on the spot, get a straight answer from him about his involvement in the murders. And instead I got distracted by tequila and tits.

Probably I allowed myself to be distracted because I can't take Mal's involvement seriously – the whole idea is ridiculous. But what if it wasn't simply a distraction? What if, subconsciously, I'm avoiding the issue? Is there something about Mal, about his *character*, that makes me question his innocence?

Just before I get out of the taxi, I make the mistake of rubbing my eye with my fingertip. There must be a whisper of haemorrhoid cream left on my skin and it's still potent enough to induce tears with its menthol sting. I try to wipe away the substance with the back of my hand.

"You alright, mate?" The cabbie asks as I hand over my fare.

"Yeah. Fucking... something in my eye."

I pat the side of the vehicle and stagger half-blind to my front door. It's been a long cab ride since my last tipple and I'm starting to get that dehydrated, late-evening head-fuzz that's always a danger if you don't fully commit to your day drinking. This eye business isn't helping either.

First things first, I need a shower and I need to change.

No, *first* things *first*, I need a whisky before any headaches think about taking up residence.

Damming the flow of tears with the back of my hand, I pluck a bottle of Hyland from the booze cabinet in the lounge, unscrew the cap and take a swig as I climb the stairs to the bathroom. I dump my shirt, my tie and my jacket on the tiled floor and step out of my trousers. There's a sheen to my thighs where the cream has been absorbed and turned to oil. It thickens to a foamy paste around my underpants, which I drop to my ankles and kick across the room. For a moment, I stare at myself in the long mirror above the sink. I stand as I would normally stand, my bad posture sagging my chest into a small pair of pointed, witchy tits, which rest above a roll of fat that seems to have taken the place of my ribcage. Below that, my belly bulges, and then there's a false tan line created by the white *Bum Hero* paste. My cock hangs dark and limp in the shadow of my gut. I straighten my spine with my hands on my hips, push my shoulders back, but that doesn't do the trick anymore. My gut refuses to flatten the way it always used to. If the body is supposed to be a temple, then mine is an abandoned chicken shed, strewn with shit and feathers.

"What happened to you, you fat bastard?" I sigh to myself.

And then, I don't know why – perhaps to really solidify this moment of self-loathing – I take hold of the underside of one of my flabby little tits and I try to bring the nipple up to my lips. Just to see if it's possible. If it can be done. And when I realise that it can, I hesitate for a moment, then I stick out my tongue and lick the nipple. It's at exactly this instant, with a sea-breeze saltiness hitting my taste buds, that my eyes catch movement over my shoulder, a blurred shadow behind the shower curtain, and I start to turn, but before I can even cry out in surprise there's a couple of rough hands around my throat, and I'm thinking that this is the second time I've been attacked from behind in the space of a few days – and I can't remember being attacked from behind even once in my life before that. The hands wrap a piece of cord around my neck and then lock behind it and I can immediately feel all kinds of pressure in my temples and in my eyes. I'm getting flashes of pain in my chest. There's a pinch in my left armpit. My attacker yanks hard, almost lifts me off the floor, and I try to get my fingers underneath the wire but it's already too tight. There's a raspy, desperate wail coming from my mouth that I'm making no conscious effort to produce. I flail and punch but I can't get a good swing. I try throwing an elbow but their stomach is tensed and they probably take the impact without flinching. A whirlwind roars in my ears. I catch a glimpse of my attacker's wild eyes in the mirror. He's dark skinned. Wiry. With his thick, pinched brow and enormous hooked nose he looks like an Arab from an old Tintin comic. My heels slip on the tiles and the wire cuts deeper into my neck. A fart rips from my arse, inflicting stinging vibrations on my haemorrhoids, and Rätsel's words about victims of strangulation pop into my head – how they have a tendency to shit themselves. And then I can feel it, the need to *go*, and I'm close to the brink, and I have to clench *hard*. Suddenly I'm fighting a war on two fronts, top and bottom. It's more than I can take. I drop both hands, reach back between my legs, behind my tensed-up bollocks to my cheeks. I get my fingers wedged right up into the crack of my arse, right to the hole and it's knotted clusters of piles, and I collect big globs of whatever shit-tainted haemorrhoid cream there is left back there. Then I slap both hands over my shoulders, behind my head, stabbing my fingertips at those furious, wide-open eyes and I keep pushing when I feel the moist softness of them giving way.

My attacker howls and the cord immediately goes slack. I fall to my knees, barking air into my lungs as the figure behind me reels into the side of the bathtub.

"Fuck!" he shouts with a thick accent, flapping his arms, grabbing hold of the shower curtain to stop himself falling over. "Motherfucker!"

There's still no strength in my body and I scrabble across the floor to the shelf where I set down the whisky bottle. I pull myself up, take hold of the bottle by the neck, willing my legs to stop trembling so I can fight. The Arab barges straight past me, hands over his face, and runs down the stairs. I tumble down after him, follow him through the front door out onto the street, bottle of whisky raised above my head, and I'm trying to shout but my throat is closed up. My voice rattles behind my Adam's apple like a half-charged electric razor. The Arab pings into a lamppost, spins, rights himself and sprints away. Even blinded he's moving too quickly for me to catch him. I wheeze with my hands on my knees and watch him disappear around a corner.

Behind me I hear the slam of my front door, closed by a breeze, the catch snapping into place.

"Shit."

I take a swig of whisky, walk slowly round to my neighbour's house and knock on the door.

"Mrs Armitage," I whisper. "Mrs Armitage, it's Jim."

The door chain scrapes across and then a wedge of darkness opens. A pale, wrinkled face peers out. She looks me in the eye, looks down at my naked crotch, looks at the bottle of whisky in my hand, looks me in the eye once more.

"Oh, Jim," She says. "Not again."

She softly closes the door.

Two attacks. Two victories. And that second attack was serious. That was an attempt on my life right there. Just a few more seconds with the cord around my neck and that Arab would've had me. Right now, I'd be dead. He'd be positioning my body, probably placing my dick in my hand.

But I'm not dead. Against all odds, I beat that bastard. I'm a fucking *superhero*.

There's a spare key to my flat hidden under a rock in the backyard. The only problem is there's no back gate – I have to climb over the fence to get to it and I've let things slide a bit as far as garden maintenance goes. A six-foot barrier of brambles lies between me and my property. I pull up a wheelie bin and climb aboard, denting the green plastic lid with my weight, and I rise unsteadily to meet the weak, trellised fence. After another swig of whisky, I hurl the bottle onto what used to be a lawn but is now eleven square feet of dandelion and burdock, then I grab the shaking trellis with both hands and swing a leg over. You don't realise how much protection a thin piece of material affords you until your genitals are pressed against untreated wood, when all of your upper body bears down on that splintered apex and presses it into the loose folds of your scrotum. Grunting, I slide the other leg over and drop shrieking into the tangled mass of weeds, the inside of my thighs grazed by the fence. Thorns prick my tender flab and rip bloody holes in it as I pull myself out of the thicket. The skin on my legs is mottled red and white like sliced salami.

I retrieve the whisky and the key and I open the patio door onto the lounge, which is filled with a sort of radioactive afterglow. A psychic residue of violent energy. Everything is more or less as it was when I left this morning but it all feels more *intense* somehow. The sofa, the TV, the half-dead fern in its terracotta pot – they all sit silently, nervously, unable to look me in the eye. My furniture is in shock.

The broken skin around my neck throbs. My throat still feels half closed. I take a cigarette from an open packet on the coffee table and light it, grab a bag of ice from the freezer, put a couple of chunks in a glass with some vodka and grapefruit juice, hold the rest of the ice against my neck and take a seat on the traumatised sofa.

I watch white ribbons untwisting from the end of the cigarette. Smoking does little to slow the exuberant rhythms of my heart. Likewise, finishing my vodka and grapefruit juice. I think about having that shower but at the moment the prospect of ruining more clothes is preferable to revisiting the scene of the crime. It's a strange feeling, climbing the stairs, walking past the bathroom vacated by carnage. It isn't terror that makes me tremble. Not quite. It's the proximity of death. The parallel universe in which I failed to survive is still close by, hanging between the veils of reality, but the escalation of events is already surging forward in that other dimension. The flies are laying their eggs. Enzymes, no longer kept in check, are breaking down tissues and fats and skin. Acid bursts through the stomach wall, corroding my guts and my muscle. My eyeballs suppurate, boiling with microbes, oozing down the parchment skin of my collapsing cheeks…

I close the bathroom door.

Across the landing, my bedroom carries the same tense energy as the rest of the house. Unnerved, I dress quickly, in clothes from the darkest recesses of my wardrobe – a limp, brown suit I never thought I'd wear again, and a creased, canary yellow shirt. The sensible thing to do would be to call the police, but I can't face the stress of it right now. The questions. Rätsel would twist the situation anyway. He'd have an angle. The prospect of a nice pint, taken while surrounded by friendly bar-folk is far more appealing. I check my watch and note that there's still an hour or so left until Barry calls last orders at *The Oath*. I'm collecting my keys and my wallet and readying myself to depart when a memory of my last visit to *The Oath* sneaks to the front of my mind.

Gerald the Farmer.

Cricket.

Ireland versus Zimbabwe.

Stilted conversation.

Drone strikes.

Terrorists.

Islam.

"You used to make dirty pictures, didn't you? I mean, what do you reckon the Taliban would think of that?"

Not that I get invited to many dinner parties: Blue's apartment is exactly what I'd hoped it would be, a quilted palace of femininity and comfort. The air is warm and scented with herbs and dry petals. The décor is minimal, but not that hard-edged kind of minimal that makes you feel like you can't sit down. There are lots of alcoves and lots of shelves, lots of cute little side tables, spaces that would be occupied by ashtrays and half-filled glasses and folded newspapers in my gaff. Here they're smartly appointed, with a long-necked vase here and a wooden bowl of potpourri there.

I'm sprawled on a cream sofa with a glass of red in my hand. Blue doesn't have any spirits but she has plenty of wine. Good wine, at that.

When she first saw the burnt ligature marks around my throat and heard the croak of my voice, I had to fight her not to call the police. They aren't on my side, I told her. I'll talk to them when it's absolutely necessary.

She was having a dinner party when I called and, from the way she's dressed in a long backless gown, I can tell it was an important occasion. I don't understand what goes into hair, what women do for those hours they lose in the bedroom before they leave the house, but the fine ripples and plaits in Blue's pinned-up doo must have taken some effort to arrange. I almost feel bad that it's wasted on me. I'd be happy with the way Blue looked if she didn't work her hair at all, or if she pigtailed it, or even if she had a back-and-sides dyke-cut, with the boots and dungarees to match. Before I arrived, she cleared out all her friends, and now she's removing plates with half-eaten desserts on them, carrying them through to the kitchen, as I sip my wine.

"You really think this is all because of terrorism?" She calls out over the sound of a knife scraping food into a bin.

"What else could it be? An Arab, a *Muslim*, just tried to kill me. The same Arab was almost certainly responsible for the deaths of Al, Keith and Dane. Guys that worked in porn. Guys that made money from *sex* and *naked women*. It's a fucking terrorist plot! Of course it is! There's nothing an Islamic fundamentalist hates more than a great big set of norks, is there? Now that I think about it, I'm amazed it hasn't happened sooner... that one of the smut factories in LA hasn't been parcel-bombed before now. It isn't just the Muslims that are capable of that kind of action either – think about those abortion clinics that get attacked by Christian fundamentalists. We should all have twenty-four-hour protection!"

"What about your friend?" she pokes her head out of the kitchen doorway. "The one you brought to Eddie's. You said the police were looking into him."

"I was thinking about that on the way over here. I was thinking about it *a lot*. And I remembered something. Mal doesn't talk about his past much, but I remember him telling me that one of his parents was an Arab. Or Persian. Something along those lines. I'm pretty sure it was his mum. And he *is* quite dark featured when you think about it."

"His hair is white."

"Yes, but it's that kind of *bright* white you only get if your hair used to be very dark."

"So you think he's a terrorist?"

"It's the only thing that makes any sense. I've been trying to think of a motive for Mal's involvement ever since Rätsel put him forward as a suspect – hey, is there any more of that wine?"

Blue brings the bottle over and fills my glass.

"It's the only thing that fits, Blue. It's so unexpected, it has to be true."

"He really, really doesn't seem like the type. When you two came to the club the other night he was very far gone, maybe even more drunk than you – and that's saying something, honey."

"Mal's quite a lush, I'll give you that. But sometimes these Muslims go deep undercover. I've read about it. I've *written* about it. They lead the kind of lifestyle that, deep down, disgusts them, seeing it as a kind of perverse penance. Some of them do it for years and they do it just to deflect attention from themselves. To make themselves the *last* person you'd expect to be a terrorist. And if it's the *last* person you'd expect to be a terrorist that you're looking for, well, then Mal starts to fit the bill."

Blue begins to sit down in the armchair opposite, but I make room on the sofa, sitting upright, and I pat the cushion next to me. She comes over.

"You've known him how long?" she asks.

"I've been working for him on and off since I stopped working with you."

"So about twenty years. And you think he's been putting up a front all that time?"

"I'm not saying that it isn't a stretch to think of Mal as some kind of... Taliban crusader. But if he's involved in this – and the more I think about it, the more I realise he *must* be involved – then it's the only conceivable explanation."

Blue pulls her skirt up past her knees, tucks her feet under herself and sips some wine thoughtfully.

"If he's been a terrorist for twenty years, why hasn't he done anything before now?"

"Who says he hasn't? It wasn't Mal that attacked me today, was it? This guy's worth hundreds of millions of pounds. He'll be bankrolling the operation, pulling the strings from a safe distance. These terrorist groups always need someone to finance them, don't they? They won't want Mal getting his hands dirty, putting their money at risk. I bet this thing goes much deeper than we can even begin to imagine."

Then I remember that there's something else.

"There's something else," I say. "Oh fuck, there's definitely something else."

"What?"

"Earlier today. Mal... I thought he was just... oh that fucking *bastard!*"

"What? What is it?"

"I heard him on the phone. I wasn't eavesdropping, it's just his voice is so loud..."

"Jimmy, *what happened?*"

"I went to his agency to see him and I was waiting for him in his... er... atrium... and the door to his office was open, and I thought he was just angry with someone about a campaign, or a client or... I don't know... something to do with the business. But I think he was arranging a hit. *My* hit. He was telling someone to *kill* me, Blue."

"Are you sure about that?"

"Think about what's just happened to me. I hear Mal saying he wants me taken care of, then, a few hours later, someone tries to *take care of me.* That's no coincidence! And it was the look on his face when he saw that I'd overheard him... He looked like he'd been caught... doing something he shouldn't."

"Okay. Suppose Mal is involved, and that this *is* terrorism – why are these terrorists choosing to attack people that *used* to work in porn? Wouldn't it make more of a statement if they just bombed a studio that was still operating?"

"Hmm... You've got me there."

"And that's another thing... why have they been murdering people silently, making it look accidental, rather than using something like a bomb? Surely the whole point of terrorism is to *terrify* people – to get maximum exposure for your cause."

Blue rests a hand on my thigh, squeezing gently. I place my hand on top of hers.

"Jimmy, you really need to go to the police with this," she says. "It sounds like they know a lot more than they're telling you. If Mal *is* a terrorist, they probably already have people watching him."

"Okay. But I can't deal with that bastard Rätsel right now. I'll talk to the police tomorrow. It's been a long day. My first thought, when I realised what's going on, was to make sure you're safe."

"I'm safe, Jimmy. Thank you."

She squeezes my thigh again.

"If you don't mind, I'd like to sleep here tonight," I say. "On the sofa. Or the floor. Just to make sure nothing happens to you."

"That'd be nice. And I think, after what happened to you today, you could probably use some company too."

I smile and finish my glass. Blue starts to get up but I stop her with a hand on her knee.

"No, no," I say, standing. "I'll get it."

"That one's empty," she says as I walk towards the bottle on the dining room table. "There's a nice bottle of Malbec in the rack above the kitchen sink. Bottle opener's in the drawer next to the fridge."

Blue puts on some music, something jazzy, a female voice that's slow and quiet and vaguely melancholy, and we sit together on the sofa, and we finish the bottle of wine. Well, I suppose I finish it and Blue helps. We open another and I finish that too as we fill each other in on what we've been doing with our lives during the intervening years.

Blue tells me how she's followed my career. She knows about my journalism awards, used to read my weekly column during that two-year period when I managed to write one. She even has a copy of my coffee table book, *Inn Vogue*, a photographic pub-crawl of the most unique boozers in Britain. She pulls it from a drawer and places it in my lap to prove that she owns it.

I tell her I've quietly been keeping tabs too, that I never watched any of the movies she made after I quit the business (a white lie) but I know every title. I tell her I had a little celebration when I found out she'd finally moved on from porn.

When I ask Blue if she'd like a fag, she tells me I have to smoke out on the balcony. I'm slow to my feet, reluctant to leave her, but she stands too.

"Mind if I cadge one?" she says.

It's cold outside and it looks like it's just been raining despite a lack of clouds, the infinite majesty of the universe unable to compete with a mustard glaze of light pollution. Puddles reflect streetlights on the tarmac below. When I lean on the railing, I soak my hands and the cuffs of my shirt. Blue takes one of my fags, holds it between her lips, and wraps a shawl around herself while I light it for her.

"Twenty years," she says, exhaling smoke. "You say you kept tabs. How come you never got in touch?"

I hesitate and stare at the shadowed office block across the street while I light my own fag, my mind working on an answer. The obvious response would be to fire back the same question but Blue answers it for me after another long exhalation of smoke.

"I waited for *you* to call but I never felt like I could get in touch with you myself."

"You didn't?"

"Jimmy, you're so successful!" she says, beaming. "I'm so proud of what you've made of your life. I never wanted you to think I was trying to use you in any way."

"I'd never think that."

"You were always going to do well. I knew that. But it happened so suddenly. You just… left. I suppose given the opportunity I'd have done the same thing."

She links her arm through mine and leans her head on my shoulder.

"We were in totally different situations," I say. "What I did… what you did… Christ, I just held the camera. I don't feel sorry for myself. Not after what I saw you subject yourself to."

"I knew what I was doing."

"Yes, you certainly did. *That* I never doubted. The thing is you were doing it for a reason. You *really* needed the money. All that trouble with your family... it must've seemed like your only option."

"And you *didn't* need the money?"

"Everybody needs money, but I could've earned mine doing something else. I didn't need to work in porn, not in the same way you needed to."

Now she puts her arm underneath my jacket and around my waist. I can feel the chill of her bare skin through my shirt. It makes me think about the last bloke Blue took to bed, probably with abs of granite, certainly with a physique more solid than my own pudding-gut. I try tensing but through all those layers of blubber it's a futile gesture.

"I got into photography when I was a teenager," I say, "My grandpa gave me this old SLR for my birthday, along with a box full of black and white film. My dad bought me a book about professional photography. And something... clicked, I suppose. No pun intended."

"Ha."

"It made sense to me, in a way that none of my school subjects ever did. So, when I finished school I took an art course and specialised in photography. Started building up a portfolio. And then I saw this advert in a local rag, a photographer wanted for a one-off job. That's how I met Dane Biggerman."

Blue shudders when I say his name.

"The following weekend I had my first porn shoot. A lone girl baring everything for an eight-page spread in *Grunters.*"

"Yeah," Blue nods. "That's how Dane started everybody out."

"The thing is, Blue, I was eighteen. Inexperienced. At that point in my life, I'd had sex a couple of times – with a couple of absolute brawlers, if I'm honest. Here I was, spending time with gorgeous women, replicating every sexual position you can name and getting my lens so close I could smell their sweat... *And* I was getting *paid*. It was the dream job."

Blue turns her head, gives me a hard stare.

"I'm under no illusions about you, you know. You weren't that different from the other letches working behind the scenes. But you were honest, at least. And you had a charm. We always got on, didn't we? Right from the start."

"It was meeting you that changed my attitude to the whole enterprise. Until then, I hadn't really talked to any of the girls. Not properly. I directed them, got them into the right positions, but I never got to know them. And even when you and I became friends I didn't feel too bad because you dealt with it all so well. You were fearless."

"I had to be that way. If I'd been anything else the business would've consumed me."

A frozen gale blows through the gorge of high rises and we both shiver and suck air through our teeth. Blue takes one last puff from her cigarette, flicks the butt out into the night. It glows brightly for an instant and wheels down to the street, sparks scattered by the wind. I throw mine, half-smoked, over the railing to join it. Blue slides back the glass door and I follow her inside, closing the door and the heavy curtains behind me. We take our places back on the couch. Blue sits closer this time, leaning into me. I try not to breathe too noisily as I take in her scent, the sickly-sweetness of cocoa butter tempered by a tang of tobacco.

"Shame started creeping in the more I got to know you," I say. "I didn't enjoy the job anymore. I suppose I'd seen so many vaginas that the novelty was gone. And then…"

I think about telling her the real reason I left, the final moment that turned me away from porn for good. But I can't quite get the words out. And there's a horrible part of me that sees the way this night is going, reading Blue's gentle touches and suggestive, sleepy-eyed glances, and that horrible part of me doesn't want to bring up anything emotional because it thinks it might get in the way of a potential shag.

"And then Mal offered me some work," I say. "And I took it. Simple as that."

Blue looks at me for a long time, half smiling as if she knows I haven't given her the whole story, then she yawns into the back of her hand.

"I'm tired," she says. "I think we should go to bed."

"So do I," I say, unable to suppress a fat grin.

But watching Blue rise from the sofa, watching the shift of her arse beneath her skirt as she transfers weight from one foot to the other, the horror of what's about to unfold suddenly becomes apparent and a hailstorm of insecurities swirls around me. It's a moment I've simultaneously fantasised about and dreaded for a very long time. There's nothing more daunting than exposing your normal-sized cock to a woman who's faced a regiment of men with a nine-inch batting average. It's impossible not to picture all the other cocks that she's seen before, of every size, shape and colour. And that's not the biggest worry – far from it. Christ, the state of my arse. The smell of it. The haemorrhoids. The toxic cream.

My cock.

My gut.

My wretched arsehole.

My whole body has been conspiring against me for years, corrupting itself in preparation for this humiliating episode. This moment should be pure. *Ecstatic*. And I feel nothing but the most exquisite terror. As for that supersonic boner I've been getting in Blue's presence recently... nothing. Not a hope. I'm about as hard as Italian meringue.

None of this is going to stop me from trying, of course. That base, evolutionary impulse overrules any and all insecurities.

I clamber up from the couch so that I'm facing Blue, place a hand on her neck, running my thumb along her jaw, and pull her towards me for a kiss. For a second, she allows it, perhaps she even kisses back, but then she pushes away with a pained expression on her face that could easily be misread as disgust.

"Jimmy..." she says. "I... er... When I said we should go to bed I meant... separately."

"Oh fuck," I say, and sit back down with my face in my hands. "Of course you did."

"I'm not saying there isn't a... connection... between us. It's always been there. But you've changed. That charm I was talking about... I still see traces of it. But mostly you're too drunk to have a proper conversation. And I don't have room in my life for another destructive personality."

Blue turns and walks into her bedroom, where I hear her opening and closing a drawer, then she comes back into the lounge and places a pile of blankets and a pillow on the couch next to me.

"Night Jimmy," she says and kisses the top of my head.

I finally raise my eyes from behind my fingers and watch the perfect sway of Blue's arse as it disappears into the bedroom, her skirt embossed by the frilled edges of her panties.

And there it is, that supersonic boner, back with a vengeance.

Saturday

Flight risk: When I wake up, I've got a headache and furred teeth and I have to roll my tongue and suck on it for half a minute before I can draw any kind of moisture into my mouth. Blue is in the kitchen, dealing with the washing up and gently putting away the dishes so she doesn't disturb me.

"It's okay," I shout. "I'm up. You don't need to tiptoe around in there."

I hear the click of a switch, then the roar of a kettle quickly coming to the boil, then the click of it turning off again. It must be one of those coiled, futuristic jobs that can fix you a brew in five seconds. She appears with two steaming mugs of tea, holding one out for me to take. My head shrieks as I sit up to accept it. The tea trembles in my hand and I take a quick sip before it spills.

"Oh… lovely," I say, gasping. "This is just what I need."

I'm lying, of course. A bloody Mary is just what I need. An espresso martini is just what I need. I'd even take a piña colada.

"Looks sore," Blue says between sips, nodding at my neck over the top of her own mug.

"Now that you mention it…" I wince. I'd been distracted by the headache but now I can feel the burnt skin cracking when I twist my neck, fissures of raw flesh opening along the scar. A crazed itch bursts from the thorn-pricks on my legs – a suitable accompaniment to the itch that's gradually returning to my arse.

"Are you going to talk to the police today?"

"I know I should…" I say.

Blue frowns.

"And I will," I continue. "But I'm thinking about getting out of here for a while, until this terrorism business sorts itself out."

"Getting out of where? Out of London?"

"Out of the country. There are always jobs abroad in my line of work. I could hide out in a jungle for a couple of months. Or on a beach."

"You're going to run away?"

I shrug, then I nod.

"You should come with me," I say. "I'm serious. If I'm right about this, then you're in just as much danger as me. Women and children are fair game for these religious nutjobs."

"I can't leave. Not without notice. I have a job. One that pays very well."

"A job's no good to you if you're dead."

"Please promise me you'll go to the police before you make any plans to disappear."

I nod.

"And Jimmy? Try to stay off the booze today, okay? This is all getting very serious. You need to be able to think clearly."

"You're right. I'll be sensible."

I take a long gulp of the tea and the heat soothes my headache.

"What are your plans?" I ask.

"I'm working at Eddie's tonight. Nothing until then."

"In that case, I don't want you to take any chances. Lock yourself inside this flat and keep the doors and windows bolted. Any problems, I have my phone. I'll talk to the police and when they hear what I have to say I reckon they'll sort out some kind of protection detail for you. But first, I need to go home. Have a shower. Change my clothes. Pack."

Blue frowns.

"Whatever happens today," I say. "I'm leaving this mess behind until somebody else clears it up. I can't force you to join me, but hopefully by talking to the rozzers I can get you enough protection that you won't need to worry."

Blue leans down and kisses my forehead.

"Be careful," she says.

She gives me the number for a minicab firm, then leaves me to wait for the taxi while she has a shower. I finish my tea, gather my clothes, and let myself out. There's a minimart on the ground floor of Blue's apartment block and I nip inside to grab a packet of fags and a half-bottle of vodka, which I transfer to my hip flask. Blue's right, I do need to think clearly today. But there's no way I can think clearly with a hungover smog behind my eyes. Have you ever had one of those moments when you go to write a familiar word like 'gentle' or 'already' or 'else', and suddenly you can't remember how to put the letters in the correct order? A sort of temporary dyslexia. That's the state of mind a hangover puts me in, if left un-remedied. Except in a hangover, this isn't a five second brain fart we're talking about – it's a full day of mental flatulence. And it isn't spelling that's the problem, it's crossing the road without getting hit by a car, or remembering to put your cock back in your trousers after you've had a piss.

Booze is a necessity.

I'm a third of the way into the half-bottle by the time my cab arrives, nicely topped up. Ready for anything.

Sport-obsessed wankers: "Forsyth, Whiteley and Holness."

"Beverly Holness, please," I say.

"One moment."

Hold music, cheap and electronic. The amount of money my agent siphons from my earnings you'd think she could afford some strings. This is why I normally wait for *her* to call *me*.

"Good morning, you're through to Liam. How can I help?"

"Liam, it's Jim. I need to speak to Bev immediately."

"Oh, *Jim!* It's been *yonks!* How *are* you?"

Liam's transparently insincere enthusiasm is another reason I rarely make this call.

"Fine, Liam. Could you put me through to Bev, please."

"Hmmm... Might be *tricky*. She's got quite a *lot* on her plate today. Let me just see if she's available to speak to you."

"She is."

"Excuse me?"

"She is available to speak to me, Liam. You're her personal assistant. You'd already know if she wasn't available, otherwise you'd be terrible at your job and Bev wouldn't have kept you in employment for the last two years. What you're really about to do is check whether or not she *wants* to speak to me. And she does. Believe me."

"Woah! Steady on there, Jim! Ah ha ha *ha*. You are *such* a card. Give me a mo and I'll put you through."

I'm stuck on hold again, no doubt while Bev berates Liam for allowing me to talk my way round him.

"Good morning, James," I hear, eventually. "What an unexpected *joy*. You're halfway through your first bottle by now, I presume?"

"Beverly, my sweet–"

"Ah, I see. You're already on your *second*. Are you calling to tell me how much you love me? Because *that's* a call I've been waiting on for a *long* time."

"Beverly…"

"Yes, darling?"

"Remember that shoot you phoned me about, the one Down Under?"

"As a matter of fact, I do."

"Is the job still available?"

"Well, I would have thought so yes, but I'll have to check."

"I've changed my mind."

"You've changed your mind, James?"

"I'd like to take the work."

"Correct me if I'm wrong, but didn't you tell me that Australia was a cultural vacuum, populated by sport-obsessed *wankers* and there wasn't a chance in hell I could get you to set foot in the country?"

"Did I really say that?"

"And more besides. You went on *quite* the tirade. Spiders, snakes, crocodiles, jellyfish… You basically accused me of attempting to murder you by sending you to the most toxic environment on earth. So, pray tell, what has changed?"

"I just feel like a holiday. Do you know how long it's been since I had a holiday?"

"I am sure every day is a holiday to you, dear."

"What sort of compensation are they offering?"

"Off the top of my head… as well as your usual fee, they'll cover your expenses, including five-star accommodation and business class return airfare."

"Not too shabby."

"Indeed. And maybe you could take a couple of weeks rest afterwards. Dodge the deadly flora and fauna long enough to see the sights – or lack thereof."

"Who's it for again?"

"My god, James. Could you at least *pretend* to take an interest in your own career? Were you really about to take on a job without knowing who the client is?

"I'm asking now, aren't I?"

"The shoot is for *Piston*. They're an upmarket high street chain. It's for their autumn/winter collection."

"Well that doesn't sound too hard, does it?"

"Precisely my point the *first* time I tried to book you for the job. Forgive me if I'm being rude, but you're slurring a bit. A *lot*, actually. I don't want to put you forward for this work, only for you to come off your latest *bender* and change your mind again. I need some commitment from you."

"Bev, trust me. I'm committed."

"I'll be calling you tomorrow to make sure. I'd rather hear all this from you when you're sober – if a sober James Stakes is even *possible*."

"Tomorrow I'll already be in Oz."

"You'll *what?*"

"I'm going home now to pack a suitcase and I'll be getting a taxi to the airport later on today. No buggering about."

"This job doesn't start for another *five weeks*. I haven't even officially *confirmed* it for you yet. Besides, you already have *other* commitments."

"I'll have to put them on hold."

"You *can't* bloody well put them on hold. What about the Satnav thing Mallory wants you to do?"

"Me and Mal have fallen out."

"*What?* When did you– What do you *mean* you have fallen out?"

"We've fallen out."

"Then you'd better *un*-fall out! Mallory Haines accounts for nearly seventy percent of your income."

"He does?"

"Yes! For Christ's sake, are you really that oblivious to the minutiae of your professional life? When did this *falling out* happen?"

"Yesterday, I suppose."

"And how bad a falling out are we talking?"

"Bad enough for me to need to go to Australia *right now.*"

The phone crackles with static as Bev sighs into it.

"Do me a *huge* favour, James," she says. "Sober up. Have a nap. Wait until the alcohol has worn off before you do anything drastic."

"You don't understand Bev. It isn't safe for me here. Mal wants me *dead.*"

She sighs again.

"Of course he does."

And with that she slams down the phone.

A tale of two princesses: There's a sizeable supermarket one street over from my gaff. I get the cabbie to drop me outside then head straight to the back of the store, to the Home & Garden aisle, with the intention of arming myself. The closest thing to a weapon I can find is a pair of hedge clippers, so I take them to the checkout and pick up a bottle of Polish vodka on the way.

Outside my pad, I open the clippers and, holding one handle, stamp on the other to snap them into a couple of blunt knives. I swig the vodka for courage, put the bottle on the front step, lean my face against the front door, breathe deeply, hold my breath, and listen for any movement inside. I pull my key from my pocket and attempt to unlock the door but refuelling an aircraft at 10,000 feet would be simpler. Christ, I really am topped up. The lock flirts with my key, leading it on. Just as the key thinks it's in with a chance, the lock – that tease – pulls away. I get down low, bring my eye alongside the key, slip it into the lock and turn it. I breathe deeply again, decide I need another swig for courage, put one hand on the door handle, raise the other above my head, grasping one of the blades tightly. I take in one more deep breath, throw open the door and roar into the darkness that greets me.

The flat feels empty.

But didn't it feel empty just before I was attacked?

How does a flat *feel* empty anyway?

I search all the rooms, turn on lights one by one, open closets and laundry hampers, my hands shaking all the time. I even check the inside of the tumble dryer.

There's nobody here. I'm safe.

I put the broken clippers down on the coffee table in the lounge and, after making sure all doors and windows are secure, I pull a heavy trunk off the top of the wardrobe in my bedroom, unsettling a thick layer of dust that sets me off on a sneezing fit. I'm a serial multi-sneezer. If I sneeze once, I'm sneezing five times. And each of these sneezes is like a dagger to my frontal lobe, bringing the headache back into play.

The trunk is your classic leather-handled travel case, so it doesn't give much leeway when you try to close it up. You're forced to pack light. I hastily stuff in towels, shirts, suits, a great big ball of underpants and socks, and a couple of ties. I don't take the time to fold or roll anything, don't distinguish between clean or dirty – I'll pay the hotel to wash and iron my clothes when I get wherever it is that I'm going. I snap the heavy brass clasps shut and heave the trunk downstairs.

Then I call Rätsel. I tell him I need to see him and he says he can be here within the hour.

With that done, I decide it's time to get in the holiday mood, treating my anus to a thorough application of *Bum Hero!* before mixing a cocktail.

I retrieve the vodka from the front step, put it in the freezer, swapping it for another bottle of vodka that's already ice-cold. After rinsing a martini glass with dry vermouth, I pour in what I estimate to be two measures of vodka. There are lemons in the fridge but when I open the door I recoil at the roiling stink of something rich and meaty that's been neglected far beyond its use-by date. I slam the door shut before it makes me puke. Ready-squeezed lime juice will have to do as a substitute. After a stir and a quick taste I decide the cocktail is delicious, knock it back by the sink, pour myself a bigger one and take that through to the lounge.

I flop down on the sofa, put my feet on the coffee table and hit the big red power button on the universal remote. Everything electronic in my flat is kept on stand-by. For convenience, obviously. Those Greenpeace wonks might as well accept that the mass population isn't going to give up their conveniences for the sake of a couple of degrees Celsius. The ice caps are done for. It's not my fault polar bears can't adapt to a changing climate. Things are *supposed* to become extinct, anyway. Survival of the fittest – it's nature's defining principle. Hippies are so hypocritical. You can't say you're at one with nature and then ignore its defining principle.

The TV wakes up and the prehistoric roar of people fucking blasts from the surround sound before the picture has fully faded in.

"Shit shit shit shit shit!"

I hammer the volume control with my thumb, worried about poor Mrs Armitage next door. What that old bat must think of me! The Beeb must be feeling ballsy, broadcasting a show with that kind of racket before the watershed.

Sound muted, I watch the screen, the figures on it, their motions and moans repeated in a 30-second cycle. Realisation squirms its way out of the dark pit of my subconscious. The skin tightens at my hairline and a cold sweat beads my skin.

Alan Girth. There he is, enormous cock waving vigorously like one of those inflatable dancing tube-men they use to advertise secondhand car showrooms. This isn't *Homes Under the Hammer*. The TV is tuned to the second AV channel – the DVD player. And I'm looking at a DVD menu screen. In fact, I'm looking at the calling card of a serial killer.

The movie was called *The Persian Princess*. No jolly puns, no humour, although the name does have a fairytale quality to it. A fairytale quality that belies the nastiness and depravity of what we filmed. As far as the shoots I was involved in go, it was one of the worst. Brutal. A rape picture. It's a depressingly popular genre. There are plenty of pervs out there that get their kicks from simulated rape.

These films have a typical structure. In reality the starlet consents, of course, but in the movie she acts like she doesn't. And then she's supposed to start enjoying it about two-thirds of the way through, so that by the end she's the one in control and on top. Concluding the film that way is supposed to go some way towards absolving guilt and washing the bad taste from a viewer's mouth.

But *The Persian Princess* was different. It was all about humiliation from beginning to end. Again, the starlet consented to what would take place, but she must have been pretty desperate to agree to the terms of this performance. Dane loomed over the production right from the start, took more of a personal interest than usual. He stayed at the studio to view every scene as it was performed, leering from behind the director's monitor.

In the movie, Al plays a nineteenth-century British soldier, shown hospitality by a Persian king as he journeys across the deserts of the Middle East. Al takes a shine to one of the king's daughters and sneaks into her room once everyone else is asleep. When she refuses his advances, he bullies her, strips her, beats her and rapes her. The princess's jealous sister catches the soldier in the act but instead of helping the princess, she gleefully joins in with the assault, holding her down. At the movie's climax, she produces a gem-encrusted strap-on to sodomise her sister with, while the soldier rams his cock down her sister's throat. The picture goes on for an hour. For anyone other than its niche intended audience, it's a tough watch.

As far as I know, the princess was a genuine Persian, certainly ethnic. She looked the part, with dark hair and brown skin and huge eyes that had a seductive, oriental slant. When she spoke, which wasn't often, her English was heavily accented. After the shoot, I never saw her again. Never saw her before, either. She was too much of a unique beauty to stay under Dane's wing for long and was probably snapped up by one of the big filth studios in LA.

The starlet playing the princess' sister wasn't quite so authentic, however. In a black wig and brown stage make-up, Blue wasn't disguised particularly well, but she was enough of a draw with her fan base that it didn't matter, and she could wield a bejewelled strap-on like nobody's business.

It's a message. *The Persian Princess*, the reason they're doing all of this. And it fits. Perhaps Al signed our *fatwās* just by ripping off the girl's hijab, but I bet the lesbianism, the incest and the buggery didn't help either. There's no doubt in my mind that if my Arabic assailant had done his job properly, I would've been found naked on this couch, a cord wrapped around my throat, my lifeless eyes staring at the horror of my own work, looped for eternity on the TV in front of me. There's no doubt in my mind, either, that that's how they found Alan and Keith and Dane.

The DVD credits only confirm my suspicions.

Sound recording and editing: Keith Rumbold.

Ah, yes, that's the fella: "Crikey!" Rätsel says when I open the door. "I don't suppose I need to ask what happened to you!"

I don't say anything, letting him follow me back into the lounge.

"Did that happen here?" he asks, pointing with a pen at the scar on my neck.

"Upstairs. In the bathroom."

"You should have called 999. They'd have made it here a lot quicker than I did."

"It happened last night."

"*Last night?* Why the hell has it taken you so long to report it?"

"I wanted to relax and come to terms with what happened in my own time, without having to deal with your shit," I say. "I couldn't face your smug presumptions."

He looks at me without blinking, then takes a seat in the hard-backed chair opposite.

"Why don't you fill me in on what took place," he says.

I tell him everything. The strangling. The nude ruckus. His little black eyes flick between his notepad and my gaze as he scribbles. He still doesn't blink.

"What did he look like, your assailant?"

"Sort of Arabic, would be my best description."

"Arabic?" Rätsel frowns. "What makes you say that? Was he dressed like an Arab?"

"No... I don't think so. Now that you mention it, I'm not sure what he was wearing. Nothing unusual."

"No dishdasha?"

"No."

"Turban?"

I shake my head.

"What was so *Arab* about him, then?"

"Dark skin, dark hair, big nose – he looked like an Arab. What more can I say?"

Rätsel shrugs.

"And you say you overheard Mallory Haines instructing someone to kill you, is that right?"

"That was yesterday as well, before I was attacked."

"Yet you still didn't get in touch with the police?"

"I didn't know what he was referring to at the time. I thought it might've been work-related. I actually ended up going on a bit of a drinking session with him afterwards…"

Rätsel laughs. It's a humourless sound, like an axe striking a tree in an empty forest.

"What exactly did Mallory Haines say that was so incriminating?" he asks.

"I can't remember the specifics."

"Of course not. I'm sure you'd already had a couple by that point."

"The basic *gist* was that he couldn't kill me himself because you guys, the police, were sniffing around his business. So he told whoever was on the other end of the line to handle it."

"Then this morning you changed your mind and decided you *did* want to involve the police. Why was that?"

"A friend of mine, a woman named Blue Darling–"

"Now that's a pornstar's name if ever I've heard one!"

"She's a *target*. I tried to warn her last night… only she wouldn't take me seriously."

"Ah! Sounds like a sensible lady," he nods approvingly. "What makes you think she's a target?"

"She was as much a part of that industry as anyone else. There's every reason to think she could be under threat."

"I suppose that makes some sense – except for the fact that all the victims so far have been male."

"That doesn't mean a great deal. Almost everybody working behind the scenes in porn is male. It might just be that the murderers haven't got round to slaughtering any females yet."

Rätsel concedes the point with a shrug.

"There's something else," I say. "There's a film called The Persian Princess, it's about twenty years old, and as far as I can tell it's the only thing that directly connects Al, Dane, Keith and myself. Blue is in it too."

Rätsel makes a long note, taps the pen against his chin, writes something else.

"Well," he says eventually. "I can see the connection between Mallory Haines, Mr Rumbold, Mr Girth and yourself. At some point Mallory has employed each of you. But I can't find any connection between him and Mr Biggerman, and I can't see any motive for the murders."

"Terrorism," I tell him.

The word exhausts Rätsel's patience. His head drops. He runs his thumb and middle finger along his eyebrows so that they meet at the bridge of his nose, then he sighs.

"Terrorism," he repeats, quietly and sarcastically, looking down at the floor.

"Listen to me, Rätsel. The guy that attacked me was an Arab. The video that links all the victims together is about the rape and humiliation of a *Persian* princess. Muslims hate porn – they hate *sex* – so imagine what they think about porn with actual Muslims in it."

"And how does Mallory Haines tie into this *terrorism* theory of yours?"

"One of his parents was from the Middle East."

Rätsel squints, rubs his eyebrows again and closes his notebook.

"Look, you've given me a lot of information here. The terrorism thing... it's a stretch, but there's still enough for me to bring in Mallory

Haines and ask him a few more questions. To be able to do that I'm going to need you to go on record. Get everything you know on tape."

"Okay. What about Blue?"

"If you come to the station with me now, I'll put a car with a couple of uniforms in it outside her house."

"Can you do that now?"

"Are you going to come to the station?"

I nod.

"Then I'll make the call."

Rätsel puts me in the same interview room as before and sends in a female detective to take my statement while he goes to collect Mal. She's about my age, fairly plain-looking, with a sturdy body in a tight-fitting grey trouser suit. No make-up. Brown hair, long and straight. She takes off her jacket when she sits down, revealing a short-sleeved shirt and biceps that'd make the average man balk at an arm wrestle. She doesn't say much beyond offering me water and stating the date and time of the interview. There's a constant surliness to her demeanour, which I put down to her thinking there are much more important things she could be doing with her time.

The lack of access to alcohol during the interview sees my hangover reassert itself. A headache thrums patiently behind my eyeballs. My body temperature fluctuates between summer in Hong Kong and winter in Franz Josef Land. I have to grip the edge of the table firmly to stop my hands from shaking and even then, I can see boisterous ripples forming on the surface of my glass of water, as if there's a t-rex practicing ballet in the next room.

The detective leads me through each step, revisits all the old connections. The mucky trade I used to ply. She moves onto Mal, and I talk about our relationship, covering everything from our first meeting at my art college to globetrotting ad shoots and dusk-till-dawn benders, finishing with the recent violence and the telephone conversation I overheard. I gulp water throughout the interview in a bid to stave off the morning fog, but it continues to roll in regardless.

After about an hour-and-a-half Rätsel comes back. He curtly sends the other detective out of the room, takes her seat and glares at me, his face red, his moustache quivering as his jaw clenches and unclenches.

"Terrorism," he hisses eventually, shaking his head.

I flinch, then I pick up my water, trying to make it look like the flinch was just part of a jerky but intentional movement.

"You are just a drunken buffoon wasting my time," Rätsel continues.

"Be fair, Rätsel. I've hardly touched a drop today."

"Mallory Haines has got alibis for every single murder and multiple witnesses for every single alibi."

"Hey, I never said Mal was the murderer, did I? I said he was involved."

"Oh. That's right." Rätsel snaps his fingers. "You said he was *involved*. As a *Muslim terrorist*. A pension-age, *white*, multi-millionaire *Muslim terrorist.*" Each word is said slowly, with considered rage.

"As I already told you, Mal's not white, he's mixed race."

"Only if you count *northern* and *southern* as different races," Rätsel shouts. "His dad was from York, his mum from Rochester. Both white. Both very much *English*."

I pick up my glass of water again.

"I could've sworn he said his mum was foreign..." I say, before taking a long sip.

"Well, I've checked, and the only foreign person related to Mal in any way was his nanny."

"Yes! That's it! His nanny! Now I remember... his nanny was the one!"

"His nanny was *Romanian.*" He stretches the word out, as if he's describing a new concept to a toddler.

"Ah... Romanian. Ah, yes, that's the fella. I knew it was *something* like that."

"Do you know what proportion of the Romanian population is made up of Muslims?"

I shrug.

"I checked. Nought-point-three *percent,*" he shouts. "And you can guarantee that tiny figure was a damn sight smaller sixty-odd years ago when Mal needed a fucking nanny!"

Rätsel glares at me, making my scalp tighten.

"What about the threat he made on the phone? You can't just ignore that."

Rätsel closes his eyes and takes a deep breath through his nose.

"What did you actually hear?" he asks. "What were the specific words that came out of Mal's mouth?"

"I'm not sure I can remember."

"Did he say *how* he wanted you killed?"

"No. He just said that he wanted them to take care of me."

"*Take care of you?* Those were his words?"

"Um…"

"So, he didn't actually say he wanted you *killed?*"

I look down at my hands, clasped together in my lap, and shake my head.

"In fact," he goes on. "It *could* be construed that he was arranging a nice little surprise for you! Did he even mention you by name?"

I don't say anything.

"Oh for fuck's sake!" Rätsel slams his hands down onto the table and stands up. *"Get out!"* He shouts and points at the door. "Get the fuck out of here. Don't even *think* about contacting me again!"

"What about Blue? The protection detail?"

"The only thing she needs protection from is you, you useless pisshead."

Sorry, boss: The taxi swings into a temporary parking bay outside Eddie Gitt's and I roll out. The evening is still warm, the sun just dipping beneath the tower-block skyline, shadows creeping long from the horizon. I spent the rest of the afternoon in a pub just across the road from Rätsel's police station, trying to work out my best plan of action, and the only thing I can come up with is my original plan to fuck off, take the job in Australia, disappear for a few weeks until everything returns to normal. There's no way I can leave without Blue, though. I tried calling her a few times, but when she didn't pick up, I realised she must already be at the club waiting to go on stage.

I stare at low clouds, bruising in the dying sunlight, turned by the wind, stretching into ribbons. The city around me disappears and I imagine looking up at those clouds from a cold desert, then from a forest glade, then from a boat in the middle of a vast ocean. The world spins as my head tips back and my eyes see through the sky until I'm not really staring at anything. I'm just staring.

I need to take Blue away from here.

There's only one bouncer on the door this time, probably because it's too early to expect much trouble. He's bulky, in an ill-defined sort of way, pork-nosed and big-eared. The brawler type, as opposed to the mixed-martial-artist. He frowns at me as I approach.

"What was all that about?" he says.

"All what?"

"*That.* Over *there*. What were you looking at?"

"Oh. I was just… imagining being anywhere but here."

The bouncer squints at me, cocks his head to one side, frowns again.

"Sorry, boss." He shakes his head. "Not tonight. You've had enough already."

"I promise you I haven't."

"You reek of it, mate. It's coming out of your pores."

I raise an arm, sniff my armpit.

"Oh *that,*" I say. "That's from earlier. This afternoon. I promise you, although I've had a couple of drinks since, I haven't been *properly* pissed for about three hours."

"Let me ask you something, mate," he says, leaning towards me. "Have you ever been refused entry to a club by a doorman before?"

I nod.

"And, after being refused entry, have you ever tried to talk your way inside?"

I nod again, slowly this time.

"And how many times did that work out for you?"

I sigh, reach inside my jacket. The bouncer tenses, anticipating a weapon. I pull out three twenty-pound notes, flash them in front of his face, place them in his hand. After a quick side-to-side glance, he slides the money into his trouser pocket, steps to one side and lets me past.

"Have a lovely evening, sir," he says with a dash of sarcasm.

"I'm sure I will."

Inside, the club is about two-thirds full. Pretty busy, considering how early it is. There's a pianist on stage, with a blonde in a long green dress poured over his grand piano, singing a smoky jazz melody. The slit in her dress cuts all the way from her heel to her stomach, so that each time she turns the audience sees the red flicker of her underwear.

I skirt the bar, weave through the tables, over to the stage door I saw Blue come out of the last time I was in here. Just as I reach out to pull the handle a bouncer materialises, planting his hand on the door to stop me from opening it. This guy has a more athletic build than the doorman outside, but he's still a brawler, with the trampled face of a rugby player.

"Where are you going?" he asks, with disinterested hostility.

"Me? I just need to get a message to one of the dancers."

"That right?"

"Yes. Blue, her name is."

"Blue? Oh, I like Blue. She's lovely."

"Isn't she just?"

"One of my favourites. Know her, do you?"

"Yes," I smile. "It's really important I speak to her."

"I'm afraid it's staff only back there, boss."

I pull some more money from inside my jacket and hold it out for him to take. He smiles and shakes his head.

"If only it were that simple," he says. "You could be a complete nutter for all I know. A *perv*. We get plenty of 'em coming in this club, I can tell you. If I let you back there and you started fondling the girls, it'd cost me my job."

"Please, you don't understand-"

"No, *you* don't understand." There's some venom in his spittle now. "You're not going back there. Take a seat, have a drink, and I'll get a message through to her on your behalf."

With a concrete paw on my shoulder, he guides me to a chair at an empty table, forces me to sit and waves over a waitress.

"What's your name?" he says.

"Jim Stakes. Jimmy, she calls me."

"Okay, *Jimmy*, I'll see what I can do for you."

The smug half-smile he gives me, along with a condescending wink, tells me he has no intention of getting any messages to Blue.

I order a cask-strength single malt from the waitress and sip it while I listen to the singer. At first, I think she's just singing one very long song, but I start to notice subtle key changes and variations in tempo as the pianist skilfully guides her from one melody into another.

I light a cigarette and order another whisky, cut it with a few drops of spring water, tainting the clear, brown liquid with an opaque cloud.

The singer finishes her set holding a long, high note she didn't look like she had the lungs for. There's an appreciative murmur from the audience and some quiet applause as she bows and exists the stage. The pianist follows her. A couple of stagehands wearing braces and flat caps wheel away the piano as the lights dim.

I stub out my cigarette, order another whisky, light another cigarette. The bouncer has disappeared for now, but he'll be watching me, or he'll have somebody else watching. The stage door is only twenty feet away, unguarded, but I can't risk being thrown out of the club or I'll never get to Blue.

The lights come up as a pattering of snare drums hints at some impending action. Slowly, a white Pegasus descends, a stylised, muscular steed of vacuum-formed fibreglass, with mechanical wings of paper feathers rising and falling and rustling, straddled by a blonde in a layered white dress. It's Blue. I try to catch her eye, raising my hand and waggling my fingers, but from her position the audience will be washed out by the glare of the footlights.

"Blue," I whisper through cupped hands.

She doesn't react. The band appears and music blasts, brassy and colourful. Blue lifts an arm and a stream of doves flies out from under it, a fucking *flock* coming out of her armpit. She lifts her other arm — more doves. This is some serious pigeonry. The audience is awed. There's a mutter of applause. Blue climbs off the horse.

"Blue!" It's one of those pointless whisper-shouts that's loud enough for everyone to hear except the intended target. A couple of nearby heads turn.

I push my chair back and head for the stage, but the table adjacent to mine suddenly sidesteps into my path. My last-ditch evasive manoeuvres fail. I trip over a chair leg and hit the deck, pulling half the tablecloth with me. An honest misstep.

"Blue," I say as I rise up. "It's me. It's Jim!"

She hears me now, turns her head and looks, then pretends she doesn't see, her eyes falling on me for an instant before moving past, over the rest of the audience.

"Blue, it's not safe," I shout. "We're both in danger!"

Her head snaps round to me again. Now her eyes are wide and stern. *For fuck's sake, Jim!* They say. *Not now!* But I have to ignore the message. She doesn't know the whole story yet.

"They're coming for us."

The people around me lean back in their seats, try to distance themselves without my drawing attention.

"We need to leave *tonight.*"

More commotion at the back of the room. Heavier. The sound of chairs being chucked aside.

The music is still playing but without much commitment from the band, who look around with crooked brows and nervous smiles.

"Jimmy, go home," Blue says. *"Please."*

"They're coming for us."

A tornado cuts a swathe through the crowd behind me. He'll be on me in seconds. I glance over my shoulder, see the bouncer coming, see the other knuckle-faced bouncer from outside not far behind. A sprint for the stage sees me crash into the front of it, breaking a couple of clamshell footlights as I collapse onto the boards. I climb up, grab Blue by the hand.

"What the *hell* do you think you're doing, Jimmy?"

"We need to get out of here. These guys… they're relentless. They want me dead. They want you dead. The police… they won't take me seriously!"

"Listen to yourself!" she shouts. "You're *slurring.* You *stink* of *booze.* You can barely *stand up.* I *asked* you *not* to drink today!"

"Blue, I'll be honest, I did have a drink earlier… I needed it to calm myself down. But that was before I found out what's going on. And now I know. The extent of it. We're both in serious… peril. You have to believe me."

As I'm saying this Blue's eyes travel to the glass in my hand, the contents of which have somewhat miraculously survived my stumbling journey through the crowd. This isn't the first time my hand has retained a subconscious grip on an alcohol container.

"Serious peril, Jimmy? You still managed to find the time to have a whisky."

"No, you don't understand. I only bought this because the bouncers would've thrown me out if I didn't buy a drink. Listen to me, Blue. *Please!*"

I pull at her arm and she reacts with an out-of-nowhere slap, a proper red-hander that puts me on my arse. The bouncers are up on stage now. They take an arm each, hoist me to my feet, start to drag me away. Blue doesn't do anything to stop them, just stares at me with a pained and maybe hateful grimace.

"It's *The Persian Princess,*" I say. "That's why they're doing this."

Her anger falters for a second but her glare quickly hardens again.

"I lied last night," she says. "I felt sorry for you. The truth is, there was never any chance for us."

The words hit harder than any slap. I think I hear anguish in her voice, but it could just be wishful thinking. She's facing away, doesn't watch as the bouncers punch me in the gut and lug me out through a fire exit, into the choking piss-stench of a back alley.

Sunday

The horrors, the horrors: The headache is there even before I'm fully awake. You know those pictures you see of an anaconda that's swallowed an animal too big for its stomach? That's how my brain feels, ripped along its flanks. The dehydration, the nausea, the emotional turmoil – it's all too much. This is a full-blown Category Five hangover and the details of where I am and how I got here have been redacted. The sudden arrival of an earthquake, tearing through the building, suggests I must be abroad, that I caught my flight to the other side of the world but, no, it's just the lactic acid spasms of my salt-starved muscles, shaking the mattress, rattling the nightstand. I grab hold of the bed sheets and ride out the horrors.

I stopped drinking, I know that much. I've gone this long without drinking before – I do it every time I sleep – but this is different. At some point before I passed out, the decision was made. I've *stopped* drinking. For good. And my body knows it, already anticipating the withdrawal. That's why it's giving me such a hard time. That's why the black pig is leaning so heavily on my shoulder.

Where did I take myself after I was ejected from the club? I must've checked into a hotel – a five-star deal going by the softness of the sheets, and the crystal chandelier hanging above my bed – but where did I go before that? I bury my nose into the arm of my shirt. Besides my own beef-and-onions body odour and the lingering fermentation of alleyway piss, there's a feminine grace note, a perfume that brings to mind dark hair sweeping over my face. A pointed nipple rubbing my nose. I must've gone to a strip club, the obvious refuge for any man suffering heartache.

As I sit up, drawing my knees to my chest, there's a nauseated yawn in my stomach that makes me dry retch into the back of my hand. Off the bed, across the room, into the en-suite, I throw up in the direction of the toilet. My accuracy lets me down, as does the closed toilet lid. It doesn't matter, it's a wet room, tiled floor to ceiling – it'll hose down without too much trouble. I throw up again, this time liberated by the fact that there's no need to aim. Dropped to my knees, I heave until there's nothing left except a sour taste in my mouth and looped strands of saliva swaying from my bottom lip.

Back in the bedroom I open the curtains, close them again when hawks of light tear out my eyeballs. Shivering, I return to the bed, submerge myself in the hefty folds of the duvet and shut my eyes, but all I can think about is Blue and the danger she doesn't realise she's in. There's too much at stake for me to remain bedridden. I need to put something in my body to help me cope, an alternative to the alcohol my fibres and membranes and cells and synapses are craving.

There's a pad of paper on the bedside table that tells me I'm staying in the *Drake & Macefield Hotel* on Shaftsbury Avenue. I grab my phone and dial the number of a man that can supply me with what I need.

An hour later there's a knock on the door. I grab a white bathrobe, tie it at the waist and look though the peephole. Standing in the hallway is a middle-aged Indian gentleman with slick, side-parted hair and a waxed pencil-thin moustache, wearing a green shirt and a suit the colour of a brain haemorrhage. He's smiling a smile so warm a lizard could bask in it.

"Mr Jimmy," he says when I open the door.

"Bahut," I try to smile back. "Sorry. I'm in a really bad way today."

"Oh no. No, no, no." He waggles his head vigorously. "That should be no problem for you today, my friend. No problem at all. I have exactly what you need, oh yes. A proper fixer-upper."

Bahut holds out a black plastic bag. I take it from him.

"I really appreciate this," I say.

"That should perk you up, lovely jubbly. Oh, yes! Lots of perkings for you, I think!"

I go back into the room, put the bag on a dressing table, pick my jacket up off the floor and get a roll of notes from the inside pocket. I give the money to Bahut.

"Please count it," I tell him. "I won't be insulted."

He looks aghast, slapping a hand over his heart.

"Oh no, Mr Stakes! I would not dream! Always I have good dealings with you. My best customer, that's who *you* are."

He pockets the money.

"Well, thanks again. I'm sure I'll be in touch very soon."

"Oh yes, I'm sure of that also," he winks. "I give you my best stuff, always, and you enjoy it. No problem at all!"

He waves and walks down the hallway.

I lock the door, go back to the dressing table and open the bag. The hot, buttery fragrance of the contents rises to my nostrils and my hangover immediately takes a step back. I just paid Bahut to open up his restaurant five hours early, cook me his chef's special Razala Gosht curry with fried saffron rice and garlic naan, cauliflower bhaji, chicken pakoras, popadoms and pickles, and deliver it all from Putney into the heart of the city. So, that's a £300 curry and, as I lift the first foil tray out of the bag, I realise I have nothing to eat it off and no cutlery to eat it with.

Adapting quickly to the situation I use the naan as a plate, spread it on top of the dresser, empty out the rice, then the lamb, then I scoop up the curry with a plastic business card I pull from my wallet. Garnished with diced naga chillies, it tastes like thermonuclear warfare. The lamb's scorched assault on my senses overwhelms any ill effects of the hangover. Sweat brims in my pores. Snot streams from my nose. My eyes bleed. A cool rush of endorphins sweeps through my body, knocks out all the shakes and the groans. I fold the naan like a Cornish pasty and chew through it until there's nothing left except a burning veneer of grease on my fingers.

It's as I'm licking the business card clean that I realise there's still another avenue of the investigation I'm yet to pursue. Brendan Hardy. *Deviant Services*. *The Persian Princess* was missing from the list of films he gave me when I visited him in *The Bunker*. Why would he lie about its existence? What exactly is he hiding?

Calls for a drink: I had five missed calls on my phone this morning, two from my agent and three from Mal. I get in a cab outside the hotel, tell the driver to take me to my apartment, and dial my agent's number. Her assistant puts me straight through without his usual pleasantries.

"So I take it this means you aren't *abroad?*" Bev says.

"Not quite."

"Sore head?"

"I've felt better."

"What about Mallory? Have you straightened everything out with him?"

"Things are still a bit... *iffy* on that front."

She sighs and says, "I hope you've given up on that silly notion that he's trying to kill you, at least."

"I'm not sure."

"Have you spoken to him?"

"No. Actually I've got a couple of missed calls from him."

"Sounds like a good sign to me. Call him back, James. Do it now. Without Mallory, your income is going to take a spectacular nosedive."

"What about the job in Australia?"

"Yes, I've put you forward for it. But remember, it doesn't start for five weeks, so there's no need to go rushing off straight away. Sort things out with Mallory, then you can concentrate on your holiday."

"Bev?"

"Yes, James?"

"I thought you'd like to know, I haven't had a drink yet today."

"At... 11.30am? That qualifies as an achievement now, does it?"

"I just thought you'd like to know."

"Well congratulations, James. You've managed something the rest of us accomplish on a daily basis."

She hangs up.

Next, I try calling Blue, partly to apologise, but mainly just to check that she's okay. She doesn't answer.

After that, I call Mal. The phone rings for a long period of time and I start to think he won't answer either, but eventually he does, with an inebriated groan.

"Jim! Thank God!" he says. "Had a spot of bother getting my phone out of my pocket. They upgraded me to this useless touch screen thing… usually hangs up of its own accord. Anyway, where've you been?"

"The police station, amongst other places."

"They got to you too! The degenerate bastards! I'll swing for them! I will! Or my lawyers will swing for them on my behalf… Pack of ravenous *wolves*, that lot. Tear those piggies to shreds. The filth won't know what's hit them!"

"Mal, stop. Please. I know what's going on. I know you're involved. When I came to see you in your office the other day I overhead your telephone conversation. I didn't know what it was about at the time, but now I know it all."

"You know what, Jim?"

"That you want me dead."

There's a moment of silence, then Mal sputters and laughs. It's a deep mucus-loosener. The laugh of an aging, forty-a-day man. I picture the flecks of spit flying from his mouth, dappling the smooth phone screen.

"Laugh if you want to, Mal. Try and brush this aside. But I was there. I heard what you said."

"You're serious, aren't you?"

"Absolutely."

"But Jim, old boy, you must've misheard me. I would never... to you... no... never. You're a treasure! One of the old sort. You're the only man I know that can keep up. I'd be lost if I didn't have you to drown a few sorrows with. *Lost*, Jim."

"I know what I heard, Mal."

"I must have been talking to a client. Or an employee. Or my *wife*. I can be pretty bloody *stark* when I want to be. Apoplectic, you might say. It might've sounded like I wanted somebody murdered but, Jim... not you. Never you!"

"I wish I could believe you, Mal. But somebody tried to strangle me later that same night. In my own home."

"Good God! And you think I had something to do with it?"

"I don't know what to believe. But I need to be on my guard. Need to work out who I can trust."

"You can trust me!"

"I used to think so. I don't know... maybe I'm confused. But for now, it'd be best if you kept your distance."

There's a long silence as we each wonder what else there might be left to say. I watch drizzle streaking across the cab's window. Putney Bridge streaks by too, and wind-sped clouds hurtle over the churning brown misery of the Thames. Finally Mal speaks.

"Well bugger me. I was just calling because I had a bit of a thirst on. I suppose a couple of swift halves down *The Black Knight* is out of the question?"

Wouldn't even be the second time: I tell the cab driver to wait and keep the meter running while I nip into my flat to grab the *Persian Princess* disc. It's still inside the DVD player. I find the case hidden among the other DVDs stacked in slanted piles on top.

The door to my liquor cabinet is ajar. One of the rare bottles inside catches a shimmered lance of sunlight, throws it back out into the room to strike the twitching corner of my eye. I pause, blink away a sudden watery blur, stuff my suddenly shaking hands in my pockets. The lights dim and an ocean starts swirling around me, a vortex of grief and sickness, and I sink, feeling the full pressure of its depths. My eardrums tighten and pop. I lean on top of the cabinet, telling myself it'll pass.

"It'll pass," I say. "It'll pass."

The room darkens. The bottles reinforce their position, clamouring for my attention as the shakes take hold with renewed fury. My heartbeat pounds in my temples, in the fat vein in my neck, in my wrists and behind my knees. Then it falls silent for long seconds, before pounding with extra pomp and vigour, booming until my eyes are wide and I'm gasping for air. I throw up, a small amount, but solid, like half a tin of dog food emptied onto the carpet. You're probably sick of hearing about me being sick by now. Well believe me, I'm sick of it too.

I wipe my mouth and splash water on my face over the kitchen sink before running back to the cab.

"The Bunker," please," I tell the cabbie.

"The Cabinet War Rooms?" he says with a strain of confusion. "Churchill's bunker?"

"No. The Porn Bunker."

He still isn't sure, thinks that my last remark might've been sarcastic.

"Do I look like I'm in the mood to stroll around a museum?" I say, leaning up to the partition, planting my lips against the microphone. "Take me to the fucking Porn Bunker on Charing Cross Road."

There's a cardboard cutout of Angus Tool, the current industry record-holder, at the foot of the stairs, with a starburst-sign above it telling everybody that Angus's new movie is released *TODAY!* and it's available *HERE!* He's naked, smirking, one eyebrow cocked, with his hands on his hips and his feet squared with his shoulders. The back of a woman's head covers his crotch. There's a list of five starlets printed down her spine, then a strap line saying 'For the first time *ever*, one of these girls takes all of *The Tool* in her ASS! But *who* will it *be?*'

Despite the fanfare, the shop is empty. Seems a starlet taking it in the ASS isn't such a big deal anymore, even if the thing she's taking could plug a black hole.

This time the sales assistant is a woman old enough to have the indefinite weathering of somebody anywhere between seventy and a hundred years old. The deep folds of skin on her neck remind me of my own scrotum. She could be your grandma, this woman. Nothing about the way that she's dressed would suggest otherwise – grey perm, bifocals, blue polka dot dress and a necklace of large, fake pearls. I suppose the term 'granny porn' exists for a reason.

"Yes, dear?" she says when I approach the counter.

"I'm looking for Brendan," I say.

"Well you've come to the right place! We have a very comprehensive buggery section–"

"No, *Brendan*. Brendan Hardy. Is he here?"

"Oh, silly me. You're looking for *Brendan.*"

"Yes. What did you think I said?"

"Never mind," she says, chuckling. "Brendan's taking a delivery in the back," then, with a wink, "That *isn't* a euphemism. I'll just see if I can get him for you."

She turns, walks with slow, hunched steps back to a heavy blast door that has *Staff Only* stencilled onto it, and slowly cranks a wheel to open the door before poking her head into the darkness beyond.

"Brendan!" she shouts. "Someone here to see you about our buggery section."

She waddles back up to the counter.

"He'll be with you in a minute," she says. "What our Brendan doesn't know about anal, you could write on a grain of sand."

Half a minute later Brendan Hardy bounds joyfully into the room, a huge grin on his face that falls slack when he sees me.

"Oh," he says. "You again. Mr *Mainstream*. We still haven't got any more Al Girth stock in, if that's what you're after."

"It isn't."

"Well, I'm quite busy. I'm sure Grace is more than capable of fulfilling your *vanilla* needs."

He begins to turn away.

"Why did you lie to me the last time I came in here?"

Hardy blinks three times in rapid succession then rubs his eye. Something glistens in his beard, like a snail trail running from his bottom lip to the tip of his chin.

"I'm sorry?" he says.

"You showed me a list of Al Girth's films and you told me it had every one of his titles on it. I double-checked with you to make sure they were all accounted for, and you said they were. Which was a lie."

"Really, I don't have time for this. Grace, could you—"

"*The Persian Princess*. That's an Al Girth film. But it wasn't on the list."

"I... I really don't know what you're talking about."

"I would've thought it was one of his standouts. His only rape picture... I would expect a man like you, with your experience and knowledge, to at least be aware of it."

I see him fighting to hold something back, lips so tight they're bruising. He sees himself as an authority in this world. An oracle of adult entertainment. I'm challenging his reputation but for some reason he won't defend it.

"I think you must be mistaken," he says after a pause. "Perhaps you're thinking of *Ali Boobie and the Naughty Thieves?* It isn't a rape picture but—"

"No. I'm thinking of *The Persian Princess*. Don't pretend you don't know what I'm talking about."

I take the DVD from inside my jacket and slap it on the counter. Hardy's eyes widen and fix on the writhing entanglement of bodies that make up the cover. He reaches for the case but I put my hand on top of it first.

"Grace," Hardy says, without unlocking his stare from mine. "Would you go into the back and start unpacking the new stock, please?"

"Are you sure, Brendan? I know you were looking forward to having a peek at that new shipment of fake arses—"

"It's *fine*, Grace. I'll look at them *later*."

"Okay then, dear," she says, eyes twinkling behind her glasses. "I'm rather excited to see what they look like myself!"

She exits through the blast door with a giddy swagger.

"Where did you get that?" Hardy asks once he hears the clunk of the closing door.

"So you *do* know what this is?"

"Of course I do. I wouldn't be much of an expert if I didn't."

"And yet the last time I came in here there wasn't a trace of it in your records."

"Because as far as anybody is concerned, that film doesn't exist. There isn't a single copy of it available anywhere on the market."

"How can that be possible?"

"Look, you're following a dangerous line of inquiry. It'd be better for you if you threw that DVD away and forgot you ever saw it."

"What do you mean, dangerous?"

"There are some very *serious* people with a very *serious* interest in that particular DVD."

"What kind of serious people?"

"The fewer questions you ask about them, the better. Trust me."

"Are these people capable of murder?"

"If I were you, I'd just leave this well alone."

"Your advice has been noted, but I've got a raging hangover and anything other than a straight answer is going to start pissing me off," I slam my hands on the counter. "Tell me what's going on."

Hardy swallows, rubs a hand over his face and purses his lips. He assesses my bulk, trying to judge how much muscle might be hidden under all the surface blubber.

"So *forceful*..." He says quietly, giving me a thin smile. "Okay. If I tell you, you leave this place and you keep that DVD to yourself. No more questions."

"Fine."

Hardy looks down at the floor, squints and strokes the crusty stripe in his beard, wondering where to begin.

"First thing that happened was about five years ago," he says, still looking at the floor. "Somebody bought out *Purple Head*, the DVD publishers of *The Persian Princess*. Not long after, the new owners discontinued the DVD's production. Now, that didn't raise too many eyebrows because it was an old picture and didn't sell many copies. But then, not long after *that*, someone started contacting all the adult entertainment shops, bulk buying *all* of the Persian Princess DVDs and any of the VHSs that were still in circulation. Some collectors noticed what was happening, started holding back their own copies, waiting for the price to rise. And it did. DVDs were going for as much as £100. A cassette was even more. Adverts appeared in the back of magazines asking for any copies of the movie that were still out there, offering relatively large sums of cash for them."

"Who was doing all the buying?"

Hardy shrugs.

"Someone with a lot of money. And someone who wouldn't take no for an answer. Stories started going round. Urban legends. A guy in Bristol responds to the advert, says he has a copy of the movie, but when the buyer goes to meet him, the seller changes his mind. Won't sell. So the buyer cuts his dick off, ransacks his house and takes it anyway.

"They... cut his dick off?"

"So they say. He wasn't the only one, either. Next, it was a guy in Aberdeen. Castrated. Then it was someone in Sheffield..."

"And this actually happened?"

"Enough people believed it did, that's the point. Nobody held back their copies anymore. They were all bought up very soon after."

"So there are no more left?"

"You'd sometimes see the odd one appear on an online auction site but it would be sold instantly. Yours is the first copy I've seen in about two years," he says, pointing at the DVD on the counter. "But the most incredible part of it? If you go online now, you won't find any mention of *The Persian Princess* anywhere. Not on a free-streaming site, not even on a message board."

"How's that possible?"

"Like I said, whoever was buying these DVDs had a hell of a lot of money. They must have somebody working full time to pull down any trace of *The Persian Princess* as soon as it comes into existence."

"Surely you've encountered this buyer, working here? *The Bunker* would have to be the starting point for anyone wanting to buy up porn in the way you're describing."

"Yeah, a couple of times a man came in here, but he said he was acting on behalf of his client, like he was a lawyer or something."

"What did he look like?"

"Big. Massive, in fact. Foreign. He had an accent."

"Arabic?"

"Could be. Very smartly dressed. He didn't look *right* in this place."

"What makes you say that?"

"Being in a shop like this makes people feel vulnerable. They either put up a wall to hide behind, scuttling around the displays all embarrassed, or they put up a front, acting brazenly, as if they couldn't give a shit who knows they're in here. Either way, nervous, confident, they appreciate what they see. You can't disguise lust."

"Right."

"This guy was different, though. He was stiff. Disapproving, if not disgusted. He didn't want to be in here at all. Walked around frowning at everything."

"Could've been a Muslim, then?"

"I suppose he could, but couldn't anyone? It's a religion, not a race."

I tap the DVD.

"What about the film itself?" I say. "What do you know about it?"

Hardy sighs like the subject is boring to him.

"Not a lot to say, really. I suppose at the time it was released it was quite extreme. You didn't see too many rape pictures back then, not produced by a mainstream studio like Biggerman's, anyway. Simulating rape for the purposes of erotica is *technically* illegal, but trying to enforce that is tricky – there's a blurred line between a cry of pain and a moan of ecstasy. As long as the girl doesn't actually say 'no' it's very hard to prove that the performance is supposed to represent rape, especially when you take into account the limited acting abilities of most pornstars. In this case, the victim's performance *is* pretty convincing. Chilling, in some ways… But beyond that, there's nothing too special about the film."

"Did the… um… *victim* star in any other movies?"

"No. But that's not unusual. Quite often a girl will have a crack at porn, realise she's overestimated her capacity to cope with the emotional demands of the job, and fall off the radar. Might take a couple of films for it to happen, might only take one."

"Why do you think this buyer is going to such extreme lengths to secure all the copies of the movie, then?"

"Ah, well, something like this has actually happened before. More than once."

"It *has?*"

"Let me show you something," Hardy says, reaching under the counter. He pulls out a little red cash box, opens it with a key from his pocket, lifts out a coin tray, takes another key from underneath it.

"Come on, I'll bring you up to my office."

He walks me over to the blast door, turns the rusted wheel, pulls it open, ushers me past, up a narrow staircase lit with the eye-straining flicker of a single eco-bulb. Grace comes to the top of the stairs before we reach the final step. She's beaming, holding a pair of clenched rubber buttocks in the palms of her hands.

"Brendan!" she beams. "Oh, Brendan, they're magnificent! They've got *real* hair! And they're self-lubricating! *Smell* that."

She pushes the quivering bum towards me. I almost fall backwards down the stairs trying to avoid it.

"Eurgh! It smells like dried shit!"

On hearing this, Hardy pushes past me.

"Really?" he says with excitement. Then he sticks his nose right into the flabby crevice and sniffs four or five times. With each sniff his beaming eyes widen further. "Mmmm, that is rather excellent, isn't it?"

"I should say so!" Grace cries.

Hardy extends his finger, pushes it past wiry bristles, against the toy's horrible, puckered orifice until his hand is juddering with the strain. The sphincter suddenly gives way and his finger slips inside with a wet fart, all the way up to the knuckle.

"How do they create such resistance?" he says. "Remarkable."

He then turns to me, remembering why we're here.

"Ah, Grace, could you go down and hold the fort for a few minutes? There's something I've got to show this gentleman in my office."

"I'm sure there is," she says with a wink in my direction. "No problem at all. I'll leave you two to it."

Hardy pulls his finger out of the hole, sniffs it, then wipes it on his trousers.

"The office is just through here," he says.

He opens a door on the other side of the storeroom, flicks a light switch and another eco-bulb slowly illuminates the bare brick walls of a medieval dungeon, with a ceiling that must've been artificially lowered. I have to stoop to enter. Chains hang from metal rings pinned into the walls, trailing across a wooden floor that's spotted and streaked with an uncountable number of stains. An iron maiden stands in the far corner. Then, entirely out of place, there's an old desktop computer, crowded by stacks of paper files on top of a cheap fibreboard desk, with a plastic office chair tucked under it. Onscreen, a slideshow of what appear to be bloody stills from horror movies is acting as a screensaver. I stop watching the gradual scroll of images when I realise that they are close-ups of something else entirely.

Hardy walks over to the iron maiden, uses the key from the cash box to unlock it, opens the heavy door, revealing a safe.

"Ever heard of Rusty Dawn?" he asks.

"Can't say that I have."

Hardy reaches into the safe and turns around, holding a cellophane-sealed photograph of a naked woman lying spreadeagled, sucking the index finger of one hand, running the fingers of the other through her coarse, black bush. Her hair is long and red, feather-cut with high flicks out to the side. The shot has a grainy, Vaseline-glow typical of the mid-seventies.

"Let me tell you about her."

Rusty Dawn: LouAnne Cheshunt was born on 15th April 1960 in Tapioca, Wyoming, a town with a population just shy of 6000. She was an unfortunate-looking child, even her parents Alvin and Moira had to admit that, with lunatic bug-eyes bulging behind thick corrective lenses, and an underbite that required significant metalwork to straighten out, giving her a smile that could shift a compass needle. Her looks, coupled with a strict Presbyterian upbringing, made her an outcast at school, so that even when she started to fill out, when her teeth were straight and her eyes were un-crossed, the other children continued to ignore her. Then, at the age of fifteen, a line of code in her DNA activated and overnight her tits were weaponised. The girls made jokes at her expense, but the boys' heads had been turned, and suddenly LouAnne was getting her first taste of popularity.

Long years as an outcast had made her naïve to the reality of what the boys wanted from her and she didn't put up much resistance when Clive, the first-choice quarterback with the thick arms, tried to get into her panties. Of course, the very instant he'd popped his load he turned cold, avoiding her embrace and leaving her without a word spoken to pick up her clothes from the damp floor of the gym locker room. Her heart was broken. Soon afterwards, LouAnne found consolation in the thick throwing arm of the second-choice quarterback, a friend of Clive's, a quick-to-laugh kid called Dale with curly brown hair and a face that seemed honest. Except Dale was just after one thing too and, like Clive, he wasn't going to hang around once he'd got it. Pretty soon LouAnne had done the rounds with the whole football team. She might've been innocent with Clive, and a little naïve with Dale, but by the time she got to Fat Joe, the pimply linebacker with a persistent sweat-rash, she knew exactly what the deal was.

And then Mr Gennero, the science teacher, took a liking to LouAnne and it was different again. He kept her back after class, not because she'd done anything wrong, he said, oh no, but because he saw *potential* in her and he wanted to help her harness that potential. Mr Gennero was old and he had a pronounced stoop but you could see he'd been handsome once, and he was kind and he treated LouAnne better than any of those footballers ever had. She started deliberating carefully over her outfits and curling her hair on days when she had science, and she made excuses for more reasons to stay behind after class, even misbehaving sometimes so that he'd be forced to keep her back. The first time she plucked up the courage to kiss him she was surprised when his hand jumped straight to her tit. She thought maybe he would have been taken aback, or maybe he would've protested, but no, his hand went right *there* without hesitation, his thumb working the nipple through her blouse. She supposed it could have something to do with him being old and not wanting to waste time. He told her a place to meet on a quiet lane, where he'd be parked in his station wagon, and she did, and that was when they had sex for the first time, in the back, on top of an old tartan blanket, the axles of the car grinding and squeaking. LouAnne took Mr Gennero's slow movements to be a sign of tenderness and she knew a mature man would be sensitive to her feelings and wouldn't be as single-minded as the boys on the football team.

Their affair continued, often in the car on top of that musty red and green and black blanket, but sometimes round at Mr Gennero's house when his wife was out playing bridge, or round at LouAnne's when her parents were at one of their prayer meetings. LouAnne started to get boastful and suggestive, confiding in girls she thought of as friends, and pretty soon everybody at school had a fair idea about what was going on. Mr Gennero saw the danger coming.

When he told LouAnne that they couldn't see each other outside of school anymore, that it was unrealistic for her to expect him to leave his wife of thirty years, first she pleaded with him, then, when she saw his mind wasn't for changing, she arranged for them to have one last boot-knocking session. A farewell fling. She told him to come over to her house on a night when her parents would be out at a dance. She was lying, of course. Her mom was away, visiting her aunt, but her daddy was only working a late shift at the sawmill and when he came home to find his daughter bent over the couch with a pigeon-chested old duffer hanging out the back of her, he threw Mr Gennero to the ground and beat him harder than a man who'd just got off a ten-hour shift cutting logs should've been able. The righteous fury of the Lord flowed through him as he pummeled feeble old Gennero. The more he kicked and punched, the closer he felt to Him. LouAnne screamed, tried to pull her daddy away, but he kept on going, stamping on Mr Gennero's crotch with his steel-capped boots, until the old man's genitals had all the flesh pulped out of them, mashed into the polyester carpet.

LouAnne's daddy was sentenced to five years by a lenient judge, who sympathised with the predicament of fathering a wayward child, but LouAnne was already long gone by that time, hopped on a Greyhound to Los Angeles before the charge of manslaughter had even been pressed, with her hair dyed red and her name changed to Rusty. In a story so clichéd that to call it a cliché is itself something of a cliché, she believed she could make it as an actress. The smooth-talking fella she met at the bus terminal licked his lips when she told him her plans. He believed a rare beauty like her could make it too – she'd just need to do him a few favours first.

Rusty's time on the streets was mercifully short. After only a month, she was picked up by a talent agent who hadn't been able to resist the sight of her strutting along the boulevard, his car headlights reflected back at him from the shiny red latex that barely contained her ass. As soon as she climbed into his car, he knew she was special – he had to get her in a picture. He passed her along to a producer and then a director, who could both see that this girl had *something*, but whatever it was, they couldn't make it work on film no matter how hard they tried. The problem was she *couldn't* act. As far as they could see, she really was only good for one thing – but that one thing she was good for she did with prodigious skill.

Eventually she came across the path of Eugene Lustig, the owner of a newly founded adult entertainment company. He saw firsthand the potential that Rusty possessed, the same *potential* that Mr Gennero had seen over the top of a biology textbook, and he started her off with a supporting role in a softcore film called *Bernard and the Babysitter*. She might not have been too great when it came to delivering her lines but that didn't matter a whole lot because Rusty's other talents were uninhibited by the presence of a camera. After a couple of other softcore titles, Lustig put Rusty in her first hardcore feature and the *Rusty* series began. *Rusty Nails* came first. Next there was *Rusty Swings*, followed by *Rusty Ploughs*, *Rusty Rails,* and *Rusty Rides*.

Michael Biscuits first encountered Rusty in an adult movie theatre just off New York's Times Square. Like Rusty, he was based on the West Coast but he had business in New York with a firm of architects, who were designing the Biscuits Plaza in downtown LA. Biscuits, you see, was a petrochemical magnate who liked nothing more than to slip into a trench coat, put on a porkpie hat and a pair of dark glasses and sneak into a porno screening late on a Friday night.

The movie was Rusty's third hardcore picture, *Rusty Ploughs*, in which she plays a farmer's daughter who acts out every sexual variation of the joke with the various travellers that pass through the farm. Biscuits was immediately entranced by the young woman on screen. Her shadowy eyes had a look of guilt to them, like she was getting away with something – something she would keep on doing until she was caught. And punished. Looking at her, Biscuits started to conceive all manner of punishments that he knew, deep down, the young whore would probably enjoy.

Within a week, Biscuits had seen all the movies that Rusty had released so far. He bought reels direct from the porn studio so that he could screen the movies in his own private cinema. When he heard that Rusty was making a new movie, he paid the studio a huge sum to allow him to watch the production, but he was thrown off the set almost as soon as they started shooting when, sick with jealousy, he tried to attack Rusty's co-star.

Biscuits festered in his mansion. He started missing meetings and ignoring calls from clients. The Biscuits Plaza project was abandoned. Eventually he was voted off the board of his own company. It barely registered. All he cared about now was Rusty.

His first move was to buy out the porn studio, paying well more than its worth so that the deal would go through quickly. Next, he started buying the reels of film for all of Rusty's pictures. He contacted every adult theatre in the US and in Europe, again paying well above the odds. Then he bought up all the magazines and the merchandise associated with Rusty and went so far as to track down any items that had already been sold into general circulation. He wanted the image of Rusty's naked body all to himself.

Rusty had been warned about Biscuits' obsession and she was appropriately disturbed, but that didn't stop her from seeing the financial opportunity it presented. Biscuits was a couple of decades older than her, but he wasn't a bad-looking guy – if you were going to marry someone for money you could certainly do worse.

She woke up early on a cold February morning and spent a couple of hours in front of her dressing table primping coils into her hair, plucking errant follicles from her eyebrows, applying liner and shadow to her eyes until the whites shone out of the darkness like headlights on a desert road. Her lips were waxy with gloss. The green shift dress she picked out set her red hair ablaze, the skirt so short that when she sat in her soft-top with the roof down her lack of underwear would be clear to see for anybody that might peer over the top of the door.

She left her cramped apartment in Korea Town, drove up the coastal highway towards the affluent suburb of Santa Esmeralda where Biscuits lived, with the wind behind her and the sun bouncing off the Pacific Ocean, sensing that finally her fortunes were going to change.

Rusty was never seen alive again.

Her car was discovered the next day, parked in a driveway ten feet from the vulgar Doric columns surrounding the entrance to Michael Biscuits' white mansion. It was Biscuits' groundskeeper that found the car, with the driver's side door still open and the keys in the ignition. A trail of blood ran from the open door into the house. As the groundskeeper followed the trail, it got wider and redder and darker until it reached the stairs leading down to Biscuits' private screening room. He hesitated at the top step long enough to lose his nerve, dialled 911 from the phone in the hallway and sat outside chain smoking as he waited for the police in the winter sun.

They found two bodies, a man and a woman. Both naked. The woman had been beaten with something long and blunt – they'd later find a nine iron tossed in the bushes outside the front door. Her body was covered in scratches and deep bite marks too, which had been received post mortem. Slumped over her, the man's body was unmarked, except for an exit wound blown out of the back of his head from the revolver he'd stuck in his own mouth.

A fellow porn guy: "Your classic murder suicide," Hardy says.

"That was… surprisingly detailed," I say. "Where did you get all that information?"

"News reports. Police reports. I may have embellished here and there for the sake of the story," Hardy says. "But the main details hold up."

"I'm surprised I haven't heard about it before. You think the same thing is happening with *The Persian Princess?*"

"Maybe not quite the same. But there are plenty of men out there that have been conditioned to believe that a woman can be *ruined* by promiscuity. By having any kind of sexual past whatsoever." Hardy's lips glisten with saliva. "When Rusty presented herself to Biscuits, the hours he'd spent watching her screwing on his little home cinema, coupled with the sudden reality that she was so obtainable in the flesh… it must have been a collision of ideas that his pathetic little brain couldn't handle."

"I'm not sure this situation is quite the same."

"There have been other instances, less extreme than what happened to Rusty, where the husbands of ex-pornstars have tried to eradicate any evidence of the work their wives used to do. Maybe your Persian Princess has found herself a sugar daddy who's struggling to deal with his wife's previous line of work."

Hardy stands up, puts the photograph of Rusty back inside the iron maiden.

"What about the photograph?" I ask. "If this Biscuits guy bought up all her merch, how come you've got that?"

"That photograph is the thing that got me into this magical industry," Hardy says, without a hint of irony. "It was my dad's. He gave it to me. Told me he could've sold it for a small fortune once. It was worth thousands... right up until the day that Michael Biscuits blew his brains out. Then its only value became one of sentiment. I get thrills every time I handle it."

Hardy sits down again and I remain stooped under the low ceiling, my back starting to cramp. He's probably getting a kick out of my discomfort.

"One thing that *is* different," he says. "We're talking about an obsession on a much bigger scale this time. Okay, Biscuits was buying up more than one movie, but home video was only just taking off, so he didn't have too many copies to track down. More significantly, he didn't have the internet to contend with. I'd wager whoever's been getting rid of *The Persian Princess* is much more than just a single-digit millionaire."

"You must have a way of contacting this buyer in case somebody like me shows up wanting to sell a copy."

"Oh no," Hardy says, shaking his head. "I'm staying out of this now. And you should too. If it's the kind of obsession I'm talking about then the person behind it all is unstable. Unpredictable. I'd say anybody that's even seen *The Persian Princess* isn't entirely safe."

"Brendan, I'm already in a huge amount of danger because of this film, whether or not I contact the buyer."

His eyes narrow.

"What are you talking about?" he says hesitantly.

"Alan Girth, the star of *The Persian Princess*, is dead."

"I know. I told you that the last time you came in here. That's why we don't have any of his films in stock."

"Well Keith Rumbold, the sound engineer that worked on it, is dead too. So is Dane Biggerman, the producer." I slap a hand on my chest. "I was the cameraman on that picture–"

"Wait," Hardy shakes his head. "Hold on. Are you telling me... *You're* James Stakes?"

I nod.

"No," he says. "No, you can't be.... You're too fa..." his voice trails off and he stares at me for a long time. "Yes. I suppose it could be..." he says, finally. "Oh my God. James Stakes. In the flesh. You're a... a legend. Your camerawork... it was... sublime..."

"You don't have to bullshit me, Hardy. I know you despise all those *mainstream* films."

"I won't deny that. But I won't deny talent, either. The way I look at it, Biggerman had a couple of gems working for him that he took for granted. Blue Darling, obviously – God knows why she didn't move on to bigger things. And then you. The *biggest* crime was that he wasted you on magazine work instead of films! There are only a handful of features out there with your name on them."

"And most of those are very low budget."

"Exactly!" he shouts. *"Exactly."*

He looks at me, shaking his head, and says, "James Stakes," one more time. Smiling now, he rubs his hands together and spins the chair around so that he's facing the desk.

"Right," he says excitedly, rummaging through the piles of paper that surround the computer.

"Somewhere hidden under all this *crap* is a business card with the buyer's contact number on it. Whether or not he's still using it, I don't know... I would've thought so... but... Aha!"

He spins back round and hands me a small red business card with one word printed onto it, along with a mobile number.

"Sova? Is that a name?"

Hardy shrugs and says, "He never told me his name, just said that I should erase *The Persian Princess* from my stock lists because I wouldn't be selling it anymore, and that I should call the number on this card if I ever found out about any more copies up for sale."

Hardy walks me back downstairs, through the shop, Grace directing a dentured leer at us both from behind the counter as we pass.

"What about terrorism?" I say when we reach the foot of the stairs that lead back to the street.

"What *about* terrorism?"

"Do you ever worry about it? This place flies in the face of every religious doctrine on the planet. Seems like a natural target for extremists."

"Well, I'm not going to lie, it is something that has been brought up as a concern at PISSTITS meetings."

"PISSTITS?"

"The Pornographic Industry's Society for Sellers, Traders and International Tycoons," he says, then quietly adds, "Between you and me, I think they just stuck the *International Tycoons* bit on the end for the sake of a nice acronym."

"It *is* a lovely acronym."

"The general consensus was that because we occupy a niche in society, we wouldn't provide a particularly high-impact target for the terrorists. They obviously don't like what we do, but it's western society's fault as a whole for allowing us to do it in the first place. So we're in no more danger than anybody else."

"And no less."

Hardy's eyes narrow.

"You think this Persian Princess thing might have something to do with terrorism?" he says. "Wait... *of course* you do! That's why you asked if the buyer looked like an Arab."

"It's just a line of thought."

"The Persian Princess," he says, a hand over his mouth. "The *Persian* Princess. Oh, Christ! What if that's it? What if this is the start of some kind of porno jihad?"

"I wouldn't jump to any conclusions just yet."

"But can you imagine it? Those bastards trying to suppress our freedom to explore our sexual appetites... It wouldn't stop *me* selling, you know. I'd stand up for what I believe in. I'd be a freedom fighter. They might plant IEDs, they might send suicide bombers, but I wouldn't give in!"

I start to climb the stairs. Behind me Hardy says, "You're one of us James. A porn guy. I can tell. You always gave the viewer exactly what they wanted at exactly the right time. Crotch zooms, fanny pans, pop-shots... face, tits, arse... You can only do that if you appreciate the art yourself. What I said earlier about you staying away from this place... forget that. You'll always be welcome here. I hope whatever it is you've got to sort out... gets sorted out. Godspeed to you, James! *Godspeed.* And good luck."

He stands with his hands behind his back and a lopsided grin on his face, watching me, a fellow *porn guy*, slowly climbing the stairs to the street.

Nobody is sova: It shouldn't be so cold. That's what everybody keeps saying. In the street, in the pub, on TV, there's always the same preoccupation.

When will spring stop fucking about and get here?

It's as if the country has a collective annual amnesia, forgetting the seasonal shenanigans of the previous year. One 'unseasonably' harsh winter follows another, with 'unseasonably' wet summers in between. People have every right to complain, but they shouldn't be surprised. Our weather is shit. It always has been. This little island gets molested by clusters of competing weather systems every season.

I don't normally feel the cold if I'm honest. Maybe it has something to do with the alcohol, all the chemical reactions stoking my central heating, because today, without the booze, I really *am* feeling it. The shivers from the subzero wind chill and the shakes from the hangover engage themselves as soon as I step outside, making me drop the contents of a cigarette packet onto the damp pavement. I scoop up any fags that aren't too soggy, put one in my mouth, return the rest to the packet, and spend a couple of minutes trying to strike the flint on my lighter with my rattling hands. The nicotine doesn't help much. Its powers are vastly diminished without a pint or a dram to back it up.

The afternoon sky is dark. The rushing air prickles with moisture. Down the street a tramp has scooped himself into a closed doorway, his hood pulled over his eyes, a cardboard sign on his lap saying 'Spare change plz'. What has this guy got going on in his life that's so important he doesn't have the time to write out 'please' in full? He makes direct eye contact with people as they walk past, pleading for their help in a downtrodden Scottish brogue, forcing them to respond, even if it's just to tell him to piss off. This is what they want, these tramps. To be recognised. To raise themselves above a subhuman existence through these brief interactions with other beings. The money isn't what's important, only the acknowledgment from someone else that, yes, *I see you*. But I can't handle it today. I'm too whacked-out, emotionally, to reject anybody's advances. I'd give him the change if I had it, I'd pay off the emotional blackmail, but my pockets are empty. So I resort to my usual ruse when avoiding the homeless – I cough into my fist, trying to get a nice convincing rattle going, and I hack and I snort. He won't want my money now. He can't risk it, not with his AIDS-shafted immune system. One drop of mucus might be all it takes to put him in the ground. And the gambit works, he doesn't make a noise as I move past, although for a moment I think I hear him call after me, saying 'Oi, Jimmy!' but I don't turn round. How could he possibly know my name?

I cross the street, duck into a bookshop, looking for warmth, avoiding the temptations of *The Royal Shepherd Inn* next door. It transpires that the bookshop has an alcohol license anyway. There's a wine rack holding various New World reds next to a display of modern classics, and there are posters for 'Book and a Bottle' offers on all the walls. Pynchon and a Pinot, £18.99. Brontë and a Burgundy. Lessing and a Lambrusco. Vonnegut and a Viognier. People sit by themselves at tables scattered around the shop floor, with a glass in one hand and a book in the other. I hesitate at the till, watching a businesswoman with felt-tipped eyebrows knocking back a hefty glass of red, the muscles in her slender neck sliding to embrace the warmth of the alcohol. Feverish with yearning, I splutter out an order for a bottle of sparkling water from the cashier and sit down at an empty table in the 'Christian books' section where I know I won't be bothered. Outside, there's an unseen collision of clouds and a great slash of rain sweeps along the street, the roar of falling water usurping the book shop's disinterested lounge music. The pavement is lost in a grey haze of torrent and spray. People take cover in doorways, or frantically open umbrellas, or try to beat the rain by sprinting through its falling sheets. The bookshop is effused with smells of damp fabrics as people crowd inside to shelter from the weather.

I chug my water, hold the bottle against my forehead, beads of condensation collecting above it, mingling with beads of sweat, running down my face. I try to call Blue again, twice, but there's still no answer. I take out the business card Hardy gave me but I can't read the number because my hands are shaking and my eyes have lost the ability to focus. I put it down on the table and dial. A deep, foreign voice answers after only one ring.

"Hello," It says.

"Sova?" I say.

"Sova," the voice repeats drawing out the 'S' and the 'oh', the 'va' arriving and finishing with unexpected abruptness.

"Are you Sova?" I ask.

"Nobody is sova. Sova means 'owl'. Is just word."

The accent doesn't sound Arab – the consonants are too harsh and there's no song in the voice – but then, aside from the attempt on my life, my experience of Arabs is limited to villains in action films. Besides, there are other kinds of Muslims out there. Who knows what an Afghani accent sounds like. Or it could be Kazakh, Bosnian, Persian, Malaysian… It could even be one of the nought-point-three percent of Romanians that Rätsel was so quick to dismiss.

"But sova tells me you have something I want," the voice continues.

"Correct. And I know how *much* you want it. And I know how *rare* it is. You name a good price and it's yours."

"What you have? VHS? DVD?"

"DVD."

"One hundred pounds is good price for DVD."

I could just accept his offer. The goal is to meet the buyer – it doesn't matter how much I sell the DVD for. But it hides my true intentions if I haggle, and this is a good opportunity to find out the kind of personality I'm dealing with.

"Maybe five years ago that was a good price," I say. "But this is one of the only copies left now."

"One hundred fifty."

"One thousand," I say. *"That* sounds like a good price to me."

"Ha! One thousand for small piece of plastic? I give you three hundred. Is final offer."

"Five hundred or I go elsewhere."

"Elsewhere? There is no *elsewhere*. I am only buyer."

"Okay, five hundred or I burn it."

"You burn it, you save me job. Please, you go burn DVD. You lose three hundreds of pounds and I am happy."

"Five hundred or I watch it right now while you listen."

Silence. Then, without humour, "Five hundred... Okay, I give you. You come now to warehouse–"

"I don't think so."

"What you mean, *don't think so?*"

"I've heard some pretty nasty stories about the lengths you'll go to to get your hands on this film. I'll meet you somewhere public, with plenty of witnesses."

"Where you suggest?"

"Do you know *The Black Knight?*"

"No. What is black knight?"

"It's a pub."

"Not pub. I don't like pub. You English live in pub. Is very unhealthy. Somewhere else."

I try to think of another public location, a place I know well enough to feel safe, but the only places that come to mind are pubs and bars and clubs and strip clubs. The Tower – would that be good? They probably force you onto a Beefeater tour... The Houses of Parliament? Can you even get *in* to the Houses of Parliament? Buckingham Palace? St Paul's? How have I never been to any of these places?

Then a memory flickers, like an image projected onto smoke. I'm talking loudly, wearing a tux and holding a champagne flute. There are attractive middle-aged women wafting around me in ball gowns and sequined dresses, gawking at marble sculptures and oil paintings. The opening night of an exhibition. Free booze.

"The Obsidian Gallery," I say.

"Obsidian Gallery? Like art gallery?"

"Yes, it's an art gallery."

"Where is Obsidian Gallery?"

"Just off Kensington High Street. Look it up online. It shouldn't be too hard to find."

"Okay. We meet Obsidian Gallery, in… one hour and half."

"Fine. Call me on this number when you arrive so I know how to find you."

"Good. You bring DVD. I see you, one hour and half, with cash."

Obsidian: I arrive fifteen minutes early at the gallery and immediately realise I've made a mistake. As far as witnesses go, it's a terrible location to make the exchange. The last time I was here it was a special event, ticketed, full of journalists and celebrities and those vacuous, tuxedoed people that somehow make a career out of attending ticketed events full of journalists and celebrities. Contrast that with the daytime, when it's more like a storage space for silence. An elegant mausoleum. The kind of place where you're embarrassed to cough.

I wander from room to room, from Italian futurism to Russian constructivism to Belgian monotonism, eventually settling alongside the sculpture that seems to have the most foot traffic – and by that I mean there happens to be one other person in the vicinity, a gawky twenty-something alternative-type, male, with a dorsal fin of bleach-blonde hair peaking above his crown. He stares thoughtfully at each piece of artwork, slowly tapping his bottom lip with an index finger, his torso bent forward at a perfect right angle to his legs. The central sculpture comprises two figures, both male, one standing behind a lectern, arms raised, face distorted with rage, while the other figure crouches beneath the lectern giving him a discreet blow job. It's made from a material that shines black all over, with a subtle rainbow shimmer like oil on water, as if the figures have been rescued from a marine tanker spill. The descriptive footnote says the sculpture was inspired by Nigerian homophobia, showing creationist hate-preacher Goodfury Andrews giving his infamous mob-riling speech before the Lagos gay-bashing rally of 2002. The artist, an ex-Muslim and human rights activist, has been exhibiting the work in galleries worldwide, taunting

Andrews by sending him a photograph of it from each new country he visits.

"What the fuck is this?"

I turn round as a light-skinned Arab the width of a tractor tyre squeezes himself into the room. His pastel blue suit must've been specially tailored to accommodate his enormous steroidal frame, but it still stretches taut at his thighs and biceps, with strained creases running out of his armpits and crotch. A red power tie hangs comically short, the majority of its length required just to circumnavigate the Arab's fat neck. The dorsal-finned hipster turns and sniffs at the Arab, purses his lips, then sashays out of the room.

"This is some kind of joke?" the Arab says, gesturing at the sculpture. "You meet me here, next to *this?*"

"You're the one that didn't want to meet in a pub."

"Is fucking disgusting! Is two men? I thought maybe short-haired woman under table but..." he bends down to look closer at the crouched figure. "No. Fuck! Is two men. Why you want to look at this?"

"I don't have any problems with it."

"Ah, yes. I see. You have no problem because you are comfortable with sexuality, yes? You are modern man, of course. They say people that hate gays do it because they are gays themself but are scared to admit, yes? So now everybody likes gays, because if you are *not* liking the gays then this means *you* must be a gay. Is gay propaganda. Is big gay Catch-22."

"That's not quite how I'd put it."

"You want cigarette?"

"I don't think you can smoke in here."

"*I* want cigarette," he says, slapping away my comment.

He reaches into an inside pocket, pulls out a yellow packet branded in an alien script, devoid of the usual government health warnings, opens it, takes out a thin, black stick, puts it in his mouth, shakes the packet in my direction.

"Go on then," I say, taking one.

He lights his cigarette first, then mine. It tastes like an overheated clutch. The smoke peels from our mouths in thick blue swirls.

"So, you have DVD?" he says.

"Do you have the money?"

He holds out an envelope, opens it so I can see the purple wedge of twenty pound notes inside. I take it, count the cash, and hand him the DVD.

"Good," he says. "And now, fat man, you come with us."

Two more Arabs appear through two different doorways, one of them wearing a bandage over his eye and the same pinched frown I saw reflected in my bathroom mirror when he was trying to throttle me. Both exits from the room are now covered.

"If you think I'm just going to walk out of here with you, that I'm not going to scream for help or put up a f–"

"Please," he says. "Don't embarrass yourself."

"Ask your friend with the eye patch about what I'll do to stay alive. A little bit of embarrassment doesn't frighten me."

"What about pain? Does pain frighten you?"

"Yes. Obviously. *Obviously* pain frightens me."

"You come quietly," he smiles. "There is less pain."

"I still think I'll pass."

"You surprise me. I thought you are gentleman."

"The options you've presented me with don't really give much scope for *gentlemanliness*. If I come quietly then you say I'll experience less pain. If I don't come quietly then it's unlikely that I'll experience any pain at all. You can't possibly think you can abduct me in broad daylight without someone trying to intervene or call the police."

"No," The Arab says, shaking his head. "The police are not problem. Anyway, you are not understanding me. Come quietly, don't come quietly... does not matter for *your* pain. Either way *you* are feeling much of pain. The choice I give is for your girlfriend, Miss Blue. How much pain do you want *her* to be feeling?"

Are we there yet: They put me in the back of a black saloon car, parked illegally in the street outside the entrance to the gallery. The Arab with the bandaged eye sits to my left, the Arab who, so far, hasn't had much of a role in this story sits to my right, stinking of stale tobacco and – of all things – parsley. Sova-Arab drives.

"How's your eye?" I ask, looking at the bandaged Arab's good eye, which, on closer inspection, isn't actually all that good. The lids are puffed-up, red, and the white of his eye isn't white at all, it's a caustic yellow.

His friend, the guy to my right, responds on his behalf, cracking an elbow into my face, knocking my head back against the parcel shelf. Pain riots around my bleeding and probably broken nose.

The driver says something angrily in a language I don't understand or recognise and the guy that just struck me responds with equal anger in the same language.

"Fucking... ow!" I shout, pinching my nose, leaning my head back. Blood pours through my fingers, down my chin and my neck.

"I would not give Nargis reason to hit again," the driver says. "He does not think before he act. I tell him I don't want blood on you before we get to destination and *now* look! Blood all over your shirt. How we explain this if cop pull us over?"

"Where are we going?" I ask.

"We are going to warehouse–"

The bandaged Arab interrupts him. There is another angry exchange in a foreign language.

"You know, that's very rude," I say. "Talking in a language I don't understand."

"Sorry," the driver says. "Velak, he hate you because of what you do to his eyes. He say I should not tell you where we go, but I say does not matter, we kill you anyway, so you tell nobody."

"Oh. Right."

"We take you to warehouse in Docklands."

"Is that where you've taken Blue?"

The driver doesn't say anything.

"She'd better be okay," I say.

"Oh yes? She better be okay? What will you do, fat man, if she is not okay?"

The car stops in traffic as two lanes are forced to converge by some unmanned road works. I look through the tinted window at a family in a people carrier idling alongside us. A boy and a slightly older girl in the back are arguing and slapping at each other over the top of a toddler strapped into a child seat. The mum turns round from the front passenger seat to pacify them. The dad, the driver, says something with a smile into the rearview mirror and everybody laughs.

"Look at that," I say.

"What?"

"That family. In the green car. You see them? Look at how normal they are. Why can't you people be like that? Why do you have to ruin everything? Why does the world have to be so fucking serious to you?"

"World is serious place," the driver shrugs. "Always people, they are dying."

"That's why you need a sense of humour, otherwise death is all you think about. That family isn't thinking about death. They're thinking about a zoo or a theme park or wherever it is they're going today. They're just living."

"So what? Why do I care?"

"You know what I'm getting at. Do you even think about the stuff you believe in? Properly think about it? *Objectively* think about it? You can't, can you? Because if you did, you'd realise it was all bollocks."

"What this fuck he talk about?" Velak with the eye bandage says, then to me, "Shut your fuck up!"

"You see? You can't accept a difference of opinion, can you? You can't even *entertain* the idea of questioning your beliefs. If it's written in an old book, then that's all that matters."

"Seriously, what kind of fuck is this?" Velak says to the driver. The driver shrugs.

"Want to know what I believe?" I say. "I believe in nothing, that's what I believe. No god, no afterlife. I don't even believe in free will. I believe a person is just a big bundle of molecules and chemical reactions that came into existence one day and will stop existing another day."

"How you believe this?" the driver asks.

"Abran, please. Don't encourage." Velak mutters.

"You want me sitting in this traffic in silence, Velak?" Abran, the driver, says. "All you are ever talking is about football. And Nargis... Nargis never say anything! Finally I have someone with conversation I am interest in. I want to hear what fat man say."

The traffic starts to move up ahead. Abran puts the car into gear, rolls forward, slows when, after travelling less than fifty feet, the brake lights in front begin to flare again. I watch the traffic in the next lane to see if the people carrier with the family in it is still nearby. It's now about three cars back.

"My mum was a sick woman," I say. "She suffered from what her GP called a chemical imbalance in her brain. It made her depressed all the time. Stopped her from getting out of bed. So, they gave her drugs to counteract the imbalance and bring her levels up to normal."

"Fuck your mother!" Velak says. "Whore-bitch."

Abran says something angrily to Velak in their language and Velak sulkily looks away, out of the window.

"Essentially, they were using chemicals to change my mum's personality," I say, calmly ignoring the outburst.

"So what?" Abran says.

"So, my mum's brain was faulty. It wasn't producing chemicals in the right proportions for her to have a *normal* personality. Which, if you think about it, means that chemicals dictate what somebody's personality is like."

"Your mother was sick."

"Yes, she was sick. Because of an *imbalance* in her brain chemistry. So, the rest of us, we all have a balance of chemistry close enough to what society considers normal that we don't have to take medication. But that doesn't mean our thoughts and our actions aren't still dictated by chemicals in the same way. For us it's just less extreme. Which would suggest that free will is only an illusion."

"Yes, I know this. Is called determinism."

"What's called determinism?"

"The thing you talk about. Is called determinism. Means no free will. Means everything start at big bang and because atoms all start at same place, they all travel same way, and they will all end at same destination. The chemicals in our brain are born in stars billions of years in past, and so every decision we make was also born in those stars. We have no more choice about where we end up than golf ball hit by golf club."

"Yes I suppose that *is* what I'm talking about."

"So what? Why you talk about this?"

"I'm just trying to make you see that these acts you're perpetrating are... um... futile. Why believe what was written down in a book hundreds of years ago when it has no relevance in the modern world? Why waste your life following a doctrine as unscientific and outdated as Islam when it has essentially been proven wrong?"

"Islam?" Abran says.

"Yes. The fact that you understand a concept like, um, *determinism* tells me you must have doubts about being a Muslim."

"I have very *big* doubt about being a Muslim."

"You do?"

"Yes! I have *one hundred percent* doubt!" he shouts, laughing. "Hey Velak! He thinks we are a Muslim!"

Velak snaps his head from the window, looks at me, laughs. Nargis, on my right, is laughing too.

"Is that what you think, fat man?" Abran says, still laughing. "You think we are terrorist?"

And I laugh too. It's a deep laugh that shakes my body – a laugh of relief, although why I feel so relieved, I'm not sure. These men still intend to kill me. I suppose now I can see the possibility of a way out of this where I couldn't before. There's no negotiating with the kind of skewed logic that would make someone commit murder in the name of a god, but money, anger, revenge… those are motives I can work with.

"You think I am Muslim, fat man?" Velak smiles.

I shrug and smile back. Velak's smile twists into a sneer.

"I look like fucking Arab to you?" he says.

He hammers a fist into my crotch, catching me square in my love-spuds. I crumple into my own lap. Air empties from my lungs along with a mist of nose-blood that speckles the upholstery and the back of Abran's suit.

"Velak!" Abran shouts, then all three men argue in their native tongue, which I now guess isn't Arabic. I keep my head down and my eyes closed and I try to breathe through the sickening, winded pain. When the three of them are calm, when the ache in my testicles has dulled, I turn, without lifting my head up from my knees, and I look at Velak.

"You know, Velak," I say. "You really do look like an Arab."

Docklands: When I wake up my cheek is rubbing against some kind of fabric. The weight and pressure of blood in my head says I'm upside down. There's pain in my head too, and it goes beyond the usual hangover headache. It's more real. More present. It has a focal point, a specific, pulsing region of origin at my crown. Beneath me; footsteps on tarmac. Behind me; voices and more footsteps. Somebody is carrying me over their shoulder. The voices belong to Velak and Abran, so Nargis must be doing the carrying. I groan to let him know I'm conscious and he immediately crouches, setting me on my feet, which, for a moment, don't seem like they're going to be able to take my weight.

When I stand up and straighten my neck the pain flashes like a stripped nerve, so I duck my head, hang it low between my shoulders. We're walking through a car park towards a warehouse that backs onto the Thames. The building looks abandoned, weeds flourishing in its gutters and between the crumbling red bricks. Some of the windows are boarded and others are smashed. A tugboat trawls past, tethered to a barge stacked with metal containers, most likely a cargo of trash heading for one of the gargantuan landfills upstream. It's a familiar sight – my photography studio can't be more than a ten-minute walk from where we are.

Nargis pushes me in the back and that pain flashes again, navigating its way through bone, from my spine to my skull.

"Move," he says.

"Alright, take it easy," I say, staggering forward. "My head is fucking killing me."

"Is your fault for saying Velak look like Arab," Nargis says. "Even if is true. Make him very angry."

"It isn't just him. You all look like Arabs. Where are you guys actually from anyw—"

Only big pain in my ass is back there: This time when I wake up, I'm sitting in a chair, with my hands tied behind my back. Blood from my nose has clotted and dried down my face. My crotch is damp and I'm worried for a moment that I might've pissed myself – except there's a strong odour of freshly grated Parmesan cheese and, since I'm always reminded of vomit when I smell freshly grated Parmesan, it stands to reason that I'd be reminded of freshly grated Parmesan when I smell vomit. I don't raise my head because the region of pain has expanded from the top of my skull out to my forehead and down behind my ears.

The room is dark and empty, except for a pile of heavy chains, intertwined with snarls of rope. There's a weird scratching and snuffling sound, like a dog that's caught a scent, coming from behind me, possibly through a wall from another room. The only source of light is a window that's half boarded up. The small section of visible glass is fogged with grime.

A door opens and an angled pathway of light cuts across the floor, up to my chair. Abran enters, stands in front of me. I don't look up but I can tell it's him from the colour of his suit.

"Where's Blue?" I ask.

"Ah, you are awake," Abran says. "Good. Boss will be here soon. He will want to talk."

"Abran. Blue. Where is she?"

"Yes... Your girlfriend. I am very sorry, fat man. I lie about your girlfriend."

"What! What have you done to her?"

"No, I mean I lie when I say we have her."

As a revelation it's a difficult one to know how to take. On the one hand, Blue is alive. Unharmed. And that can only be good. On the other hand, I needlessly gave myself up without a fight. Actually, it's not that hard to know how to take it.

"Idiot!" I shout, bucking and straining against the rope binding my hands to the chair.

"You should have ask for proof that we have her before you agree to come," Abran says.

"Yes, Abran, I know that *now*, don't I?"

"If it make you feel better, Nargis and Velak have gone to collect her."

"How could that in *any* way make me feel *better?*"

"I don't know. Maybe you get to see girlfriend one last time before you die." Abran sniffs. "Did you vomit on self?"

"I don't remember doing it but, yes, I suppose I did. I think I might be concussed."

"Smells bad. Maybe is not so good you get to see girlfriend, huh?"

"Abran, listen," I ignore the rocketing pain in my temples and lever my chin up to look at him. "What's going on here? Have I got any way out of this?"

"Boss will talk when he arrives."

"How about *we* talk, you and me, before your boss gets here. You must know I'm quite a wealthy man. Maybe we could cut ourselves a little deal."

"You are not wealthy, not compared to boss. Compared to boss you are pheasant. Anyway, is not just money. Boss is powerful man. I cut deal and let you go and tomorrow I am *dead* man. But boss is reasonable, you will see. Maybe when you talk to him, he listen."

The snuffling sound behind me gets louder, becomes a sort of barking and groaning. There's a series of metallic thuds, then more sniffs and groans.

"Is there a dog back there, or something?" I say.

"Ha! *Dog!* There is no dog. Only big pain in my ass is back there."

"What is it?"

"You would not believe even if I say."

Shaking his head, Abran walks back out of the room and closes the door.

I try pulling at my restraints again, but my hands are tied fast. I can't even get halfway towards making a fist. My feet aren't tied but when I try to stand the chair doesn't budge. Either it's bolted to the floor or it's too heavy. I push backwards instead, against the rest, to see if I can get it to rock that way, but it won't rock. As I push more the wood flexes with a vulnerable creak. I push again, harder, and the creaking gets louder, but so does the heat and the pain in my head. Gritting my teeth, I tense my calves and my thighs and I stamp at the floor and the creaks in the chair become snaps. Abran might have the intellect to understand a concept like *determination*, or whatever it was called, but he failed to consider how easy it would be for a man of my substantial heft – a man he consistently refers to as 'fat man' – to break an old chair. I stamp again and the snaps become splinters. The splinters become loud cracks. The loud cracks become me tumbling backwards into a pile of destructed wood.

I lie on the floor with my hands still tied but the rope loosened, a warm flow of blood spreading back into my forearms. The exhilaration of freedom only lasts a few seconds. Find me like this and they'll give me more than just a bad headache.

I roll onto my side, then I roll onto one knee, then I'm kneeling, then I'm standing. Without the chair to hold it in place, the bondage unravels from my hands easily. I start to run for the window, but a blinding fissure opens in my head when I'm about halfway there and I swoon, before collapsing back to my knees. I crawl across the floor and grapple with the windowsill until I can lift myself up to it. The unboarded section of the window is too small for me to fit through. I wouldn't want to draw attention to myself with the sound of breaking glass anyway, so I focus on the plywood board, which covers the two larger sections below the mired glass. The board is fixed on the outside of the window frame and any broken glass has been cleared from the near side. I put my hands through the frame and push. Without much strain, the nails holding the board in place come loose from the crumbling mortar and it topples forward. The noise it makes when it lands is too loud. The time it took for me to hear that noise was too long. I poke my head out of the window and see that it's at least thirty feet down to some weedy, pot-holed tarmac. I'm thinking about the pile of chains and rope, tying them together so I can climb down, when I see a flash of sunlight bounce off an approaching windscreen. A car slides into the car park, a shimmy and a wiggle in the tail hinting that the driver isn't in full control, the vehicle powering over to a parking bay near the warehouse entrance, before a wrench of the handbrake flings it into a screeching turn and an abrupt halt. It's one of those sports cars with a six-figure price tag and bodywork somewhere between an aeronautical prototype for space tourism and a bike helmet. The two-tone green and yellow paint job shifts and blends depending on the angle it's viewed from, as if someone tried to recreate the precise hue of an infected sneeze. It's an ugly car, and that ugliness is part of its ostentation, and the ostentation is what makes it so spectacularly ugly.

The driver's gull-wing door clicks, then rises.

Out steps Mal.

The buyer: Mal looks a bit booze-bothered, unsteady, with a wandering five-pint stare. His off-kilter gait sets him zigzagging to the warehouse entrance, which he hammers with both fists. A few seconds later the doors open and he saunters inside.

In desperate need of a weapon, I collect one of the broken chair legs and smash it through the small pane of glass. The larger fragments pour outside, leaving me with nothing but shards the size of grit and sand and dust. I try the pile of chains, running the hefty links through my fingers, and I start to swing a length of about five feet. It's the best thing I've got.

Footsteps outside the door. Abran must've heard the shattering glass. I brace myself, knees bent, swinging the chain, ready to launch it. Abran kicks the door so hard one of the hinges pings against the wall behind me. It's the first time I've seen him properly enraged, his tendons stuck out like plastic seams along the sides of his neck. His face is flushed crimson, tightly creased, a frown so deep I can't see his eyes.

"What the fuck is this, fat man?" he shouts.

I spin the chain at my side, throwing ripples of turbulence across the room.

"You found a chain?" Abran says. "So what! I eat fucking chain!"

He lunges towards me, diving straight into the path of the chain as I sweep it round in a wide arc that catches him on the chin, and knocks him to the floor. But it doesn't knock him out. He rises, mouth gaping, his lower jaw hanging broken, an inch or two lower than anatomically correct, giving him an appearance of cartoonish bafflement. I swing again and he takes a step back.

"You did eat that chain, didn't you, Abran!" I say, the sudden surge of adrenaline apparently making me want to quip like I'm in a third-tier Sylvester Stallone movie. "Want some more? Because I've got plenty to dish out."

Abran peels off his suit jacket, wraps it up in both hands, stretches it between them like a pair of oven gloves. He comes forward again, slowly this time. I throw the chain overhand so that it falls on him from above. He reaches with his jacket, catches the chain before it strikes his head, but fails to get a tight enough grip on it as I pull it back out of his hands. I whip the chain quickly at his side, thrashing his ribs, breaking them with a dull crunch. Somehow, he ignores the pain, slaps his arm down, trapping the chain between those ribs and his enormous bicep. I pull the chain again but this time it holds firm. Abran's eyes narrow. He'd be smiling if he could. He drops the jacket, grasps the chain with both hands and yanks me towards him. I release my hold and allow myself to fall to the floor, grazing my knees on the dust of broken glass. Abran hurls the chain with enough force to smash the floorboards as I roll out of its way. He throws it again. This time I'm not fast enough and it glances my shoulder. An exquisite shard of agony travels down my arm to my fingertips. As Abran throws the chain again, I scoop up a handful of broken glass and throw it in his face, at the same time rolling away from the falling metal. Glass in his eyes and in his throat, Abran lurches off balance and the chain smacks harmlessly into the floor. He totters, blinking furiously, choking, spinning the chain at nothing. I run at him, throw a fist up at his dangling chin, clattering it into the roof of his mouth, ripping the tendons in his jaw. He falls backwards with a wail, clutching his ruined face in his hands and I snatch away the chain.

"What the fuck am I supposed to do now, Abran?" I say.

I take the chain in my good arm. My other arm is stiff, unable to move. The shoulder might be broken. Abran sits on the floor, trying frantically to put his unhinged face back together. And I suddenly have the terrifying realisation that I'm going to have to kill him.

There's no way round it.

If I don't, I'll be no better than one of those squealing blonde birds you get in horror films – the ones that don't take the chance to finish off the villain when it's given to them. The ones that have me shouting 'kill him, you silly bitch' at the TV. But she never kills him, does she? No. She legs it. And she's inevitably murdered once the villain has had chance to regroup.

Trembling, I start to spin the chain. With one hand, it's hard to control the weight of it. Abran doesn't move, doesn't flinch from the punches of air. Perhaps he's in shock. Perhaps he's accepted what's coming.

Under my breath, I say, "I can't do this," and Abran makes a spluttering sound that might be 'Don't' and holds up his hands in surrender.

If I make it out of this warehouse, I'll be hearing that 'Don't' again in my nightmares.

I try to end things quickly, aiming for the top of Abran's skull, but throwing the chain one-handed fucks with my coordination and it thumps into his shoulder. He wails and rocks forward, clutching the top of his arm.

"Jesus. Sorry, Abran."

I try again, but this time miss completely, and the poor bastard flinches as the chain smacks against the floorboards.

My final attempt is a direct hit, cracking the top of Abran's skull like the shell of a hard-boiled egg. He falls backwards, eyes open, bloody saliva bubbling from the twitching pink mush of teeth and bone that used to be his mouth.

One second a man, the next a corpse.

I close my eyes.

How are you supposed to feel after you end someone's life? Indigestion seems to be my body's immediate response. I bend over and grip my knees against the pain in my stomach.

Somewhere in the future, a therapist just hit the jackpot.

I run to the door, out onto a suspended walkway that stretches the length of the warehouse. There are several rusted staircases descending to the concrete floor. It's a vast space, mostly empty, except for a couple of large steel shipping containers and a few wooden crates, the dim, granular light of the room dissected by mote-filled sunbeams from a series of skylights. Mal stands alone in the middle of it all, facing away from me towards the door. I sprint along the walkway, down the first set of stairs, and across the concrete. He hears me coming, turns, fixes a bleary squint on me that slowly becomes moon-eyed terror. He twirls, trips over his own feet, scampers towards the door.

"Oh no you don't, Mal!" I shout.

His pace falters and he looks over his shoulder with confusion. Then he stops and I slow down, walking towards him until there's only ten feet separating us.

"Jim?" he says. "Oh, thank God! I thought you were a bloody *zombie!*"

I frown at him and he attempts to explain, "You know, one of those *scary* new ones… one of the ones that can run."

I continue to frown.

"Because of the blood," he says. "All around your mouth."

I touch a finger to my mouth, then to the crusty black snot-blood combo that clogs my nostrils. Mal wheezes. The ten-yard jog has done him in.

"Christ, Jim. Are you alright? You look a bit of a mess, if you don't mind me saying."

"I just had a tussle with your boy, Abran."

"Abran? Who's that then? Do you mean the big fellow… in the blue suit? He ran off after he let me in… said he had to go and check on something."

"He was checking on me."

"I'm sorry, Jim, I don't follow. What was he checking on you for? What are you *doing* here?"

"Can you drop the act, Mal?"

Mal shakes his head, mouth open, brow still lined with drunken confusion.

"Is it because of your wife?" I say.

"My... wife?"

"Is that why I've never met her? Because you think I might recognise her? Is *she* the Persian Princess?"

"Is my wife... a Persian princess?"

"I'll admit, I was wrong about you being a terrorist. Your boys weren't at all happy when they found out I thought they were Muslims."

"A terrorist? My... boys? Why do you keep talking about *my* boys?"

"Go upstairs. See what's left of one of them."

"Jim, *please*," Mal slaps a hand to the side of his head, rubs it down one of his jowls, "I had a couple of glasses of calvados after lunch... to aid digestion, you know how it is... and I had one or two carafes of wine *with* lunch... My brain's taking a little bit longer than usual to process... info. You really are going to have to spell things out for me. As far as I'm concerned, I'm just here to meet Anton."

"Who's Anton?"

"How on *earth* can you be in Anton's warehouse and not know who Anton is?"

"Who is Anton, Mal?"

"Anton Zlody. He should, er... he should be here by now," Mal says, looking first at his watch, then around the deserted warehouse. Following his gaze, it's at that moment I notice the noise coming from inside one of the cargo containers, a steady pattering of feet, which travels from one end to the other, turns around and paces back.

Mal starts to speak but I silence him with a raised finger.

I walk over to the container, press my ear against it. The patter continues, reverberating through the rusting metal. Quick steps. Something with four legs. I knock on the container and the pattering stops.

I knock again. There are a couple of bounding thuds over towards me, followed by a feline roar that echoes within the steel and knocks me backwards.

"Is there a fucking *lion* in there?" I say.

"Could be," Mal shrugs and says, "Sounds like some sort of big cat, anyway."

And then, with a metallic squawk, the warehouse doors are thrown open and Anton Zlody steps inside.

Anton: Anton Zlody is the scariest man you've ever seen. The *scariest* man. He must be about seven feet tall, the sort of height when the advantages of being tall start to become outweighed by the disadvantages, when the body's proportions are so misaligned that it looks deformed. Not that you'd notice much with Zlody – he's got more deformities than all the Bond villains combined. The skin on his face is reptilian rather than human, roughly textured by a lattice of intersecting scars, arranged in a way that suggests they were caused by design rather than accident. The scars continue all across his bald scalp, his cheeks, right down past his chin and his neck, to the collar of his shirt.

I've seen something similar before. About three years ago I worked for *Bloke* magazine on an article about scarification, an extreme alternative to tattooing that creates body art with cuts and brands, rather than ink. Through the assignment, I met a charmless Austrian violinist with sheet music sliced into his chest, the notes of his favourite piece of Wagner drawn out in the hot red of raw flesh. I also interviewed a teacher from Wakefield, who'd had her star sign branded onto the left cheek of her arse (*Bloke*'s editor pithily captioned the photo with *'Ass-trological'*). Both artistic renderings were intended for the purposes of beauty. Zlody's scars are something quite different. They are all about intimidation.

He's flanked by a couple of suit-wearing bruisers that must have been hired from the same dial-a-henchman agency as Abran and his buddies. He points at me and the scars on his face twist into a scowl.

"Why are you not tied up somewhere?" he says to me, and then, looking at Mal, "Have you been helping him?"

His accent is almost flawless, but that only serves to heighten the *foreignness* of it, emphasising any little imperfections that do exist. There's a loose rattle in his throat that says he's a forty-a-day man.

"I have to say, Anton, I'm rather *bamboozled* by all of this," Mal says. "I'm not entirely sure what you mean, asking if I helped him. Are you talking about Jim? Why is *Jim* here anyway?"

Zlody ignores him, turns his attention back to me.

"Where is Abran?" he says.

He walks past us into the warehouse, shouting Abran's name.

"He's upstairs," I say, quietly.

Zlody dashes the length of the warehouse in long freak-show strides, up the buckling stairs, taking them three at a time, ducking through the broken door, into the room that served as my cell. Five seconds of silence follow, before his lungs eject a gallon of fury and there's an explosion of breaking wood.

One of the hulks by the door shifts uneasily from one foot to the other, fiddling with the links of his watchstrap. The other hulk stares hard at me without blinking or moving.

"What exactly did you do up there, Jimbo?" Mal whispers behind a cupped hand.

I don't respond.

Zlody erupts from the room and crashes back down the stairs, leaving a trail of blood on the railings behind him. There's blood on the front of his shirt too. The savage design of his face is scrunched up like a ball of paper.

"You must have pulled some dirty fucking trick to take down Abran like that!" he shouts. "No way he would lose in a fair fight with a fat piece of shit like you."

"What's fair? Breaking my nose when I can't defend myself? Knocking me unconscious without any warning?"

"No. Not Abran. Maybe Velak or Nargis. But Abran... he has principles."

"Not anymore, he doesn't."

Zlody smiles, which is probably the most terrifying response he could have given me, far more unnerving than any angry rebuke. He gestures at his henchmen, says something to them in the same language I heard Abran speaking earlier, and they march towards me.

"Hey now!" Mal says. "I'm not sure I like what's going on here!"

The larger of the two men, the one that wouldn't stop staring at me, grabs my lapels and clatters the top of his skull into my face. My legs go limp but, amazingly, I don't black out. Not quite. I suppose I sort of *grey* out. I'm aware of him holding all of my weight and I can hear Mal shouting, "Jim! Are you alright? Jim! Jim!" and then Mal is saying, "What have you done to him, you rotten bastard?" and then Mal is throwing punches at the back of the guy's head and suddenly I'm on the floor because his attention has been diverted and he's let go of my jacket.

"Run, Jim!" Mal shouts. "Run my boy!"

But I'm not running anywhere. My head has taken too much of a beating. All the sounds are coming from the end of a long tunnel. The light is muffled. The only thing that feels real is the pain, which is so dizzying it makes me throw up again.

They've got Mal, I can see that, and they're looking to their boss to see what he wants them to do.

"Take them upstairs," Zlody says. "Both of them. Put them in the other room."

The other room, I think, as I'm dragged up by my collar. The room next to the one I was held in before. The room that had snuffling noises coming out of it – the snuffling noises of a very large animal.

The snuffler behind door number two: I'm starting to come out of my daze when they get me to the top of the stairs. They drag me along the walkway, with Mal grunting and doing his best to resist them somewhere behind me. The two rooms are alongside each other at the back of the warehouse, where they probably served as the owner's office, and the office of a foreman, when the building was in full use. We pass the first room I was kept in, the doorway open on Abran's body and the splintered carnage we wrought on the wooden floor.

I hear Mal saying, "Oh good God!" when he catches sight of the corpse.

The walkway turns at a right angle and continues up to the entrance of the next room, which is closed. Zlody walks up to the door, a solid piece of metal about four-fifths his height, painted green, with a small viewing hatch cut out of it. One of his thugs throws him a huge hoop of keys and he unlocks it.

"Honestly, gentlemen, I have never done this before," he says. "It will be interesting to see what happens."

They shove me in first, with an excess of force that lands me in a corner on the opposite side of the room. Mal follows, falls next to me, and they lock us in. We squint in the grey light, which is strained through a tarpaulin-covered skylight. Damp trouser material is cutting into the fat on my thighs, a chafing that could very quickly become a nappy rash.

"Christ Almighty, Jim. I don't mean to be rude but there's one hell of a vomit-y pong coming off you—"

Mal cuts himself short when something shuffles in the darkest part of the room – a plump mass of fur that looks like it's rearranging a pile of blankets. I hear that snuffling noise again, but much louder, along with a steady vibration that could be a purr or a growl.

"Mal, I think there's a high probability that I'm severely concussed, so you're going to have to confirm that what I think I'm looking at, is what I'm actually looking at."

"You aren't mistaken, Jimbo."

"What the fuck is going on? What is a *giant fucking panda* doing in an East London warehouse?"

Mal ignores me, starts to get up, softly saying, "Hello little chap. How are you then?"

"Mal, don't go near it, for fuck's sake! It'll tear your bloody face off!"

He looks at me for a second, then looks back at the panda.

"Oh, I'm sure it'd be sensible to exercise a certain amount of caution in this situation, but he wouldn't want to do us any serious harm," he says. Then, quietly to the panda, "Would you? Hey?"

Thankfully Mal stops moving forward when he gets within about eight feet of the beast. He squats on his haunches, holding his hands behind his back.

"What a magnificent beast," he says.

"That thing could turn on us. Any second. Look at its *claws*, Mal. They're massive. We need to get out of here."

"And how do you propose we do that, with those brutes guarding the door?"

Zlody peers in through the window, his jagged lips spread back in a grin, displaying huge pink gums and tiny flat teeth.

"I don't know, Mal. But there are two of us in here. We need to think of something. We can't just roll over and let them feed us to a panda."

"Feed us to a panda?" Mal laughs. "Jim, these lovely creatures are omnivorous."

"I'm not much of a biologist, I'll grant you, but doesn't omnivorous mean they eat *everything?*"

"They might snaffle the odd rodent or insect here or there, but nothing bigger than that. And, as I'm sure you're aware, they spend most of their time harmlessly munching on bamboo."

"Will you please leave it alone and come back over here? My head is pounding. We've got enough on our plate, without throwing a pissed off bear into the mix."

Mal holds up his hands in a pacifying gesture and sits down with his back to the wall. He takes a hip flask from his inside pocket, unscrews the cap and holds it out for me to take.

"They confiscated my phone," he says, "but they left me with this, which is something."

I grab the flask. There's a hollow plunk of liquid inside it. Even at arm's length I can smell the cherry-oak barrels. The peat. The ocean spray.

"Algablanden," I say. "Eighteen years."

Mal nods.

"Hell of a nose you've got there, Jimbo," he says.

"I've been trying to give up booze," I say. "Haven't touched a drop since... What day are we on?"

"Sunday."

"Haven't touched a drop since... yesterday."

Mal frowns at me and leans closer.

"Why would you want to put yourself through something like that?"

"It doesn't matter now, does it? We probably won't be alive tomorrow. If we're going to go out, might as well go out supping on some of Scotland's finest."

"Amen to that."

I put the flask to my lips, tip my head back, pour the fire and the smoke into my mouth. It hits my throat, burns down my gullet and sparks a furnace in my belly. The heat radiates and my whole body slumps a few inches as the rising temperature massages the strain from my muscle fibres. My chest expands. My heart races. My breathing slows. Popeye, a cork pipe, and a can of spinach spring to mind.

"Oh, Mal. I needed that," I say, my eyes closed. "I really did."

"So I see."

Realising something, I look at Mal's wrist.

"If they didn't take your hipflask... did they take your watch?"

"As a matter of fact, they didn't. But I know what you're thinking, Jim."

"What am I thinking?"

"You're thinking we could use the built-in satellite SOS beacon thingamajig to signal for help."

"Mal, that is *exactly* what I'm thinking."

"Won't work, I'm afraid."

"Why not?"

"Because I kept setting the damn thing off. Remember that time we were sitting out on the wine terrace at *Veliki Pić* and that bloody great helicopter landed in the car park?"

"Not really, no..."

"You'd been doing a shoot with that rapper fellow?"

"Collizion?"

"That's the one. You brought a couple of the models out afterwards. A pair of muscular Nubians with big hair doos."

"Oh, *right!* Yes! The girls were mightily pissed off because the downdraft from the rotor blades messed up their afros!"

Mal nods.

"That helicopter was responding to *my* distress signal," he says. "I'd set it off earlier when I got stuck in the toilet cubicle and had a panic. The rescue team were rather irate, as it happens... Well, if they don't want you using the button, they shouldn't make it so big and so red and so damn tempting to push!"

He flutters his wrist at me, and the watch appears from beneath the cuff of his shirt. The emergency button is indeed very big and red and ferociously tempting.

"What will they do if you push it now?" I say.

"Nothing… It's been deactivated. To be fair to them they did allow me another couple of *transgressions* before they cut me off."

"Brilliant," I say with a sigh. "Is Zlody still watching us?"

"Um… no. No, I can just see the back of his bodyguard's head through the window."

"The big one?"

"They're both big buggers, Jim. But, yes, the *bigger* one."

I take another swig of the whisky and hand the flask back to Mal. The pain in my head dulls, becomes less tangible. It's now more an *idea* of pain. A loose concept of discomfort.

"Who is he then?" I ask.

"Who is who?"

"The lizard-man. Anton Zlody."

"I suppose *Russian mafia* is how you'd best describe him."

"What are *you* doing meeting the Russian mafia in a warehouse on a Sunday afternoon?"

"I'm afraid it has quite a lot to do with that little chap over there," he says, pointing his hip flask in the direction of the panda. "Anton is a smuggler, you see, with a special line in endangered species."

I stare at the panda while I take in what Mal just said. It doesn't seem bothered by us, still fussing in the darkness with the heaped blankets, scrabbling at them with those huge claws. It's the first time I've noticed how much pandas, with their black-and-white face-jobs, look like fat French mimes.

After a few minutes of careful consideration, I say: "Are you telling me that you're here to buy a *panda?*"

"Indeed I am."

"Fuck off, Mal."

"It's the truth, Jim."

"No. Fuck off. That's ridiculous."

Mal sips the whisky, clicks his teeth and winces. He passes the flask back to me.

"I'm sure it probably does sound ridiculous to you," he says. "But when you're in my position, when you have as much money as I do, the number of things you can't have is close to non-existent. The excitement the average man on the street feels when he's set aside enough cash to buy a flash new car, or a 70-inch flatscreen, simply isn't there for a man like me."

"So you just think *fuck it, I'll buy a panda?*"

"It's not as frivolous as that. I've always loved pandas, Jim, ever since I was a little boy. My mum loved them too. She *adored* them. But she never got to see one in the flesh before she died…"

Talking to myself more than anything, I say, "The sculpture of the panda in your house… I just thought it was some weird ethnic decoration…"

"Had it specially commissioned."

"And that silly necklace you wear…"

Mal nods.

"And the first time we ever met… my exhibition… photos of a fucking—"

"Panda," Mal says.

"No. I can't accept this. After everything I've been through… a panda. I mean… it can't be… it can't be *that fucking stupid.*"

"I don't know what else to tell you."

"Hold on… is this what all the excavation work is for, in your garden?"

Mal nods again and says, "A new home for Pì Pì. His main accommodation is finished. His bathing pool and exercise area should be sorted by the end of the month. I was supposed to be taking delivery of him earlier this week but, with this asphyxi-wank business and all the fuzz sniffing around, it seemed too risky. Anton's been pestering me since Wednesday, says he doesn't have the men to spare to take care of a panda any longer. But what was I supposed to do?"

The phone call I overheard after the meal at Mal's house and the phone call I overheard in Mal's office; he must have been talking to Zlody.

"This is fucking *ludicrous*, Mal. I just... I can't..."

I try to form a sentence but my brain can't come up with the words to create an appropriate response to this absurd situation. Eventually, I manage: "How the fuck did you find out about this animal smuggling racket?"

"Oh, it's something the über-wealthy have always done."

"Of course it is."

"Goes back to big game hunting, except now instead of killing the animals, we keep them as pets. One of ADHD's founding partners, John Aldridge, has got a silverback gorilla living in his basement. John Dawes has converted one of the barns on his farm into a bloody great aquarium that's now home to a hammerhead shark and a shoal of barracudas. I was comparing notes with the chairman of Levinson Razor last month – that's probably his Siberian tiger you heard in the shipping container downstairs."

"How much does a panda cost then?"

"Ah, you'll be disgusted with me, I think..."

"How much, Mal?"

"Thirty million."

"Jesus—"

"Plus two million a year for every year that it lives after that."

"*Jesus Christ*, Mal! You could buy a fucking top-rate Premiership footballer for that..."

"But, Jim, don't you see? That's why we're going to be alright, you and me. Zlody isn't about to write off thirty mill', is he? And he knows that if he does anything to you, then I'll be going straight to the police. His only option is to let us both go."

"I wouldn't be so sure about that."

I fill Mal in on *The Persian Princess* and my trips to *The Bunker*. About Rusty Dawn and Brendan Hardy's obsession theory. About my own theory of terrorism.

"You thought I was an Islamic extremist?" Mal says, laughing.

"Looking back at it now, it seems ludicrous."

"I would've thought it would seem pretty bloody ludicrous looking *forward* at it as well!"

"More ludicrous than purchasing a panda for thirty million quid?"

"Hmmm... I suppose you've got me there."

"Anyway, I had this memory of you telling me that your mum was an Arab, or Persian or something, and I got a bit carried away... but then it turned out it wasn't your mum I was thinking of at all – it was your nanny."

"My nanny was Romanian."

"Yes, I know. I suppose I thought they had Muslims in Romania."

"They do!"

"Not very many, though."

"No, but Maida was one of them!"

"She was?"

"Oh, yes. Lovely girl and all, but a smidge too quick to bring religion into the conversation. It was always *Inshallah* this and *Mashallah* that. Gets a bit tiresome after the third or fourth time, and they say it every bloody time they open their mouths. I mean what are you supposed to do when you ask someone if they'd like a cup of tea and they respond with *God willing?* Do they want you to just put out a mug and a teabag and let the Holy Father get on with it?"

"I don't think Muslims call him the Holy Father."

"Who really gives a shit, Jim? As we've just discussed, this Islamo-bollocks has zero bearing on our current predicament."

"It does explain where I got the idea from, though. So that's something."

"Do you follow this Hardy chap's line of thought, then? Do you think Zlody's obsessed?"

I shrug and say, "He's definitely the buyer."

"So what are we going to do?"

I look around the room for inspiration, but there's even less for us to make use of in here than there was in the first room they kept me in. The skylight is too high for us to reach. All we've got at our disposal is the panda and a pile of blankets.

"You aren't going to like this, Mal," I say.

"What am I not going to like?"

"We have to kill the panda."

Black and white and red all over: "We are *not* killing Pì Pì, Jim. Not a bloody chance."

"It's our only option."

"Do you know how many pandas there are left in the wild? Not even two thousand."

"And now, thanks to you, there's one less."

Mal sighs.

"How could killing Pì Pì possibly be of any help to us?"

"We need a weapon. He's got weapons. Those claws of his could do some damage."

"Maybe, if you got in close and managed a direct hit to someone's eyeball, *maybe then* you could partially blind them with one of those claws. And that's pushing it."

"I've already blinded two of these goons – I'm getting to be a bit of a *dab hand* where blindings are concerned."

"From what you've told me, you've just been tremendously lucky. What are we supposed to do once we've killed Pì Pì anyway?"

"You get their attention," I say, pointing at the guard through the window in the door. "I'll lie on the floor thrashing around with the panda's body on top of me. Tell them to let you out, that the panda is ripping me apart. Then, while their guard is down, I'll come at them and stick a panda claw in somebody's eye."

"And *then* what?"

"We run."

"Where would we run? They've got my car keys."

"My studio isn't far from here. We could hide out there and call for help."

"It's a terrible plan, Jim. Very *loose*. Rather than cover every eventuality, it doesn't cover *any* of them."

"We have to do *something*. Before I had my little tussle with him, Abran said that his buddies were on their way to pick up Blue."

"That nice bit of totty you were talking to at the burlesque club?"

"Yes. Remember how I told you she used to be a pornstar?"

"*She's* the Persian Princess? I don't remember her looking very Persian."

"No, Mal. She played the princess's sister."

"That would still make her character Persian though, wouldn't it? Seems a bit of a stretch…"

"She was wearing a black wig and brown make-up."

"Oof. Sounds a smidge *problematic*."

"The cultural insensitivity of a twenty-year-old porno isn't our most *pressing* concern. I need to warn her before they get to her."

"You think they're going to kill her as well, do you?"

"That would fit in with the prevailing pattern, wouldn't it? If Zlody *is* obsessed with the Persian Princess, he isn't going to want to let the girl who raped her on screen with a gem-encrusted strap-on get away with it, is he?"

"A gem-encrusted… strap on…"

Mal sips some whisky, watching the panda, which has finally managed to make itself comfortable, lying on its stomach with its eyes open. He whispers something that I don't quite catch.

"What?"

"How would we kill Pì Pì?" Mal whispers again, slower this time, and slightly louder. "You said it yourself – he'll tear your face off if you try anything."

"I thought you said they were harmless?"

"I said it would be sensible to be careful. He's still a bloody great bear, isn't he?"

"I was thinking we'd wrap its head in one of those blankets. To confuse it. And then we'd just sort of... beat it to death."

"Beat it to death? With what? *Our fists?* He's a 300-pound beast, Jim. Even if we could get one over on him, it'd take us quite a while. Don't you think the guard would notice?"

"I'll bash it with your hip flask. There's got to be a weak spot somewhere – like punching a shark on the nose."

"Punching a shark on the nose repels it, it doesn't kill it. Animals don't have self-destruct buttons."

"Alright then, one of us will wrap a blanket round its neck and strangle it, while the other smothers it. We don't have time to argue about this, Mal."

I stand up and take a deep breath. The panda's eyes follow me sleepily.

"Jim, please. *Don't*. It's... it's a waste of a panda."

"Bollocks to it."

I leap across the room, on top of the panda, grab hold of the sheet folded between its enormous forepaws and pull it up over its head. The panda bucks, flexes its back legs and kicks up off the floor. It makes a noise like a yawning dog, but with an angry base tremor that I can feel vibrating through its firm flesh and coarse fur. I wrap my arms around the sheet, drawing it tight over the panda's head and its neck. I try to squeeze but the panda's ostensibly cuddly appearance hides a solid framework of muscle. It rears up onto two legs, swiping at the air with its boxing-glove paws.

"Mal, you were right. I don't think this was a good idea."

I continue to hold on, and the panda lurches across the room.

"Jim, what should I do?" Mal shouts.

Hearing his voice, the panda lumbers towards him, pedalling its front legs. Mal ducks, crawls across the floor in an attempt to get out of its way, but the panda follows.

"He's got my scent, Jim! The bugger's coming for me!"

There's too much commotion. The guard hears what's happening, sees me struggling through the window. He opens the door.

"What fuck you are doing to panda?" he shouts.

Deranged by the new sound, the panda charges at the guard, swats at his face with those claws, slicing crimson gullies into his cheeks, through his lip, across his chin. The guard throws frantic punches at the panda's torso but he can't hold off the brawny animal's momentum and he's pushed back through the door. I see what's about to happen and release my grip, sliding from the beast's back as the guard smashes against the walkway railing, his upper body bent backwards. The panda continues over the guard and flips beyond the rail, falling onto the concrete warehouse floor. A thunderclap echoes around the huge warehouse as the guard's back is pushed too far and his spine breaks. He sighs in pain, unable to move, balanced precariously on the handrail with his torso at a severe tangent to his legs.

Mal runs to the handrail, peers over at the unmoving form of his £30-million pet. The expression on his face is thin and beaten. I grab his arm, pull him towards the other room.

"No time to grieve. *We need to get out of here.*"

Down in the warehouse Zlody and the other guard are already running towards us, shouting to each other in Russian.

"Jesus, Jim. *You* did that?" Mal says when we he sees Abran.

"He was going to do worse to me."

I pick up the rope, which is frayed, but looks like it should hold long enough for us to make our escape.

"Are you any good at tying knots?" I say.

"I can tie my shoes."

"Right. You hold the door, I'll sort the rope."

The door doesn't close fully because of its busted hinge, so Mal just props it over the doorway and leans his weight against it.

"You'd better be quick, I think they're at the stairs," he says.

I tie a double knot around the middle section of window frame, throw the rope out of the window and watch it uncoil. It barely makes it halfway down the side of the building.

"The rope doesn't reach all the way, Mal," I say, with a leg already out the window. "We'll have to jump the last bit."

Mal lets go of the door as I start to abseil down one-handed, my wounded shoulder still too tender to take much weight. Mal is just climbing out when I reach the bottom of the rope, and there's a crash from above as the door is kicked off its remaining hinge.

I let go of the rope, hit the pockmarked tarmac with a thud that jars my shins, and roll over broken glass. Mal still hasn't reached the end of the rope. I can see Zlody at the window, working furiously to untie the knot, but Mal's weight is pulling it tight, preventing Zlody's banana-fingers from prising the loops apart. Zlody disappears back into the room for an instant, then a foot shoots out, kicking through the wooden frame. The rope falls and Mal falls the last fifteen feet with it, landing in a seated position next to me.

"Bastard!" he shouts. "I think I've broken my arse, Jim!"

"Can you stand?"

He rises shakily. The broken glass has punctured the seat of his pants. Bloodstains darken the fabric. I put his arm around my neck, and we start to jog across the car park at a speed that wouldn't suggest we're running from any danger. It's more like a token gesture, like the little skip you put into your step to let a driver know you're doing your best not to inconvenience them as you cross the road in front of their car.

"How far is your studio?" Mal says.

"About five minutes if we run, maybe a little more."

"They're faster than we are. They aren't injured. Let's just stop at the next building and ask whoever's inside for help."

"Most of these factories are derelict. Even the ones that aren't – it's Sunday. There won't be anyone around."

"Shit."

"We're going to have to sprint for it, Mal. Forget about your broken arse. This is a real run-for-your-life kind of deal."

I don't have to say anything else. Mal snatches his arm back from my shoulder and bolts forward. His strides are laboured, with an uneven hobble that comes straight from that potential fracture in his coccyx, his right leg bending smoothly, while his left is thrown out to the side in a jolted step. I struggle with my own injuries, but I catch up, tell him to follow me down a path that takes us along the river, out of sight of the warehouse. And suddenly, without that visual reminder of danger, the quiet normality of pigeons and clouds and crumbling red bricks and floating nests of garbage is starkly surreal.

I urge Mal onwards when he starts to slow down by squeezing his shoulder, while dealing with my own body's stern protests against the exertion. There's a tightness in my chest that deep breaths can't suppress. The pain spreads, feeling its way through my body with long fingers, prying apart sinews and tweaking nerves. I taste iron. The red smell of it is in my nose, conjuring memories of school cross-country, racing up a frosted peak, lungs freshly seared by a lunchtime fag behind the cricket pavilion, always one of the stragglers, with Mr Capstick drill-sergeanting behind me in his tiny red shorts.

Every few seconds I glance back over my shoulder. There's still no sign that anybody is following us, but they must be out of the warehouse by now. It's only a matter of time before they discover this path.

A canal branches away from the Thames and the water shifts from the swirling brown of the river to glassy black, disturbed only by the slow ripples of an empty polystyrene takeaway box sailing in the breeze. We take the narrow towpath, through an overgrowth of weeds, until a building looms over us, its ground floor windows fitted with iron bars, its sooted red brick scrawled with gang tags and rude-boy cartoons. My studio is on the top floor. There's no entrance on the canal side, but there is an external fire escape that hangs over the towpath. Using the bars on one of the lower windows as a foothold, I climb up to put my hands on the bottom step of the metal staircase.

Mal pushes my feet from below so that I can haul the rest of my body onto it, then I turn round and help him to climb up behind me.

"Everything hurts," Mal says.

"I know."

"Everything, Jim. Running... climbing... *standing...* I'm fucked. I can't do much more of this."

"Believe me, I know. Once we get inside, we'll be safe. We can rest. It'll all be over."

At the top of the stairs there's a closed door, lacking a handle.

"What do we do now?" Mal says, panting, one hand on the door.

I motion for him to step back, then I throw my weight behind my good shoulder and barge through.

"The catch is weak," I say. "Doesn't lock properly."

"Lucky for us."

"If I'm working with people that object to me smoking, I'll prop open this door and come out to the fire escape. It's closed on me a few times before but that catch is so weak I can shove it back open, no problem."

"What if somebody broke in? You should get it fixed."

I shrug. "I get it fixed and next time I go out for a fag it'll blow shut behind me. Sod's law."

"Well let's just hope Zlody and his pals don't try and get in this way."

"They won't. If they didn't see us come in, then they won't have any idea we're up here."

My assistant hasn't cleared up the dressing room yet, so there are still huge stacks of empty boxes left over from the most recent shoot. I push them aside and walk straight to my desk. The dressing room has a landline installed in it, and a retro Bakelite telephone with a rotary dial. After the shoot I got Blue to complete a pay form, filling out all her personal details including her telephone number. The sheet of A4 is laid out handily on the desk next to the phone. I call the number but there's no answer. Thinking about it, there's been no answer from her for the last couple of days. I try calling two more times.

"Shit. She isn't answering."

"So what do we do?" Mal says.

"First, I need to change out of this suit."

"And not a moment too soon! You smell like bloody *Parmesan*. How many times *have* you puked on yourself today?"

"Twice, I think."

"That has to be some kind of record."

"Not even close. Remember that tampon commercial we shot on Mount Vesuvius?"

"Ah, yes. How could I forget?" Mal laughs.

"Shat my pants more than once as well."

"Those were the days, Jimbo!" Mal says. "So, you're going to put on some new clobber… Then what?"

"I'll try calling Blue again. If I still can't get through, I suppose we'll have to go to the police."

"Ah," Mal says. "Now, that might not be the best idea."

"Why not? I don't think they can charge me with Abran's murder. That was clearly self defence. And we can come up with a story that'll put you in the clear too – they don't have to know you were at the warehouse to buy a panda."

"That's not what I mean," Mal says. "Zlody has a great deal of influence. There are a lot of policemen on his payroll."

"Do you think Rätsel might be one of them?"

Mal shrugs. "Possibly."

"Hmm. He might be a prick, but he came across as a man of integrity. He was pursuing the case a tad too aggressively to make me think he's dishonest."

Mal frowns.

"You were willing to believe I was a fucking terrorist, but you have reservations when it comes to Rätsel being bent?"

I unbutton my trousers and let them fall into a heap around my ankles.

"Fair point," I say. "We trust no-one, then."

The suit I changed out of on Wednesday, the one with the vomit-flecked jacket, is hanging on the back of the office chair. The orange spots have lost some of their fast-food luminescence as they dried, but they still stand out against the dark grey, like splashes of highlighter ink. I might be exchanging one vomit covered outfit for another, but at least this suit doesn't smell. At least it isn't damp. I change quickly, using a towel from the shower room to dry between my legs, then I call Blue's number again. There's still no answer but only a few seconds after I put down the receiver the phone rings.

"Blue?" I say.

"Oh. I suppose I thought it might be you." Her voice is flat. Detached.

"Blue, where are you?"

"With a friend."

"Are you at home?"

"No, I'm at his place."

As much as I don't like the sound of that, it should make it harder for Velak and Nargis to track her down.

"Okay," I say. "You need to listen to me. I'm not drunk. Listen to my voice. Am I slurring?"

"No. You aren't slurring."

"Please, Blue. Don't dismiss what I'm about to tell you. I've been through a lot today and I probably would've given up already if it wasn't for you."

"Oh, Jimmy. Can we just forget about it all? Pretend we never ran into each other? This is getting painful now. We missed our chance. Whatever relationship we had… I think it was meant to stay in the past."

"Okay. If that's what you want then I'll accept it, even if I really, *really* don't like the idea. But you need to listen to me. You are in danger.

Real danger. This isn't some wild theory of mine – this is happening. Me and Mal just escaped from a warehouse where we were being held captive. We jumped out of a fucking third floor *window.*"

"I thought you said Mal was the one trying to kill you?"

"Yes. I did. And I was wrong about that. But I've been beaten up enough times today to know that I'm not wrong about the rest of it. People want us dead. And they're outside right now, looking for us."

"Who?"

"The Russian mafia."

"Why do the Russian mafia want you dead?"

"Not just me and Mal, Blue. They want you, too. And I haven't worked out the *why* yet. All I know is, it's got something to do with *The Persian Princess.*"

"Please, Jimmy… I don't want to think about that movie."

"Neither do I, but that's what it all ties back to. Al, Keith, Dane – they all worked on it. So did I. So did you. If I hadn't managed to fight them off, you'd be the only one left alive."

"What about Anna?"

"Anna?"

"The Persian princess. I suppose you don't know whether or not *she's* still alive?"

"No. I don't know anything about her. Nobody does. The only thing that's certain is that she never made any more porn."

"That's not a surprise. She was in such bad shape after we made the film… A girl that fragile… she must've been very desperate to resort to porn work. I got the feeling Dane had something over her, as if she owed him something. And the weird way that he separated her from us between takes…"

"Yes. It wasn't the most *comfortable* production I worked on."

"Why don't you call the cops? You obviously have a phone."

"Mal says this Zlody guy, the Russian, has bought half the police. We don't know who we can trust. We think maybe that detective, Rätsel, is clean, but we can't be sure."

"What are you going to do?"

"We're going to, um… Mal, what are we going to do?"

While I've been talking to Blue, Mal has wandered through to the main studio. He comes back to the dressing room and walks through the door with a half empty bottle of whisky in his hand.

"Jim," he says excitedly. "There's a dead stag on the floor through there. Ripped to bloody shreds, it is. Guts and blood all over the shop. I don't know how it got there but it might be a message. A mafia sort of thing. Like the horse's head. You know, *'he sleeps with the fishes'* and all that business. Except perhaps the Russians do it differently to the Sicilians… There might be some significance in the antlers… *Did I read about that somewhere?* Anyway, if it is a message, then Zlody must know about your studio after all. So we aren't safe here. We need to bloody well *go.*" Mal looks at the bottle in his hand. "This whisky is absolute *piss*, by the way," he says, before taking a lengthy swig.

"Mal," I hold up a hand. "You don't need to worry. That stag is a prop. It isn't *real*. I had a shoot here on Wednesday."

"Oh. A prop. Of course. We're still alright then, aren't we? False alarm." Another swig of whisky. "Sorry, what was it you wanted?"

"Blue. She wants to know what we're going to do."

"Right," he says and points at the phone. "Is that her?"

I nod.

"Hello Blue!" Mal says, waving.

"She says 'hello' back," I reply, without actually giving her the chance. "What are we going to do, Mal?"

"Hmmm… Good question. Normally if I was in a pickle like this, I'd give my contacts in the underworld a call and get them to help me out but…"

"But Zlody is your contact in the underworld?"

"Quite. Yes. Him and his associates."

I hear Blue sighing.

"I could come and pick you up," she says. "I've got my car with me."

"No. Absolutely not," I say. "That would bring you right to them. For now, you're safe. The guy you're with, is he big?"

"One of the bouncers from the club."

"Oh."

"It's not like *that*. I did take some of what you said seriously. I mean, you couldn't have made up that scar around your neck, could you? So I asked Bernie if I could stay with him for a little while. Just as a *precaution*."

"No. Right. That's good. Means you're safe. That's what I wanted to check. That you're *safe*."

"He's gay, Jimmy."

"Right. Is he? Good. Okay. Um..."

Blue laughs.

"You sit tight, Blue," I tell her. "We'll figure something out."

She hangs up, which seems a tad abrupt. Then there's a sustained beep, like a heart monitor registering a cardiac arrest.

"Someone's cut the line," I tell Mal, still holding the phone to my ear.

"What line?" he asks.

"The phone line."

"Oh. Hers or ours?"

I shrug and ask, "Is there a way you can tell?"

Then the building's intruder alarm starts blaring.

What's a suitable derogatory term for a Russian? "We need to make sure the front door is locked!" I shout over the shrieking klaxons.

I sprint across the studio, leaping over the deer carcass, slipping off my shoes when they get stuck in the tacky fake blood. I push the door and rattle the handle. It holds firm.

Mal catches up to me, starts to push the oak liquor cabinet against the door and I help him by pulling from the other side. Outside the door, there's an echo of feet slapping against concrete that travels up the stairwell, getting louder.

"We continue to underestimate you, it seems!" Zlody shouts once he's reached the top of the stairs. He isn't even out of breath.

The door shudders with the impact of a kick.

"You killed one of my men. Two, if you count poor Zvekan, but I think you could argue it was the bear that got him."

The door shudders again, louder this time. I crouch down and place my back against the liquor cabinet, bracing with bent knees, signalling for Mal to do the same. Each wail of the intruder alarm thumps against the sore point on the back of my scalp, filling my eyes with white light.

"But for every one of my men that you put down, there are ten more to take his place. The only advantage you have is that I won't let them kill you. I want that satisfaction to be *mine.*"

Another boot slams into the door. Each kick is louder than the last.

"Come on, James," Zlody says. "Did you really think you could hide from me in your studio? It took us less than a minute to find the address listed on your website."

Mal gives me a hard stare, at the same time upending the whisky bottle and tipping more booze into his mouth.

"I didn't even know I *had* a fucking website!" I say to him. George, my assistant, must have taken the initiative, trying to bring in more business and secure himself a full-time job. The sneaky little prick.

"A lot of planning went into all of this," Zlody continues. "A huge amount of effort. You are a stubborn bastard, I grant you, but that is only going to make things worse when I finally *do* get my hands on you."

"You hear that alarm?" I shout, aware of the unconvincing waver in my voice. "Well so does everyone else around here. The police will be on their way soon. If I were you, I'd clear off before they arrive."

Zlody laughs. The sound of his laughter disappears into the roar of the alarm as he backs up to kick the door again. The force of it shakes my gritted teeth.

"You know as well as I do that this part of London is empty," he says. "There might be a few houses across the street, but the crackheads that live in them won't pay much notice to any alarms. Even if they do, I have got the police in my pocket – your buddy Mallory must have told you that. A quick word to the right person and they will leave me to get on with my business. So, it is just a question of time. This door is not going to hold forever, especially when my deputy Marko gets here with his axe."

"Anton, isn't there some sort of *financial* arrangement we can come to that'll straighten all of this out?" This is from Mal.

"I have not got a problem with you, Mallory," Zlody says, the tone of his voice softening. "You can still walk away if you want to. But no amount of money is going to make me give up your friend. James Stakes is *mine*. And if you don't step aside, unfortunately you will be assuming the role of collateral damage, a very undignified way to go, in my opinion – not even important enough to be the target for your own murder."

"Oh *fuck off*, you pompous *Ruble-fucker!*" Mal says, hitching up the bottle of whisky once more, tugging at the rim with his lips, flicking out a hollow boom of escaping air.

Zlody furiously attacks the door then, landing a flurry of stamps and shoulder barges, until the wood vibrates inside the doorframe, and the liquor cabinet jumps against our backs.

"Ruble-fucker?" I say to Mal.

"Not my best," he admits. "Still, it seems to have done a decent job of pissing him off."

Suddenly, the burglar alarm cuts out. My head continues to throb to the rhythm of the absent sound, while a boiled kettle whistles in my ears. I gradually realise that the distant sound of ringing isn't tinnitus. It's coming from the dressing room telephone.

"Maybe you should answer that," Zlody says with threatening calm. "It might be important."

Mal squints at me, one eye closed, lips pursed. "I thought you said the line had been cut?" he says.

I run around the carcass this time, skipping to avoid the blood, and I land my hand on the phone just as the ringing stops. The caller is anxious – I only have to wait a couple of seconds for it to ring again.

"Blue?"

"I... I don't know how they found me but they're here, Jimmy," Blue says. "They're outside the door."

On the other end of the line, past Blue's voice and her short, terrified breaths, there's the sound of a human battering ram. The door sounds thinner than the one in the studio. Each bang is supplemented with the snaps of breaking wood. Men are shouting, perhaps three or four. One of them is pleading with the others.

"Is there any other way out of the flat? A fire escape or a window?"

"No. Nothing. We're on the fifteenth floor. There's nowhere to go... Jimmy, I think they might have killed one of the neighbours."

"Okay, you just try and hold out for as long as you can. Call the police. Someone in the block has probably already done it, but just in case...."

"You said not to trust the police."

"Too many witnesses now. It doesn't matter how much money they've got behind them, there are some things even a bent copper can't ignore."

"It's too late. The door won't last another five minutes."

"Put something against it. Block it up."

"We *have!*"

And then the door explodes and the shouting intensifies. Blue is dragged away from the phone and she's screaming and there are male screams too, and Blue is shouting, "Please! Please, don't," and she's sobbing, "He doesn't know what this is about. He doesn't know how serious this is. *Please!*" And the man's scream rises, strangling itself when the pain reaches a note too high for his vocal range, and Blue carries the mantle of his scream, crying out desperately as she's carried away and out of the room.

To the death: "What are you doing?" Mal says when I start to push aside the liquor cabinet.

"They've got Blue," I tell him. "It's over."

"You're just giving up?"

Zlody has stopped kicking the door. He can hear the scraping of the cabinet as I shunt it across the floor. Mal stays seated, hunches forward slightly to compensate for the loss of back support.

"What else can I do?" I say, and I put a hand on his shoulder. "Mal, I'm sorry I ever doubted you. I jumped to some pretty daft conclusions and I know I let you down. I should have trusted that a friend like you—"

"Jim, don't be stupid," Mal says, swatting away my words like wasps at a picnic. "What right-minded person would guess that I was buying a fucking panda? And from the Russian mafia, no less."

"Still. I *am* sorry. And I want you to get out of here."

Refusing to look at me, Mal shakes his head.

"Not a bloody chance," he says.

"Go back out the fire escape. It's a bit of a walk, but if you keep following the canal it'll eventually take you to the DLR station."

"It's not bloody happening, Jim!"

"Listen to me. They *are* going to kill me. You heard what he said – nothing is going to change that."

"But *Jim*, we almost beat them last time."

"No, we didn't. We riled up a panda and somehow we were able to use that to our advantage. And there were only three of them then. God knows how many men Zlody will have with him now. At least four. And he's got a hostage. I'm not doing anything to risk her safety. Or yours."

"I didn't even throw so much as a tantrum," Mal says, clambering to his feet, hooking a couple of wild shadow-punches. "You watch me this time. I'll show them what happens when you mess with Mallory Haines!"

"If you stay here, we all die. Zlody wins. But if you go, maybe you can get to Rätsel. Maybe you can get us help before Zlody's turned us into lion food."

"There isn't *time* for that," he says, quietly. "After all your escapes, Zlody will want to put an end to this quickly, so you don't get another chance. You'll be dead the second you open the door."

I shake my head.

"Zlody is very close to achieving his goal. After all the time and money he's invested in these murders, he'll want to savour his victory. Even if that means torture, it'll drag things out and give you some time. And if you *are* too late to save us… at least Rätsel will know the truth. Zlody won't get away with what he's done."

Mal slugs back another mouthful of whisky and stares at the floor. There's only a vague smear of amber left in the bottom of the bottle.

"Jim…" he says. "I would've stayed, you know. To the death."

"I know. But this makes the most sense."

Mal hops from one foot to the other.

"Have I got time for a piss before you open the door?" he says. "Been holding it in since the panda…"

"Bathroom's next to the dressing room," I try to smile. "Be quick."

Mal dances past the deer and disappears into the dressing room. I put my hand on the door handle.

"Okay, Zlody." I shout. "I know you've got Blue."

"Velak and Nargis had to work hard to find her," he says. "Eddie Gitt's will be missing a few employees tonight, I think."

"If you give me assurances that she won't be hurt then I'll unlock this door."

"I will be through this door in a few minutes anyway. But, fine, you can have your assurances. I have no interest in killing your girlfriend."

Mal pops his head back into the studio, attempts a smile but manages nothing more than a nervous flutter of his lips. He throws me a thumbs-up instead. Coming from Mal, it's a hand gesture that feels as authentic as Christian death metal. He disappears again and a few seconds later I hear the fire door slam shut.

I wait five minutes, give Mal some time to get away, then I unlock the door and take a couple of steps back.

Zlody gives the door a gentle push and smiles victoriously with his hands on his hips as it slowly swings open.

"This was only ever going to end one way, James," he says.

He frowns, turns his head, eyes sweeping the studio.

"Where is Mallory?"

"He's gone," I say. "You said you'd let him walk."

"I was lying, of course. You must be naïve if you think I'd give him the opportunity to raise the alarm."

He slides a flip phone out of his pocket, taps it a few times, holds it to his ear and barks some Russian into the mouthpiece. Then, after snapping it shut, he turns to me and says, "It is of no consequence. I have told Marko not to come here. Instead, he will take his axe and look for your friend."

Trans Siberian: "At last count there were just under sixteen hundred pandas left in the wild," Zlody says. "Sixteen hundred... in a forest bigger than Belgium. Do you have any idea what it is like, tracking a panda in that kind of environment? To find one that has not already been tagged by conservationists?"

"Not easy, I'd imagine," I say.

"The WWF carries out a panda census every three years. That is how long it takes them, with a team of specialists working full time. And *they* have the permission of the Chinese government. Imagine going in there without any official support, lugging your equipment up mountains and through dense forests. It took my men eight weeks just to *locate* that fucking bear!"

Zlody paces in front of me, his heels clicking a precise rhythm on the smooth concrete floor of the warehouse. They're holding me out among the shipping containers, strapped to one of the steel struts that hold up the raised walkway. My hands are stretched and bound above my head so that only my toes touch the ground. This presents my ample belly as a target for Zlody – a soft mound of blubber in which he can bury his fist when his monologue gets him worked up.

The panda lies on a white sheet ten feet way. It isn't dead, but it isn't making any great strides either. Its chest rises and falls. Occasionally it utters a feeble, childlike cry. There's a vet attending to it, a blonde-haired, straight-shouldered ex-military type, working in blue jeans and a tight white t-shirt, attaching drips and clamps and pads and bandages to the stricken beast. Every so often he'll call out an update to Zlody in a soft West Country accent. Broken leg. Punctured lung.

Fucked-up pelvis. It's ridiculous, really. I've heard of a mob doctor – but a mob *vet?*

"And then, once they found the panda, they had to get it out of the country," Zlody continues. "They had to pump it full of tranquilizers, stick it on a stretcher and carry it down the side of an extinct volcano. Two men hauling the equivalent of a dazed heavyweight boxer between them, sliding down slopes of mud and loose rock. After they finally get off the mountain and they have trekked through a hundred miles of jungle, where are they supposed to go next? The obvious answer is the border. Get across to Russia, where everything becomes easier because Russia is *my* country. *My people,"* he jabs at his chest with his thumb. "Except the border is 2000 kilometres away. 2000 kilometres through police checkpoints, army checkpoints and visa checkpoints. 2000 kilometres driving on highways, then A roads, then B roads, then F roads... X roads, dirt roads, dirt tracks, then just *dirt*, like following a river back to its source, each branch getting smaller until there's nothing in front of you but a mountaintop.

"There's a reason Russia's western border with China does not have any patrol points. You could die a thousand times trying to reach it from the nearest village, and another thousand trying to find civilisation again once you have crossed over into Siberia. A truck can only get you so far. There are times when it is just the two men again, hefting that stretcher between them, the weight pushing their feet deep into the snow. And you have to think about the panda too, you have to keep it warm, keep it fed, keep it *alive*. Do you know what a panda eats?"

"Bamboo."

"Yes, of course. But how much?"

"Shitloads?" I say.

"Thirty kilos of it, every single day. It is not just the panda they are carrying, then – they are dragging sleds behind them loaded with food as well. And you know what else? Pandas shit. They shit *all the time*. They can shit forty times a day. No exaggeration. They shit while they *sleep*. The shit just pops right out of them – they don't even stir. It is amazing their fur isn't black, white and *brown*. You might be thinking, *so what?* Everybody shits. Animals shit. People shit. What is the big problem? Well panda shit is something special. Panda shit is big and round and full of mashed up bamboo. You see panda shit and you know it is panda shit. Especially if you are Chinese. The Chinese fucking *know* panda shit when they see it, let me tell you. They *prize* it. The most expensive tea in the world is fertilised with panda shit. You cannot go dropping off little parcels of dung forty times a day because if you do, some Chinaman is going to follow that trail, even if it takes him into a blasted, icy wilderness. So, these two men, their burden is swelling. They have got the panda, they have got the panda's food, and now they have got a great big ever-increasing sack of the panda's shit."

"Why don't they just bury the shit?"

"In the snow? What happens in the summer when the snow melts? Someone finds a big trail of shit, that's what happens. Questions are asked. Investigations are made. And suddenly our smuggling route out of China gets cut off."

The vet attaches a mask over the panda's snout and twists the cap on a canister, releasing a fuss of air. Condensation coats the inside of the transparent plastic as the panda breathes.

"Eventually the two men make it out of the mountains and into Russia, where they are met by a truck full of supplies, as well as an animal doctor. Things *do* get easier from here. The terrain levels out, the roads become drivable. There are still police officers to deal with and immigration checkpoints to clear, but in Russia, if you have money, these problems are not insurmountable. They travel across the country, all the way west to Saint Petersburg, where they load the panda onto a cargo ferry bound for Felixstowe. In England – more customs officials to bribe, and bribing is not quite so commonplace here, so the bribes have to be of a persuasive size. But then, after that, after four months of very hard, very dangerous, very *expensive* work, they finally get the panda here, to this warehouse, and, almost miraculously, it is still alive."

Zlody stops pacing, approaches me and I try to tense my gut, anticipating a punch.

"And then?" he says, balling one of his gigantic paddles into a fist.

"And *then*," he shouts, drawing back the fist.

"Your *friend*," he drives the fist into my belly. With my reflex to double-over restrained, my arms stretch, popping at the shoulders and elbows. "Your friend thinks he can tell me to *wait*. After everything my men went through, he has the *gall* to say that *he* cannot take the risk."

He grabs my face, tilts it up, squeezes my cheeks hard.

"And *you*," he says. "You throw that panda, that thirty-million-pound *asset*, over a fucking *railing!*"

He punches me again and my gut implodes. The way this is going, at some point my stomach is going to give up and dump all its contents onto the floor. The only uncertainty is the exit point.

"The panda..." I say, gasping and sucking air. "I'm... I'm sorry for what happened to it. It didn't deserve... *that*. But this isn't about the panda, Zlody. I mean, maybe it is a little bit *now*... But that's not why Al Girth is dead. That's not why you killed Keith Rumbold and Dane Biggerman. Those guys didn't hurt any pandas. This is about *The Persian Princess*... And I can feel a twist coming."

"A what?"

"A *twist*. A great big fucking rug-pull. This whole... um... series of events... It's heading towards some sort of big reveal. It's been building for days. I'm strapped here, looking at you, with your horrible crocodile skin and I'm thinking about what purpose all those scars could possibly serve..."

Zlody tilts his head, frowning.

"What if... what if it's to hide your true identity?" I say. "I mean, people don't just disfigure themselves for fun. So maybe... maybe your identity is the sting in this tail. And if that's the case, it means I must already know you. Except... I don't know any seven-foot monsters. Never have done. But what if... what if you *weren't* seven feet tall when I first made your acquaintance? What if you weren't even a *man* the first time we met? What if the reason none of us ever heard from the Persian Princess again is because *she* became an enormous *he?* What if *Anna* became *An*-ton?"

Ah, not that, then: Zlody's laughter hits like an earthquake. The building rattles with it. He hunches over and grabs his knees, roaring, tears streaming downs his face, snot popping in his nostrils.

"Oh, fat man," he says as the laughter subsides. "You make a terrible detective. You're scrabbling around in the dark, with no clue, looking for a what... a *twist?* First you think we are... what? *Islamic extremists?* And now you have settled on the idea that I used to be a *woman!*"

He bends over again, great hacking retches of laughter exploding from him.

"Look at me. Look at the *size* of me," he wheezes. "You think there's *any* possibility that I was once female?"

"Um..." I cough. "I've read some things about artificial male hormones – what they can do to trannies, post-op. You know, kickstarting dramatic growth spurts, that sort of thing."

"You've read some *things*, have you?" Zlody says. He turns to the vet and sarcastically says, *"He's read some things."*

The vet acknowledges him with a thin smile.

"I didn't do this to myself to *hide* anything. Quite the opposite. I did it to *stand out*, to show everybody exactly how far I was willing to go – what I was willing to sacrifice, to succeed. Twenty years ago, I instructed three of my men to hold me down, cut my skin with hot razors, and rub salt into the wounds to stop them from healing. I paid them to do this. Every day for weeks afterwards, I had to rub in more salt, so that the marks wouldn't fade."

"Oof. I've eaten my fair share of salt and vinegar crisps in my time," I say. "Putting your hand in a packet is a horrible way to find out you've got a paper cut. So... I can imagine how much that must have hurt."

Zlody flashes a humourless smile and blinks slowly.

"When I first started out in this business," he says. "I had a lot of climbing to do."

"Smuggling endangered species? That was an established business, was it? I assumed you were occupying a niche..."

"The animals are a small part of my operation. I make most of my money in more conventional ways."

"Somehow, I doubt that."

"I grew up poor. My grandparents were Tajik immigrants–"

"Ah!" I say.

"Ah? *Ah*, what?"

"Tajik! That explains why you all look like Arabs."

"We don't look like Arabs. We look *Tajik.*"

I shrug, which is quite a painful manoeuvre when you're strapped up by your wrists and doesn't really convey the intended sentiment of a shrug either.

"Being Tajik made things difficult for me," Zlody says. "It stopped me from being accepted into any of the traditional brotherhoods. The only way I could compete was by forming a *Bratva* of my own, bringing together other Tajik and Kazakh and Uzbek and Afghani outcasts. I did not want to share my power with them, though. I did not want there to be any question about my authority, so I showed my men that I could go further than any of them by decorating my body with the proof of my capacity to endure pain, and they respected me for it. My enemies feared me. When they looked at my face, they saw the agony I had put myself through and they understood that whatever I did to them could only be worse."

"Well, you're a big scary bastard, I'll give you that," I say, shifting my weight from the toes of one foot to the toes of the other. I'm getting twinges in my calves from supporting my body, flushes of cramp that I can only relieve by relaxing the muscles – but if I relax too much it creates a torsion in my shoulders that might pop them out of their sockets. "And I'm starting to sympathise with these enemies of yours."

"I could not tell you how many people I have killed," Zlody says. "I am not saying that to frighten you, it is just a statement of fact. I have lost count. I remember the ones that matter, the ones that really got under my skin. Slashing the throats of traitors – that is what I remember. But I do not think about the others, the soldiers that were just doing a job for the wrong side, making money for the family like any other working man. Those people were nothing except unlucky. They could have just as easily been on my side except for... I don't know... an accident of birth, I suppose. I do not feel bad about them, but I certainly do not feel good either. Not like my real enemies."

"Al Girth was a real enemy, was he?"

Zlody sneers at my interruption before continuing, "My first enemy was a man named Yul Usy. When I was a child, he was the big man in Perekrestok, my hometown. And he was someone I grew to hate. But he was not the first person I killed."

The big man in Perekrestok: "The first thing anybody would ever tell you about Yul Usy is that he was a hairy man. The *hairiest* man you have ever seen. He had coils of black hair all over his body, bursting out of sleeves and seams. If he wore a shirt with a loose enough weave, the hairs would poke through the material, like fingers through a chain-link fence. He could not stay clean-shaven without visiting the barber twice a day, so he did not bother going at all, grew a beard so big people used to joke that it was where he hid all his money. And Usy had a lot of money. He controlled everything in Perekrestok and took his cut anywhere he was not directly involved. Protection, gambling, sex, drugs… the money ran like sand through his greasy fingers.

"In the centre of town, he had a coffee shop, a respectable enough establishment if you ignored all the dealings that came and went through the back door. When my sister was thirteen, she got a job there as a waitress. Vanya had seen Usy swaggering around town. She knew he was a big shot, knew he had money, but she did not know what he did to get it. My father knew well enough. He told Vanya he did not want her working there, but by that time it was too late – Usy had taken a liking to her. There was nothing my father could do. So, Vanya served coffee and she tamped tobacco into the tops of hookah pipes and took coals from the fire to light them. She was a pretty girl, and she earned a very good wage in tips.

"After my sister had been working there a couple of years, Usy started using her at his poker nights. Crime bosses would visit from surrounding provinces to wager enormous sums and she would serve their needs. Nothing sordid – Usy liked Vanya too much for that – but he would get her to wear a pretty dress, pour a few drinks, light a few cigars… things like that.

"Now Usy… he had this one tournament he had been building up to for a long time. Two tables. Twelve men. Winner takes all. Usy saw it as an opportunity to impose his authority on the other bosses by taking their money, but as the night wore on it became obvious to some that the hairy old bastard was playing with extra cards up his sleeve. Nobody said anything because to do so might provoke a war – nobody except for Zim Ispravit, a man who could afford to lose ten grand, but not at the cost of his principles. He was a high-ranking member of the brotherhood, down all the way from Moscow, with even more heft than Usy. Maybe that was why he felt the need to call Usy out. 'What the fuck is this?' he said, laughing, trying to keep things light. 'Yul, you have got the cuffs of a magician. We can all see it. Take off your jacket and let's play this game without any more bullshit.'

"Usy did not like that. He did not like the accusation, he did not like the dismissive tone, he did not like the way Ispravit thought he could carry on dealing cards after being so bold. He did not like the fact that such disrespect had been shown in his home within earshot of my sister. So, Usy climbed across the table, pulled a stiletto from his boot and drove the blade through Ispravit's neck. As you can imagine, that put an end to the evening. The other bosses cleared out, scurrying back to their districts. Usy had upset the balance of power, and he could expect Ispravit's allies in Moscow to come looking for revenge."

Zlody looks at his watch, checks the screen on his phone. It's been almost half an hour since Blue was taken and he hasn't heard anything from Velak or Nargis. I wonder how far Mal has got – the amount of booze he put away, he probably hasn't even made it to the DLR yet.

"Let me guess," I say. "Both sides fought a war so long that it weakened them enough for you to step in and take over?"

Zlody shakes his head.

"I was not interested in crime back then. I was still at school, on course to becoming a doctor."

He pauses, pinching his chin thoughtfully. "You *are* right, though, when you say that a long war would have been detrimental to both sides. And at that time, they relied on each other – Perekrestok, in the East, controlled all the contraband coming into Russia from China and Southeast Asia, while Moscow handled everything coming from the West. Yet, despite the strength of the Moscow families, Usy was confident. Perekrestok was *his* town. He owned everyone in it. If some big city gangsters were going to try and fight him on his turf, then they would be in for a long war.

"On the surface at least, business had to continue as usual. So, the boys in Moscow got creative. And they broke rules. Specifically, the biggest rule there is."

"Don't go to the police?"

Zlody nods.

"Moscow put pressure on the cops in Perekrestok to investigate Ispravit's murder. They out-bribed Usy's bribes. The problem was, there wasn't much of a case to work because Ispravit's body was never found, and the crime bosses that *had* witnessed the murder would never testify, no matter how much it might benefit their own interests to see Usy in jail. But there was one witness the police *could* squeeze, somebody present at the murder who was not an affiliate of any crime syndicate."

"Your sister," I say.

"They put all kinds of pressure on her. On my family. They promised protection, and the protection was worth more than usual because it came with assurances from the Moscow brotherhood. With my father pushing her, Vanya made her statement and ratted Usy out. She had no other choice. And then, only a couple of days later, while we were all sleeping, Usy came for her. His men took apart the police protection detail. They shot my father in the stomach. They beat me. They beat my mother. We never saw Vanya again."

"Oh," I say. "I was starting to think Vanya might be the Persian Princess."

Zlody hurtles over, winding up a right hook that he lands on my cheek. My head strikes the steel column behind me like a hammer striking a bell. The vet's head jolts when he hears the clang but he doesn't look round, continuing instead with his work on the panda. My legs go limp for a second but the pain of my arms stretching as I slump stops me from passing out.

"This isn't a story for your entertainment. This is my *life!*" Zlody says, his meaty breath coating my face. "If Vanya hadn't been taken, I would not look like *this.*"

He slaps his crinkled cheeks.

"So you wanted Usy to pay?" I say, gasping, trying to draw his attention back to his story and away from inflicting more injury.

"No. Not just Usy. I wanted those bastards in Moscow too. They abandoned us, even though my family had sacrificed so much to help them. My father never fully recovered from the gunshot wound. He lived for another seven years without getting out of bed, shitting into a plastic bag through a hole in his gut. I had to forget my future in medicine and drop out of school to support the family. I started stealing, just food to begin with, but later things I could sell on the street. Electronics. Pirated movies. And eventually drugs. After a few years I got myself a nice little racket going, started paying other people to steal for me, so I could concentrate on fencing the goods. Soon, I had the beginnings of a criminal empire, and I was getting businesses in my neighbourhood to pay me protection instead of Usy, undercutting him with cheaper rates. When Usy sent men to collect what he thought he was owed I castrated them and rubbed bleach into their eyes, sent them back to him dickless and blind – beyond impotent. Usy sent more men, and I sent them back the same way. Pretty soon, he was struggling to find anybody willing to step into my little enclave. It is one thing to fear death, it is something else to fear castration. I fed on the fear, turned myself into a monster, expanded my territory. Every time there was resistance, I made an example, lopping off dicks left, right and centre."

There's a twinge at the base of my own penis. My piss-tube constricts and my foreskin tightens.

It is one thing to fear death, it is something else to fear castration.

"Castration seems a tad extreme," I say, almost choking on the words.

"Extremely effective," Zlody grins. "There is no better way to demoralise your enemy and make them submit. Sex is a powerful weapon. It is the biggest impulse, the ultimate goal for every single human. So, when you face an army of men that cannot fuck, you face an army totally lacking in conviction. And the men you have not got to yet either step aside or they join your team. In less than two years, I cut a swathe straight through Usy's organisation, but the wily old bastard managed to slink off before I got my hands on him. Still, I had his town. I had his power. I could afford to be patient because I knew a man like Usy would turn up sooner or later."

"Was Dane Biggerman Usy?" I ask.

"Was Dane Biggerman the hairiest man you ever saw?" Zlody says, slamming his left fist into my belly. "Was he *Russian?*" he says, punching me with his right. I feel like a cheap cut of meat being prepared for the table. *"Think* before you open your mouth, fat man! Stop obsessing over the need for a grand revelation!"

He grabs my face, squeezing my cheeks so hard my incisors start cutting into them. When my eyes well with tears he lets go.

"With Usy gone, I turned my attention to those rats up in Moscow. I left Perekrestok in capable hands and took some of my best soldiers up to the capital. We established ourselves in the foreign quarter, using the same tactics as before, feeding on the resentment that comes with being an outsider, undercutting the local protection prices, recruiting those people the brotherhood rejected – the minority citizens and non-Russians – into our fold, establishing a new enclave. As our numbers grew and we began to draw attention I sent instructions home, told them to cut off the East Asian supply routes to Moscow. The brotherhood still had heroin coming in from Afghanistan, but that chain was volatile, and this was back when the Golden Triangle was the world's biggest heroin producer. Denying the brotherhood access finally provoked them. They could no longer avoid war. They sent men to wrest the eastern province from my control, a huge contingent, an *army*. But that left them weak at home. They failed to understand that for me this was not about business. This was personal. I was willing to risk my hometown if it meant taking theirs. The battles in Moscow were swift and they were brutal. I cut off more dicks. Hundreds of dicks. In the end it was easier than taking out Usy had been. And, although the brotherhood had taken Perekrestok in my absence, they were weakened by the fight, and disheartened by what had happened to their brothers and sisters back home. They wanted a truce. A power share. But I know how revenge works. How it has a tendency to fester. So I finished the war and I wiped them out. Moscow was mine and very soon after so was Perekrestok once more.

"As for Usy… I made no effort to look for him. I did not want him to feel the need to keep moving. If he started to get comfortable, he would settle somewhere, perhaps become attached to a place, reluctant to move on. That would make him easier to track down later. For the time being, I concentrated on Moscow.

"Russia was a mess after the death of the Soviet Union and there was plenty of flesh for a man like me to pick from the carcass. I bought and stole from the military. Took control of munitions factories. Auctioned off missile stockpiles, tanks, gunships… there was so much to take, so much to sell. Africa was hungrier for guns than it was for food. It still is. I sold to dictators, to terrorists, to the opposing sides in civil wars. I sold to Arabs and Persians… Muslims, Christians, *Buddhists*… Whenever you see a militiaman on the news firing his Kalashnikov into the air, chances are he got that gun from one of my agents. The ammunition too. My business expanded throughout Europe and then the US, where I supplied submachine guns to gangbangers, assault rifles to neo-nazis and hand-canons to Midwestern soccer mommies.

"It was on a business trip to New York, during a meeting with three crime syndicates, that I got my first lead on Usy. The head of a Greek crime family from New Jersey told me a story about a small island back in his home country that had been turned into a haven for sex tourists by a very hairy Russian, who seemed to have appeared out of nowhere. I asked if I could get more information about this Russian and a few days later an envelope was left for me behind the reception desk of my hotel. Inside it, a colour photograph of Usy, sprawled on a sun lounger, piña colada in his hand, sweat sparkling on the thick hair covering his flaccid breasts. His beard had been cut back to a moustache and thick black stubble. There did not seem to be a single grey follicle amongst any of it, on his face or his body, and, considering how long it would take to apply colour to all that hair, you had to assume it was natural even though Usy must have been in his seventies.

"I knew I would not be able to get near him myself, so I sent a dozen of my men ahead to scout the place out, gave them free reign to enjoy themselves so they did not rouse any suspicions. They drank and whored for a fortnight, spending their money in Usy's bars and in his brothels, all the while tracking his movements. I waited in Turkey for their signal and then, under a full moon, I crossed the Aegean in a powerboat, anchored it offshore, and swam to a beach where I met my men. Usy had bought a ruined cliff-top chapel and turned it into a home. The high vantage point made him overconfident. His security was full of holes. We scaled the rock wall in the silver light, crashing through his bedroom window before an alarm could be raised."

"And you cut his cock off?"

"Oh, we did much worse than that," he says, leaving the words hanging in the air between us.

"It was as I was pulling the nails from his fingers that I realised he didn't know who I was, or that my motive for destroying him back in Perekrestok had been anything but business. He could not understand why I had not just let him disappear, why I had to torment him. His destruction of my family was such an insignificant footnote in his life that he had almost forgotten it ever happened. So, I told him *exactly* what he meant to me. And suddenly he looked hopeful.

"'I did not kill your sister,' he told me. 'I couldn't. She was special. But she betrayed me. She had to be punished.'

"He told me if I killed him, I would never find out what happened to her – and that was when I took a pair of rusty shears to his balls."

"Zlody, please…" I say. "This is just… gratuitous."

"What is it they say? *Actions speak louder than words?* Be grateful, then, that these are only words. The actions are yet to come."

I choke at that, swallow down a big viscous ball of saliva.

"I told him, 'I am going to cut off one of your balls, and then you can decide whether or not you want to keep the other one.' With a man holding each of his limbs, spreading him like a starfish, I sliced open his scrotum, plucked out one of his testicles and slapped it onto the floor next to his face. To his credit, he did not pass out.

"'London,' he told me, gasping. 'Sergei Svodnik.'

"I cut out his other testicle and then I spent my time working on his penis, taking it away from him in painful increments."

"I think I'm going to be sick," I spit an arc of saliva onto the floor.

"As I would quickly discover, Sergei Svodnik was a sex trafficker. He brought girls from Eastern Europe into England to work in his brothels. Some of the really pretty ones made it into the grainy, illegal pornos he used to shoot."

"So I *was* right. The Persian Princess. Your sister."

"Does that satisfy your need for a twist?" Zlody spits.

"Did you find her?"

"Somebody cut Svodnik's throat outside a bar on Brick Lane – a territorial dispute, by all accounts – so I never got the chance to talk to him."

"Sounds like he was lucky."

"Yes, I think you are right," Zlody smiles. "It made tracking down Vanya more difficult, though. It did not help that all of my photographs of her were about fifteen years old. I used some of my contacts in the police to see if anyone in vice recognised her and eventually had some luck with an informant, an old tart from Lithuania with black teeth. She said she had been housed with Vanya when my sister first arrived in London. According to her, Vanya never worked the streets or any of the private rooms above Svodnik's clubs. She was given special treatment, ring-fenced until the day she was passed on to the head of a legitimate porn studio."

"Dane Biggerman."

"She only made one film," Zlody says, "before she killed herself."

I do not think you are quite following where this is going: Zlody is back to pacing, the furious exchange of air from his nostrils blasting in a rapid tempo, synchronised with the rubber squeak of his heels.

"Christ, Zlody," I say. "I know it'll sound inadequate, but... for what it's worth... I'm sorry."

If my hands weren't restrained, I'd be cradling my genitals, trying to massage some reassurance into my cock and balls.

Zlody stops pacing.

"You are correct," he says. "It is inadequate."

"It sounds like she went through hell."

Zlody sighs.

"I think of the happy girl I knew as my big sister. And then I think of this woman that threw herself in front of a train. They cannot be the same person. What frame of mind must she have been in to do that to herself? If I really allow myself to think about it... the wheels churning... the flesh tearing... Can you imagine ever being so low that you could do that to yourself?"

"If it was an intercity train, it would have been over in an instant."

"Is that supposed to make me feel better?"

"I don't think anything I say is going to change the outcome of all this."

"On that, at least, we can both agree."

"So, what happens next?"

"Really, this should all be over by now. But it is thanks to your struggles that I have developed a punishment far more fitting than the one I had originally intended for you."

"What does that mean?"

"Well... the whole asphyxiation setup... it seemed perfect. Suitably humiliating, particularly for Al Girth, given his fame. The media speculation. The tarnished reputation. It works on a personal level too – the news of Keith Rumbold's demise did not make it into the national press, but it appeared in his local paper, and you can bet his family have been torn apart by the squalid revelation of his death. Not only will they have perceived his perverse masturbation experiment, but they will now know firsthand about the filthy little business he used to be involved in."

"A bit different from your usual methods, though."

"No castration, you mean? I did not need to send any messages this time. And cutting off somebody's dick would result in a homicide investigation, something I would obviously want to avoid. Once a police investigation crosses county lines, paying people off becomes much more difficult."

"It hasn't made that much difference, though – you didn't avoid a police investigation for long."

"And I have *you* to thank for that, don't I?" He says. "That being said, I am glad Velak bungled the attack on you. If that had not happened, I would never have known about your relationship with Blue... I had men watching her apartment the night you went to visit her. They got photos of you two cuddling up on her balcony. That gave me some food for thought. Blue was always going to be a problem for me. If a man kills himself masturbating, it is humiliating. But a woman? It would probably turn her into some sort of... I don't know... feminist symbol of sexual liberation."

"I think you're being just a *tad* optimistic about the way women are portrayed in the press, Zlody."

"Well, anyway, Blue Darling is the one, more than any other, that did something terrible when she made that film. She betrayed another woman. She raped–"

"It *wasn't* rape."

"Then what else can you call it? My sister was *forced.*"

"By Dane! Not by Blue. Or Al. Or *me*. From our point of view, everything that happened on that set was consensual."

"Did you watch the movie? Did you hear my sister's whimpers?"

"We thought she was acting."

"The way she curled up on the floor after those two *animals* finished having their fun... You thought that was acting?"

"*Yes.*"

"Did any of you ever – even once – check that she was okay? Did you stop what you were doing long enough to find out?"

I don't say anything.

"When Velak and Nargis get back here with Blue, we are going to stage our own reenactment of *The Persian Princess.*"

"No," I say. "Please, Zlody... you said you wouldn't hurt Blue."

"And you believed me?"

"You can't do it to her... She's a victim too. She was traumatised by the porn shoots... Zlody, she was so *young*. Barely an adult. You've already dealt with the people responsible. Biggerman – he's the one that deserves this. Not Blue."

"I agree that Dane Biggerman deserved a harsher punishment than he received... but it is too late for that."

"Putting Blue through that... making her relive what your sister went through... it won't bring back Vanya."

"I do not think you are quite following where this is going."

He locks eyes with me.

"I am not going to make *Blue* relive what Vanya went through. That woman has sold her body more times than any of us could count. Sex is just currency to her. It would be next to meaningless."

Zlody smiles and he flutters his eyelids.

"No," he says. "I want Blue to experience what *I* felt when *I* watched that film."

"I don't understand."

"Really?" Zlody says, with a look of genuine astonishment. "You still haven't figured it out?"

And then I do figure it out. And my body temperature rises a couple of degrees. And droplets of sweat burst on my skin like condensation on a champagne bucket. And the haemorrhoidal itch that's been vexing me for days suddenly pales into insignificance.

"You, fat man," Zlody says. *"You* will be our princess."

Gun: Zlody leaves me and takes a knee next to the vet and the panda, involving himself in a lengthy discussion about the animal's wellbeing. I could use a lengthy discussion about *my* wellbeing. The recent revelation of my impending *punishment* has elevated my stress levels a tad. Couple that with the extremely uncomfortable position in which I'm being held, and I'm starting to feel rather unwell. My arms are completely numb, and that absence of feeling is drifting down my back, as if my body is slowly sublimating into the air. There's a strain in my heart as its faltering beat struggles to push blood up to those raised extremities, and a strain in my lungs as they fight to expand against the cushions of fat hemming them in. A cold, paralyzing wave sweeps down the left side of my body.

"Zlody," I say. "I think I'm... I... um... I don't feel well."

My lips are tingling. My left leg jerks against the duct tape. And my head... my head feels twisted inside, as if my brain is a dirty old sponge that's been rung out.

Zlody looks over his shoulder at me, raises an eyebrow, turns back to the vet, resuming their hushed conversation.

"Zlody, I think I'm... I think I'm having a heart attack... or a stroke... or something..."

I throw up, which is quite an achievement when your stomach has been pummelled as much as mine has. Convulsions rattle my body against the steel upright. The walkway shakes overhead. Vomit seeps from my mouth, dribbles down my chin.

"Oh no, fat man." Zlody says, approaching me with a Stanley knife in his hand. "Only *I* get to decide when you die." He slices the tape around my ankles and wrists, and I flop onto the floor, still retching, my heart prickled with cramps. My hands and my fingers buzz as blood rushes back into them.

"Vet!" Zlody shouts. "Make sure he does not die."

The vet whispers something sweetly to the panda, rises from his haunches and strides over to give me a quick examination. He smells like a dog basket in a hot room, with the underlying alcoholic sting of a teenager's aftershave. He breathes on the stethoscope to heat it before he places it against my chest and his lips pucker as he listens.

"His heartbeat is discordant," he says to Zlody eventually.

"What… the fuck… is that supposed to mean?" I rasp from the floor. "Discordant? I don't think… I don't think you know what that word… means. How can my heartbeat… be fucking… *discordant?*"

"The rhythm is wildly irregular," he says, still to Zlody. "He's clearly an unhealthy man."

"He is a fat piece of shit, is what he is," Zlody says.

The vet nods.

"Keeping him with his hands raised like that has put more strain on his heart than I think it can cope with. Although I don't think he's gone into cardiac arrest, he's come very close. If you want him to survive much longer, I'd let him lie down… but he should really be in a hospital."

I cough up a couple more rounds of stomach porridge and allow it to ooze onto the floor from the side of my mouth.

"I wouldn't worry about him trying to go anywhere," the vet continues. "His body is in terrible shape."

He's right about that. A stringent *do not move* order has been put in place throughout my anatomy, enforced by spasmodic threats of anguish and life-changing injury. My head rests on its side, lips squashed against the cool concrete.

"How can you just… stand there… and let this happen?" I say to the vet, clutching at my chest, bunching my shirt in my fingers. "Don't you have to… take an oath… or something?"

"My patients are animals. There's no point taking an oath that your patients wouldn't understand. Besides, *you* may very well have killed that beautiful creature," he flaps a hand at the panda, "so you're getting nothing less than you deserve."

He says this with tears in his eyes, his voice breaking, then he returns to his patient, laying a forlorn hand on its flank.

"Where... the fuck... do you find these people?" I ask Zlody.

He laughs.

He's still laughing when Mal shoves open the warehouse door and staggers through it, wearing just his underpants, holding a pistol. His stance is one of drunken confidence, back straight, feet spread wide apart, but his shoulders are loose, causing the gun barrel to weave dangerously for everybody inside the room.

"I told you I wouldn't leave you, Jimbo!" he shouts.

The gun's sight spends most of its time hovering over Zlody, but I'd say there's still a better-than-fair chance Mal would miss his target if he pulled the trigger. He crosses the warehouse with a feline swing in his hips, brimming with alcoholic confidence.

Moving towards Mal with his arms outstretched and fingers splayed in a placatory gesture, Zlody says, "Mallory. Look. I have a vet working to save your panda's life. We might still be able to salvage something here. If you put down the—"

Mal laughs, pausing to slouch against a wooden crate, his pale love handles folding like uncooked dough, the gun still twirling in Zlody's general direction.

"If I put down the... *gun?*" he says. "We can all bury the hatchet and laugh about today's events over a couple of pints? Not bloody likely, is it, Anton? You just stay there and shut your bloody mouth. Jim? Are you alright down there?"

"I might've had a small heart attack. Apart from that... right as rain, Mal. Where the fuck did you get that gun from?"

"Ah, well, that's a fine old question, isn't it? Got a bit *lost* on my way to that DLR station you told me about... Decided I wasn't going to be much use to you if I went wandering off... Started doubling back. And then I saw some young chaps passing a joint around in the back yard of one of those frightful terraced houses. They looked a bit rough – you know how they are around here. Hooded tops and all that. The sort of fellows you don't want to see when you're trying to flag a taxi at four in the morning. And that got me thinking... *I bet these lads have got a fair old arsenal on them.* So, I nipped over and explained our predicament. Asked them for some help. Some weaponry. As you'd expect they told me to *fuck off*. But I was undaunted. I offered them cash and then, remembering I didn't have any cash because Anton's boys had relieved me of my wallet, I offered them my watch instead. They like a bit of *bling,* don't they? The cheeky little bastards haggled, ended up taking my suit and shoes as well. But boy was it worth it for this *beauty!"*

Mal gives the gun a celebratory shake above his head, then brings it back to bear on Zlody.

"Just fucking shoot him, Mal," I say. "Shoot the bastard."

"Now, Jim... I'm a big advocate of non-violence, as you know..."

"What are you talking about? I've seen you punch a woman in the face before!"

"Ah, yes, but those were special circumstances."

"The only special *circumstance* I can remember is that she was pregnant."

"She wasn't pregnant, she merely *appeared* to be pregnant."

"You didn't know that at the time!"

"Jim, look... those priority seats... people should take into account how *far* you're travelling on the Tube, not just how old or infirm or *pregnant* you are—"

"We're getting sidetracked."

"Right. Yes. *Sidetracked."*

"Shoot Zlody. And shoot that fucking vet while you're at it."

"I think it'd be better if we brought this all to a *non*-violent conclusion."

Zlody's hands fall to his sides and he grins.

"You don't have the balls to shoot me, do you, Mallory?" he says, taking a step towards Mal.

"You just stay *right where you are*, Anton!" Mal says, jabbing the gun forwards. "I *will* shoot you. I bloody well *will*."

"No, I don't think so," Zlody takes another step in Mal's direction. "I know what it takes to kill a man, believe me. In a way it is a bit like an extreme sport. *Yes…* it is a bit like bungee jumping." He takes another step. "Some men are fearless, able to take the plunge without a moment's hesitation." He pauses, giving Mal the opportunity to take just such a plunge, stretching the pause to emphasise his point when Mal fails to fire, before raising his eyebrows and continuing. "Other men take their time, staring into the abyss, grinding down their anxieties before they step over the edge. Others *want* to do it, but their impulse for self-preservation is so strong that they have to be pushed." Another step. "Then there are those men that find another man's desire to jump from a great height incomprehensible…"

"Anton I will pull this *fucking trigger* if you take one more step!"

"And *then*," Zlody says, taking one more step, "there are those men that think they can bluff their way out of a hostage situation with a *fucking BB gun.*"

Mal's eyes widen. The pupils dance to the gun and back to Zlody. He pulls the trigger. A ball bearing pings against one of the shipping containers, ricochets off a wall, taps its way across the floor.

"Bugger," he says.

Zlody charges and Mal pulls the trigger again, but the wasp-sting of the pellet hitting the middle of Zlody's forehead does little to slow him down. Mal gets one more shot off before he's floored by a palm strike to his chin. Zlody gives Mal a swift kick in the ribs as he hits the floor, at the same time spanking a hand to the circular bruise that's already distorting the scarified lines above his eyebrow.

"Zalupa!" He shouts.

Fucking nutcase: Zlody winds tape around Mal's wrists, hoists them up against the same support column he had me strapped to earlier, winds out more tape to secure them in place. Mal's head lolls forward, and he mutters something about cheques, or Czechs or maybe chess, his eyes half open, showing only the yellowing whites.

"What does *zalupa* mean?" I ask from the floor.

After cutting the tape from the roll with his teeth, Zlody peels a fragment of it from his tongue, scrutinizes it on the end of his finger, looks down at me and says, "Dickhead."

Zlody secures Mal's ankles next, crouches down to bite the tape again.

"Are you calling me a dickhead or..?"

"Zalupa means dickhead."

"Zalupa... I'll remember that one."

"Why? You won't be alive long enough to use it."

Zlody slaps Mal's cheeks until he's roused from the stupor, then he punches him in the stomach, simultaneously hitting me with a phantom punch of recognition.

"Christ," Mal chokes. "Was that entirely necessary?"

Zlody responds by tapping a finger angrily at the bull's-eye welt on his face.

"I'll be pissing blood tomorrow," Mal says, still exhausted of air.

"You won't be pissing anything tomorrow," Zlody says.

"Well what the *bloody hell* is that supposed to mean, you cryptic bastard?" Mal says, managing to muster some indignation.

"He means you'll be dead tomorrow, Mal" I say, rolling onto my back so that I can look up at him.

"Ah," Mal nods thoughtfully. "Right."

"I do not have anything special planned for you, I'm afraid," Zlody says to Mal. "I will leave it for Marko to deal with when he gets back here with his axe."

"Hmmm…" Mal says. "Can't say I'm particularly *enamoured* with the sound of this *axe* you just mentioned. Do you have anything more in line with me slipping off peacefully in my sleep? You Russkies must have a few bottles of vodka rattling around."

"Unfortunately not."

"Lethal injection, then? Perhaps the… er… *vet*, was it? Perhaps he can put some sort of drug cocktail together."

Zlody shakes his head.

"Marko is strong. It will be quick," he says, then he nods at me. "Just be glad you are not in the same shoes as your friend down there."

He winks, takes out his phone, then walks to the far side of the warehouse where he makes a call.

"Bloody hell, Jimbo," Mal whispers. "I think we've had it now, unless you've got any bright ideas?"

"My tank is empty, Mal. And my ideas weren't that great to begin with. Anyway, I'm not sure I could get up off this floor even if I wanted to."

"No… So you weren't joking about the heart attack, then?"

"The vet checked me over. Thinks I *nearly* had one, whatever that means."

"He's a bloody vet, Jim. What does he know about human anatomy? I bet it's just acid reflux or a bit of trapped wind."

I shake my head.

"This has been coming for a while. All the garbage I've been putting in my system… it was bound to catch up with me sooner or later."

With his arms raised up as they are, Mal's stomach has flattened and the chubby deposits around his breasts have been lifted, giving an illusion of shape and vitality. There's a thicket of grey hairs in the very middle of his chest, halos of darker grey around his nipples, grey patches under his arms, but otherwise his skin is smooth and white and unblemished. Thirty years older than me, and he's in better shape. He cranes his neck, stares unblinking at the ceiling, sighs.

"Mal," I say. "Does your wife know where you are?"

"My wife?"

"Yes. Any chance she might raise the alarm?"

"Oh, no," he says with a smile. "No, I wouldn't have thought so. I'm not sure what Maria will make of any of this, to be quite honest with you."

"You're a great big fucking bundle of red herrings, do you know that?"

"Sorry, Jimbo?"

"The panda. The Muslim nanny. Your wife…"

"My wife?"

"I've known you for nearly two decades, yet not once have I met her."

"Oh… Oh, I see."

"*Why*, Mal?"

"Well, that's a rather difficult question for me to answer…"

"I don't think there's much point beating around the bush now, is there?"

"No. No, you're quite right."

Mal wriggles and fidgets and breaks eye contact with me.

"The problem, you see, is that you're a thoroughly likeable chap, Jim."

"Ah, I see. Yes, my likeability *has* always been one of my greatest failings–"

"Which *means* there's every chance she might like *you*. Platonically, I mean."

"I'm still failing to see any problems with this scenario."

"The *problem* is we'd be stuck with her then. She'd want to come out with us whenever we met up. And, frankly, *you* wouldn't like *her*. She isn't fun, Jim. No fun *whatsoever*. You'd resent me for forcing her upon you. She's *psychotic*, is what she is. I'm being serious. In fact, I *do* know what Maria will make of all this. I can picture it now. She'll get a call from the police saying little hacked-up pieces of my body have been dredged from the bottom of the Thames, there'll be a five-second blank stare as she digests the information, a trace of a smile, then she'll hang up and carry on painting her toenails, or watching *Trisha*, or whatever it was she was doing before the telephone rang."

"Oh. I'm sorry, Mal. I didn't know things had got so bad."

"Got so bad? Things have always been that way."

"Why would you marry a woman like that?"

"If you saw her, you'd understand. She's terrifying, but in that terror, there is something powerfully erotic as well. The first time she took me to bed I wasn't entirely sure I'd make it out *alive*. Some things in life … they are worth that risk. Heightened by it, even."

"I've never even seen a picture of this woman."

"Oh no. No pictures. She won't allow that. I once made the mistake of complimenting the way she looked in a picture. Somehow, she thought I was insinuating that she looks better in photos than she does in real life and it sent her into a marvellous rage. She burnt all the wedding photographs, set fire to every single photo I had framed around the house, and now if anybody goes near her with a camera… there's a *scene*."

"She sounds like a fucking nutcase."

"Yes. Well. There's a reason people say love is a drug, Jim. And the most potent drugs bring you to your *knees*. They hollow you out, steal away your health and your reputation… but none of that matters when it's placed against the few precious minutes of unfettered euphoria afforded to you in return. It must sound crazy… I know, but she makes me *happy*."

From outside comes the sound I've been dreading – the heated purr of a car's engine, the crunch and pop of tires on weathered tarmac. Zlody hears it too.

"Ah!" he says, hanging up his phone call and clapping his hands. "Perhaps your heart won't have to hang on for too much longer after all, fat man!"

There's the click of car doors opening, the clunk of them closing, the groan of the boot being raised, then the hollow boom of it dropping. There's an energetic tussle as they bring Blue in. She isn't coming easily. If this were a cartoon there'd be a rolling dust cloud with fists and legs emerging from it. She sticks a vicious boot into Velak's nads, buckling him to a hands-on-knees position, and spits in his bandaged face. Nargis grabs her arms, locks them behind her back, hoists her kicking into the warehouse as she unleashes a guttural scream.

She calms down when she sees me, lets Nargis frog march her across the room.

"Jimmy," she says. "What have they done to you?"

Nargis throws her down by my side before a conversation breaks out between the three Russians, with Velak still hunched and sucking air. Blue hustles over, kneeling, stroking my cheek. She looks like she was dragged straight from her bed, wearing a tiny pair of shorts and an oversized yellow T-shirt that bears the logo for what I assume is a fictitious bakery called *Big Baps*. Her make-up is more understated than I've seen before, almost non-existent, just eyeliner and a pale smudge of lipstick. She hugs herself against the cold of the warehouse.

"Here," I say, sitting up and shrugging off my jacket. "Take this."

"Are you sure? It's freezing in here."

"I run hot, as they say."

"Okay, thank you," she says, slipping her arms into the sleeves. Specially tailored for my bulk, the jacket looks like a super-king duvet when wrapped around her petite frame.

"I'm so sorry I didn't believe you, Jimmy" she says. "If I'd listened, we could be on the other side of the world by now."

"It's okay, Blue... I don't blame you. How could I? You were right about my drinking." I grab her hand. "I haven't had a drink in two days, you know. Really. Not one drop. That would never have happened if I hadn't met you again–"

"I bet you wouldn't say no to a drink now, though, would you, Jimbo?" Mal snorts. "I know *I* wouldn't."

Ignoring Mal, I say, "That scary looking bloke, the one that looks like a cenobite–"

"A what?"

"Have you ever seen *Hellraiser?*"

Blue shakes her head.

"Doesn't matter. You know who I'm talking about, right? Well, that guy... that's Anton Zlody. And the Persian Princess... she was his sister."

"Oh," Blue says.

"She was a sex slave, Blue. Dane Biggerman *bought* her."

Blue's hand rises shakily to her mouth. Her eyes shimmer.

"And after we made that film, she threw herself in front of a train."

"Oh God," Blue says, her voice torn down the middle.

"Jim," Mal says. "Hey, Jim!"

Still ignoring Mal, I say, "Zlody has killed a lot of people, all in the name of revenge. And he's going to kill us."

"Jim," Mal says. "I just thought of something, Jim. *Jim!*"

"He holds us responsible. He wants us to suffer. Blue, he's planning to do terrible things–"

"*Jim!*"

"*What?* For fuck's sake, *what is it,* Mal?"

"You changed your clothes, didn't you?" he says. "Earlier? At your studio?"

"Yes. So what?"

"Well, if I know you as well as I think I do, you'll have a naughty little hip flask tucked away in one of those inside pockets."

"So?"

"I was just thinking it might help take the edge off the impending axe murdering."

"Axe murdering?" Blue says, now with a warble of alarm.

"Oh, don't worry yourself, dear," Mal says. "By the sound of things, I'm the only one getting the axe. Anton hasn't really specified what he's got in store for you two… Jim, is there a hip flask in that jacket or *not?*"

"No, Mal, I don't think so."

"You don't *think* so? Have you checked?"

"For fuck's sake," I say, turning back to Blue. "Sorry, Blue. Can you have a look?"

She pats the pockets from the outside and frowns.

"I don't feel a hip flask, but there is something…"

She reaches inside and struggles to pull out whatever it is she's found.

"Well?" Mal says.

"It feels like a pen, or… I'm not sure…" Blue says. "It's wedged against the lining at the bottom of the pocket. I can't get it out."

"Not a hip flask, then?" Mal says.

"No. It's not a hip flask. Sorry."

Velak and Nargis approach, their conversation with Zlody finished. They pull me up off the floor, while Zlody unrolls a blanket in a patch of sunlight at the centre of the room.

And then Mal says, "Oh bugger."

And then I say, "What?" And I turn to see what Mal is looking at.

And then I see what the problem is.

Marko is back, and he's brought his axe.

And his axe is fucking massive.

The Dane: I'm not sure what sort of axe I expected. A survival axe, perhaps, or an axe you'd use to chop firewood. This looks more like something from a museum, forged in the Dark Ages. The kind of weapon a Norseman would wield two-handed as he rampaged through northern settlements. Marko rests the blade on the floor and leans on the long handle.

It takes Zlody some time to decide the order he'd like things to happen next. Who he'd like to torture first. Velak and Nargis walk me over to the sheet and sit me in the middle of it. Zlody looks from Blue, to me, to Mal. He stares at Mal the longest.

"Vet," he says. "You should leave. Something extremely violent is about to happen, and I don't want you to incriminate yourself."

"But the panda..." the vet says. "He'll die if I leave him now."

"He will die anyway," Zlody says. "You have done a good job, but you are only prolonging the inevitable. We both know that."

The vet lowers his head and nods into his chest.

"I'll give him an injection, then, to help him on his way."

"No. I would like to put him to sleep myself. After everything it took for me to get him here, it only seems right."

The vet hesitates.

"Trust me. I have injected people before," Zlody says with a grim smile.

The vet gives a sharp nod, an unhappy submission, then he rummages inside his leather hold-all, producing a steel-tipped syringe, which he fills from a vial. Zlody takes it from him, watches the vet's back as he crosses the warehouse and exits through the double doors.

Zlody waits for the sound of a car's ignition, then he turns, looks at Mal, drops the syringe to the floor and slowly treads on it until it crunches.

"Marko," he says. "Put that panda out of its misery."

Gleefully brandishing his axe, tapping its nape against his flat palm, Marko approaches the bear.

Mal's face droops in horror, his lower lip curled back onto his chin exposing his crooked, fag-stained lower teeth.

"Please, Anton," he says. "Don't do this. Pì Pì doesn't deserve any of the things that have happened to him today. To end it like this is of no benefit to anyone."

"That is where you are wrong. It benefits you, Mallory. I told you Marko would be efficient with his axe. Now you can see for yourself."

"I believe you. There's no need for a demonstration."

"How about I let Marko decide? After all, he is the one that transported that expensive animal all the way from China."

Marko first acknowledges Zlody with a nod, then Mal with a broad sarcastic smile, before raising the axe above his head with both hands.

What happens next is violence at its most grandiose. Marko dances with the axe like a grim majorette, spinning it with flourishes of the wrist and fingers. The blade swoops and soars, lashing the room with whips of blood. And that blood – it's so *real*. There's no mistaking it. There's no confusion. This isn't a film set. This isn't a manmade deer carcass. This blood isn't edible or mint flavoured. It isn't even red. It's a rusted, arterial orange, rich, vibrant and oxygenated, fast flowing, straight from the beast's heart. Or it's venous purple, thick and dark, seeping, pooling, fanning outwards across the concrete, quivering in syrupy ripples around Marko's leather shoes. The panda writhes and twitches, making a low noise like an old boiler struggling on the first day of winter. The blade sinks into the soft flesh between hip and thigh, splits it like slow-cooked chicken, snipping an artery to unleash a volcanic jet that stripes Marko from hip to chin. Hacking and thrusting, he breaks off one of the huge rear legs, launches it across the room to crash at Mal's feet.

I look up at Mal. He's watching everything, staring hard, staring murder, his lips white, almost invisible.

Blue watches too, flinching each time the axe falls and the creature groans, her open-mouthed expression one of distress, but also intense confusion. The sight of a giant panda being butchered isn't something anybody ever expects to see, and the bizarre circumstances that led to this moment are yet to be explained to her.

Marko keeps going long after Pi Pi is dead, until he's too tired to stand, kneeling in a dark puddle next to the split pink-and-black bag of fur, leaning his weight on the axe handle, his hair slick with sweat and panda blood.

"You're done?" Zlody asks.

Marko nods and Zlody applauds.

"Even for me, that was hard to watch," he says. "Almost worse than seeing it happen to a human."

Marko rises, panting and shaking his head, a stringy black clot dangling from his ear, his grey suit now an expressionist mural of crimson shades.

"It is okay," Zlody says to him. "I can see you have tired yourself out. No need to go straight to work again. Mallory can stick around a while longer. I think he might enjoy part two of our show."

Zlody turns to me and says, "That is *you*, princess."

Push out: "On your hands and knees," Zlody says calmly.

So, this is it, then.

This is how it's going to happen.

Classic doggy-style.

Arse in the air.

I roll onto my front and I'm already trembling. As I push myself up, the intensity of the trembling increases. The thin layer of cotton under my kneecaps does little to soften the pain as my weight presses them into the hard floor.

"Jimmy," Blue says. "What's going on?"

"That should be obvious," Zlody spits at her. "To you, especially."

"Anton," Mal says. "You can't."

"Please." Blue again. "He doesn't deserve this."

"You all deserve this!" Zlody roars.

He tugs my shirt over my head and tosses it across the room. I picture myself through Blue's eyes, my enormous gut criss-crossed with stretch marks, my quivering, dimpled boobs – all the gross curtains of flab hanging beneath me – and I want to cry.

"Bozhe moi! You really are disgusting," Zlody says, reading my mind. "Looking at you, I think we will need some chemical assistance."

Laughing, he pops a couple of blue pills from a blister pack, hands one to Velak and swallows the other.

"Now, your trousers," he says.

I fumble to unbutton them, but my fingers are shaking too much. I take a moment, try to control my breathing. From behind, Velak reaches round my waist and effortlessly rips the fly apart before peeling the trousers down my legs.

Zlody stands in front of me. His thighs are so thick with muscle that he has to unroll his trousers from them inch by inch, exposing more scarred skin as he goes. He almost trips when he gets them down to his ankles and for a fleeting moment his aggressive demeanour is overcome by a virginal awkwardness. He composes himself, removes his tie with a single tug of the knot, throws off his jacket and his shirt. He pulls off his socks, hopping from one foot to the other, and finally removes his underpants, revealing a flaccid cock that's hard to judge, size-wise, when measured against the scale of the rest of his body. Proportionally, it appears small, but it's probably still some way above that of the average man. Preoccupied as I am with the horrors about to be visited on my body, I can't help noticing that the razor marks extend all the way to the very tip of his penis – further proof of Zlody's fierce commitment to his cause.

My heart pounds. There's a familiar pinch under my left armpit, stronger than before, more insistent.

"Zlody," I say. "My heart."

"It does not matter now, fat man," he says. "If this is what kills you, even better."

Behind me, I can hear Velak undressing too, but I don't turn to look. I don't want to see more than I have to. And the reality of it, the proximity of rape, tightens my throat as Velak's fingers slip inside the waistband of my underpants. My mental association with that feeling, the exciting intimacy of someone's hands stroking the sensitive skin near my genitals, is juxtaposed harshly against the thought of the thug that's currently doing it. I shudder as Velak slides my pants down my thighs and I feel the cold warehouse air touching my cheeks and my balls and the rim of my arsehole.

Never have I been more hideously exposed. I think about the number of people that have been able to take a good look at my arsehole before this moment. My mum. My dad. My grandparents. Maybe a few aunts and uncles during nappy changes. Certainly, nobody since I was a small child. But here I am, in the middle of this cavernous room with six pairs of eyes fixed on my unwashed, unwaxed, unbleached ringpiece. And Velak, for one, doesn't like what he sees.

"Yech!" He shouts. "What the fuck is this?"

"What?" Zlody says.

"Is not normal! Something is... hanging out."

Zlody joins Velak behind me for a look.

"My god, fat man," he says. "What is wrong with your ass?"

"Haemorrhoids," I say quietly.

"Anton," Velak says. "I know I said I would do this... but..."

Zlody sucks air through his teeth like a car mechanic assessing a costly repair.

"I'll give you one hundred thousand more," he says.

"Not for *one million more* would I do this!"

Zlody sighs.

"No. You're right," he says, eventually. "It isn't fair for me to ask. You take the front instead."

"The *mouth?* What if he bite?"

"Fat man," Zlody says to me. "He does not need to worry about you biting, does he? Because you know what I will do to your girlfriend if you misbehave, don't you?"

He gives my arse a light slap.

"Don't you?"

"Yes," I say.

"Say it," Velak says. "Say you will not bite."

"I will not bite."

"You're lucky," Zlody says. "Velak is a big boy. That is why I chose him for your ass. Extra painful. But maybe it is better if we do it this way. More poetic if I am the one fucking you."

"Yes," I say. "Poetic."

"You bloody animals!" Mal shouts.

"If we are animals, then we are no worse than your friend here."

"He never did *anything*," Blue says.

"My *sister* never did anything," Zlody says. "Anyway, this is not so much about him. This performance is all for you, Blue Darling."

"Don't worry, Jim," Mal again. "I won't watch any of it!"

Nargis strides purposefully over to Mal, grabs his head with both hands and, using index finger and thumb, holds Mal's eyelids open.

"You will watch all," he says.

As Velak comes round to stand in front of my face, I can see Zlody wasn't lying about his cock. He isn't quite in the same monstrous category as Al Girth, but the appendage hanging at my eye level is still comically huge. Or it would be comical, if there hadn't just been a discussion about it going in my mouth.

"Jimmy," Blue blurts out. "There's an old trick. For... um... For anal."

I stare straight ahead. At the huge cock. I stare *through* the huge cock. I can't look at Blue. I can't acknowledge that she's here. That I'm here. I'm *not* here. I'm a leaf on the wind.

"As it goes in," Blue says. "Push out like you're having a poo. It'll hurt less."

I'm a fucking leaf.

"Marko!" Zlody shouts. "Shut her up! She will share no more of her *old tricks* with him!"

Marko lays the axe on the floor and holds Blue with one of his arms around her neck. He clamps his free hand over her mouth.

Push out like you're having a poo.
It'll hurt less.

A memory resurfaces. It must be two decades old. Dane Biggerman is giving that very same advice to a starlet before her first anal scene. I'm watching them through my camera as I set up the shot. The expression on her pretty young face is heartbreakingly earnest as she listens to his instructions.

I didn't bother to retain the information.

I didn't think I'd ever need it.

Velak strokes his cock and it immediately gets hard. Mercifully, it doesn't get much bigger. Knowing as much as I do about erectile dysfunction, those pills shouldn't be having any effect yet. Which means it's my shame that's turning him on.

And there's nothing I can do now.

It's going to happen.

I can rationalise this.

It's all about perspective.

It doesn't have to mean anything.

It doesn't have to change me.

I'll still be the same person.

The murder after it's over – that's the bit I should be worrying about. This is just the preamble, designed to humiliate me and punish Blue. This is all about power. Zlody wants to feel power over me, and he wants Blue to see me crushed.

Push out like you're having a poo.

I need to think about this the same way Blue would have thought about a porn shoot. My body is about to pay a price. That's all. This is just a means to an end. A transaction. Give and take.

It'll hurt less.

They're going to kill me soon, anyway. Once I'm dead, I won't be aware any of this ever happened. The psychological scars might only last for a few minutes. Seconds, even.

Push out.

I've been overpowered before. I've lost fights. I've had the shit kicked out of me more times than I can count. This is no different to taking a beating, there just happens to be a couple of cocks involved. When it comes down to it, what's the difference between a punch on the chin and a cock up the arse?

It'll hurt less.

One day, you haven't been fucked by a man. The next, you have. You're still the same person. Nothing changes on a molecular level.

Push out.

And yet.

There is a difference.

Push out.

The instant that cock goes in, that cock will *always* have gone in. You can't be un-fucked. You can't be re-virgined. Once you've earned those brown wings, they're yours for life. Is it a spiritual thing? Does it mark your soul? Life is more precious than anything else, so why does this seem worse than death?

Push out.

Velak's cock is centimetres from my lips. Its unmistakably masculine funk assaults my nostrils. Sweat and pubic hair. Cheese and onion. The idea of it in my mouth, the saline flavour on my tongue, might even be worse than what happens from behind.

I can't rationalise this.

With two fingers under my chin, Velak tilts my face up so he can look into my eyes. His unbandaged eye sparkles. He smiles and blows me a kiss.

"He is crying," he says to Zlody.

"Good," Zlody says.

I feel the rough skin of his hands on my back.

And I push out like I'm having a poo.

Callback: An intense new pain, but weirdly familiar too.
Inverted.
Outside in.
Searing pain.
Splitting.
Raw.

And then.

Then there's a sound of a dog hacking up phlegm.
In the corner of my eye, Marko stumbles and releases his hold on Blue.

Am I the only one that's noticed?

Marko grabs at his own neck.
There's blood pouring from his hands.
Something stuck in his throat.
Did Blue stab him with the pen she found in my jacket pocket?

When have I ever kept a pen in my jacket pocket?

My mind flashes back to what I was doing the last time I wore that jacket.
And my heart rate kicks up a notch.
The orange flecks of vomit still staining the lapels.

Their significance.

I remember it then, the sound it made when it fell to the floor.

The clatter on the pavement.

I remember that moment of victory, crouching down, snatching my attacker's weapon from him, turning it to my advantage, sending him back into the night.

The knife.

The mugger's flick knife.

In my jacket pocket all this time.

Free of Marko's grip, Blue turns and pushes the knife deeper, twisting it, shredding the wound, severing veins and capillaries.

Marko drops to his knees and she pulls the blade out.

She stabs his throat again, this time tearing through the vital stuff, the air passages and the fat veins, and he guzzles his own blood as it fills his oesophagus, coughing and gargling and spitting for oxygen. The gash ejects a spray like a nicked garden hose and Marko clutches at it, trying to stop the flow, but he's too weak to apply pressure and the blood spurts through his fingers unabated.

This is it.

Our one chance.

I take a deep breath.

Velak's rigid cock in front of my face – I lunge at it.

Over half its length goes into my mouth – more than enough to trigger my gag reflex – and I bite down, choking and heaving, saliva frothing at the corners of my lips.

He screams as I clamp my teeth together.

He's smacking the back of my head, which makes me bite down harder, grinding my jaw, gnashing and tearing as I whip my head from side to side like a terrier that's caught a rabbit.

The taste of iron.

Blood mingles with the spit pouring down my chin.

Velak's body is rigid now.

He's still screaming but he's stopped hitting me, his back arched in an unthinking ecstasy of pain, his muscles seized by an electric current.

"Release him!" Zlody shouts, punching my fat naked back.

No chance.

My jaw is possessed.

My spirit animal is the saltwater crocodile.

I barely feel Zlody's fists pounding me.

All of my focus is in my mouth.

I am teeth.

Incisors. Canines. Molars.

There is nothing else.

Blue leaves Marko on the floor, near dead, the knife staked in his throat. She claims the axe from his side and runs at Nargis.

She is a glorious shield-maiden.

Savage.

Berserk.

Magnificent tits.

Her clothes are drenched, the *Big Baps* obscured by a stain of red treacle. She leaps at Nargis, goes at him overhead, with both hands. He tries to dodge her, but it only stops the axe from hitting his skull. Instead, it chews into his shoulder, cleaving through his collar bone, driving him onto his knees.

My teeth meet and Velak's scream segues into a silent gasp of disbelief.

I yank back my head.

There's an elastic snapping sound as the stretched skin at the base of his penis is torn apart.

He falls onto his back, hands circling his vacant crotch, fingers desperate to assess the damage but unwilling to face the reality of castration.

I cough up a bloody purple lump, which slaps onto the floor.

The axe is so deeply lodged in Nargis that Blue can't pull it loose. She wiggles it and he screams. She wiggles it again, puts a foot on his chest, tugs the handle but the blade still won't budge. She lets go of the axe and Nargis hovers in front of her, silently staring, a death glaze shining in front of his widening pupils. He swallows a couple of times, blinks, smiles, then topples onto his side.

Velak is writhing, pissing blood all over the floor, shouting, 'Bastard,' with an increasing anger that might quickly coalesce into something lucid and dangerous. Blue snatches back the flick knife from Marko's throat and throws it to me, smiling briefly when I catch it.

We're really doing this.

I climb on top of Velak and, without hesitation, I drive the blade through his good eye until the yoke pops and only an inch of the hilt remains. Velak's legs thrash with the random aim of a reflex, the rubber heels of his shoes squeaking as they scribble black marks onto the concrete.

Zlody's attention has switched from me to Blue. She's crouched over Nargis, her fingers inside the massive gash in his chest, clawing the flesh apart, trying to slip the blade out.

Zlody runs at her.

Naked.

Huge.

Ridiculous.

An anthropomorphised tree, bounding.

And now I'm struggling to retrieve *my* blade, which is slippery with gore.

There isn't enough time.

Blue still can't release the axe.

Another surge of adrenaline gets me to my feet.

I launch myself at Zlody, onto his back, and wrap both arms around his neck.

My cock squidges against his bare skin.

He throws his weight from side to side, attempting to buck me off, but I cling on.

Meanwhile, my heart's clockwork is *fucked*.

It's all ticks, and no tocks.

That's messing with the rhythms of my breathing.

I can't take a single deep breath – it has to be two or three broken rasps, followed by an exhaled wheeze.

I can't get enough air into my lungs.

And even with all of my considerable mass on top of him, Zlody stays on his feet. His back doesn't even bend.

But I've slowed him down.

And that's enough.

Because, finally, Blue has the axe.

My heart is trampolining.

A lightning bolt flashes down my left arm.

As Blue swings, I let go and crumple to the floor.

The axe is rising, then falling, then sinking into Zlody's chest.

He doesn't make a sound, skids back on his heels, totters, drops into a seated position next to me.

His head turns, and he fixes me with a stare, his mouth gurning awkwardly, the flayed lips overlapping each other and pursing to one side as if reaching to suck from an invisible straw.

"Zalupa," I say.

Zlody stares at me, breathing furiously.

"You're a joke," he says, eventually. It comes out less as an insult, and more as a statement of disbelief.

"No," Blue says, kicking the axe handle, putting him on his back. "He's the punchline."

My heart swells in my chest, bouncing like a lunatic against the walls of a padded cell.

There's a waterfall of noise tumbling inside my head.

Black specks.

A swarm of fruit flies multiplies and blocks out the light.

As the darkness takes over, I hear Mal shout:

"He's the punch line? Damn bloody right he is!"

In which a lady's face appears: An ambulance turned up, and a couple of paramedics beat the shit out of my chest. They really went to town, pounding their palms, turning my sternum outside in, popping ribs, scuffing my innards. It felt like they were carrying out the kind of DIY repair job you might use on an old TV, smacking the wooden sides to free the picture of static. Whatever it was they were doing, however painful, however primitive, it worked. My knackered heart mustered a feeble rhythm, enough for them to strap an oxygen mask to my face, sling me on a stretcher and stick me in the back of their van.

As they shunted the doors of the vehicle open and slid my stretcher across the floor, I could see through the mask, through the fog of my own breath, a hazed silhouette climbing up alongside me.

I tried to pull the oxygen mask away from my face so that I could talk but strong hands behind me put it back in place.

"Blue," I said, and the person behind me, the paramedic, said "Shhhh."

"Blue," I said again. "I'm sorry. I'm sorry that any of this ever happened. I'm not just talking about today. I'm talking about all of it. That terrible fucking business... I wish I'd seen it from the start..."

Those powerful hands gripped the sides of my head and pushed it back down onto the stretcher.

"That's enough now, Jim," the paramedic said. "You need to rest."

But I couldn't rest. I had to get this stuff out.

"It was that horrible fucking Viking orgy film we made… you must remember it… Eight hours we were filming. And when it was over I came looking for you. I heard you crying in the dressing room. So raw. So much pain. Hearing those sobs… It made me question all of it. I mean, watching someone I cared for putting themselves through that… how could I do it?"

"Shush now, Jim. It's okay."

"I got blind drunk that night. Didn't show up for the shoot the next day. Never went back to work for Dane ever again."

There were tears running silently down my cheeks.

"I think I love you, Blue," I said. "I think I always have."

And then a ladies face appeared, one of the paramedics, the hazed silhouette coming into focus, a raw face, a face with too much experience. Her brow creased with a genuine concern that would never fade no matter how many times she saw somebody lying in my position, and she told me that I needed to relax, that everything was going to be alright, that my friend was safe and sound, that I'd be seeing her soon enough. Then she leaned over me and, holding my hand firmly, she told the other paramedic to give me more gas.

Surgical spirits: I went to visit a colleague of mine in hospital once, a travel writer and survival expert called Logan Spudly, who'd undergone surgery on both his knees. Spudly is the kind of bloke that describes himself as an 'adventurist' in the bio that accompanies his articles. The kind of bloke that wears out his joints climbing mountains. The kind of bloke that doesn't own a TV and doesn't sleep for longer than five hours a night. He'd been in bed for a week, and he was borderline insane by the time I visited, a squirming mass of kinetic energy, more fidgety than a seven-year-old that's been chowing down on fistfuls of jelly babies. I remember looking at Spudly and marvelling at the strain it took for him just to lie still. The constant tension in his muscles. Relaxation – it was really wearing this guy out. I tried to put myself in his position, to empathise with his predicament, but all I could think about was the rolling TV, and the drugs on tap, and the nurses fussing around him in their tight blue uniforms. Some people don't know how to appreciate a good thing.

A week after a triple heart bypass I'm thinking the same thing but for different reasons. All they did was fuck about with that miserable bastard's knees, move around some cartilage to stop it from rubbing together, so he could go back to climbing his mountains pain-free. Me, I've had my breastbone buzz-sawed. I've had my ribs cracked and my heart tickled and poked. I've got tubes coming out of my nose and my arms and spiralling out of my bellend. I don't remember that last tube going in but I'm damn sure I'll notice it coming out. There's a piss bag hanging off the side of my bed that gets changed once a day. I feel like apologising every time the nurse has to touch it, even though I know she's been desensitised by the thousands of piss bags that came before.

I've got my own room, which is something to be happy about, I suppose. Mal checked me into a private hospital on Harley Street, said he'd cover the tab and get me the best surgeons money can buy. Since the operation, he visits me every day, harassing nurses and making them give me more pain medication than I should probably be allowed. He contravenes the laws of the hospital by bringing in a bottle of whisky and he stays by my bedside until he's supped it down to the bottom of the label. I can't touch the stuff yet, not that it would have much effect when put up against the military-grade morphine I've been prescribed.

Mal told me that Blue came and sat with me through the first night after my surgery. The hospital staff would only let one person into the intensive care unit and she persuaded Mal to let her take the position. He stayed outside, in the corridor, asking nurses for updates on my condition, looking through a window into the ward where he could see Blue sitting silently, touching my arm. Minor complications during the surgery meant they kept me sedated for a further two nights and Blue waited through it all, until the danger passed, and I could be moved back to my regular room.

Then she left.

It's over a week since I woke up. She hasn't been back.

Saturday

A thousand angels: "That nurse... what's her name?"

"Nancy."

"Phhhhhhhh..." Mal puckers his lips and blows air through the gaps in his teeth.

"I know."

"Remarkable," he says, slowly shaking his head.

"I know."

"How does she stay upright? How does she get out of *bed?*"

"She's married."

"Oh yes, of course. Has to be. Very homely woman. Don't get me wrong, that's a marvellous set of Mitchells she's got on her, but you don't get a low-swinging pair like that without a bit of suckling. She'll have nipples the size of a squid's eyeball, that one."

Mal shifts in his chair, puts down the magazine he's been pretending to read for the last ten minutes, picks up the whisky bottle and fills his tumbler two thirds of the way.

"What was she doing anyway?" he asks.

"Checking my piss bag, I think."

"What for?"

"The fill level? I don't know."

Mal nods.

"I got the results from my liver biopsy earlier."

"Oh?"

"Would you believe, they said I've got the liver of a twenty-five-year-old."

"Ha-*ha!*" Mal shouts, beaming.

"They seemed annoyed when they told me. Like I didn't deserve it. Like it wasn't enough that I'd fucked up my heart."

"Of course they're pissed off, Jim. Of *course* they are! You've beaten the bloody system. They don't like it when you do everything they tell you you shouldn't, and it all turns out alright anyway."

"I wouldn't say it all turned out alright for me," I say, stroking the gauze-covered scar running down the middle of my chest.

"No. No, I suppose not."

"And even if my liver *is* fine, that doesn't change the fact that I'm an alcoholic."

Mal's hand freezes with the whisky glass in front of his face, lips duck-beaking mid-sip. He looks at me from the corners of his eyes and rests the glass gently on the bedside table before standing.

"Oh," he says, his voice pitched up like a well-spun cricket ball. "An *alcoholic*, are you? Well, I think there's an important distinction that needs to be made here."

"And what distinction is that?"

Mal leans heavily on the metal rail that runs the length of the bed, making it creak.

"You aren't *merely* an alcoholic," he says. "You aren't a fucking *pedestrian*. You, my friend, are a *functioning* alcoholic. Look at what you've accomplished in the last twenty years of your life. You're a renowned figure. Your services are sought after by the biggest brands on the planet. A normal man couldn't have achieved half what you have. Creative people like you – like *me* – we exist on another level. We require external stimuli. Booze, drugs… anything to free our minds from the boredom of reality."

Mal takes his seat again, takes up his whisky again, and sips slowly, with great concentration.

"A couple of years ago I came to realise just how beautiful it is to be in our position," he says. "To be able to handle a drink properly. I was staggering between pubs, a bit boozed up. A bit *rowdy.*"

"I've heard this one before, Mal," I say, but he continues regardless.

"I'd had a stressful day at work and I felt the need to lash out. To kick something. To stick my boot *right into it*. And I spied a traffic cone," Mal squints and points with his whisky glass, as if the traffic cone is right *there,* on the other side of the room, "and I thought to myself, 'hell*ooo,* there's the fella!' and I ran up to it and gave it a great big *hoof*..."

"Yes, I remember this one, Mal."

"My foot *exploded.* I dropped to the floor in agony, my toes naught but bloody *smithereens.* Some bastard – do you know what they'd done?"

"They'd put a plastic traffic cone over the top of a concrete bollard."

"They'd put a *plastic traffic cone* over the top of a *concrete bollard.* The *bastards!* The rotten *shits!* I broke my big toe, and a bone in my foot. It's a good job I was always a toe-poker – If I'd side-footed that fucking thing my instep would've been properly... fucked."

Mal finishes his glass of whisky and slowly pours out another, maintaining reverent silence as he angles the bottle.

"Now the reason I'm telling you this, Jimbo, is that it led to my longest period of sobriety in recent years. You see, the impact betwixt toe and *concrete fucking bollard* had shattered my big toenail and driven the shards of it deep into my toe – a horrible mess that quickly became a microbial gangbang, festering and oozing with snotty yellow goo. I was put on a two-week course of high-strength antibiotics, which meant no whisky. And for those two weeks I felt *awful*. Obviously I was in pain because of my foot, and *obviously* for the first couple of days I was dealing with a monstrous hangover, but after that had passed, I started to remember what it feels like to be sober – what being *stone cold sober* actually means. And it *is* cold, Jim. It's a cloudless, windless, *feckless* winter morning. Everything becomes *clear*, all the way to the horizon. But *too* clear. *Painfully* clear. Quiet and loud at the same time. All the things you shouldn't hear, and none of the things you should. You notice the muscles in your back, the little ones around your spine, and how much they hurt, even when you're sitting down. Even when you're lying down. There's no warmth. No cheer. There's no *life*. And all it takes to slip back into that soft, blissful, cotton-walled state is one… little… sip."

Mal dips his top lip into the whisky and winks.

"And then," he says, closing his eyes, inhaling with gusto. "Then you feel them, a thousand angels running their delicate fingers over your skin, massaging the pain out of your muscles, massaging the warmth in…"

"A thousand angels? Really?"

"Did I over-sell it a bit?" he says, sobering for a second, sitting up straight.

"You were overselling it by the time you got to the *feckless winter*. And despite that, despite all this crap hanging out of me, all these liquids zooming in and out of my body, the only thing on my mind right now is sitting down in *The Oath* with a nice pint of ale…"

"Ooh yes. And maybe a little whisky on the side for some added *vibrance*. Sounds delightful," Mal says, patting my arm. "Soon enough, you'll be there, old chap. Soon enough."

He finishes his glass again, fills it again, takes another swig.

"Anyway. How's the arse?"

Jesus Christ.

A trigger warning should have preceded that change in topic.

How's the arse?

"The arse is…"

The arse is sore, even with all the pain medication.

"I think…"

The arse is throbbing, now that you mention it.

The arse is all I can really feel.

The arse might be all I can ever feel ever again.

The arse hurts so much, I don't even know if it actually hurts.

The drugs should be cancelling out the pain, so maybe it's just in my mind.

Is it just in my mind?

"I think I'd rather not talk about it, Mal."

Mal bows his head.

"In fact," I say, choking on my words. "I think I'd rather nobody other than you, me and Blue knows about… um… everything that went on. The murders are enough. Can we keep… the rest… to ourselves?"

Mal gives me a solemn nod and stares at the floor. Then he frowns as if he's weighing something up. Then his eyes widen, and he looks at me, and he smiles.

"But nothing did happen, Jim," he says.

I try to smile back at him.

"Thanks, Mal."

"No. *No*, I mean it. I think you've got the wrong idea. I think *you think* that Anton did something to you that he *didn't* do."

"Mal–"

"No, hear me out–"

"Please–"

"I'm *serious*, Jimbo," he says, slapping his thigh. "I didn't realise you'd been torturing yourself with this these last few days. My god, I wish we'd talked about it sooner!"

"Mal, you don't have to–"

"I don't have to what…? *Lie?* But Jim – I'm not lying! I think I know what's happened here."

"Mal–"

"Listen to me."

So I listen.

"They had you bent over, didn't they? Naked and vulnerable. *Arse in the air*. And they were going to do something awful to you. *Beyond* awful. And the anticipation of them doing that awful thing was so great that it was a trauma in itself. In your head, it's as if they actually did it."

"I felt it, Mal–"

"Did you? Are you *sure*? I had a clear view from where I was strapped up to that post and I can tell you, hand on heart, that what *you* seem to think happened *isn't* what happened."

"I–"

"It never went in, Jim."

"Mal–"

"It never went in."

We sit in a silence that Mal intensifies by glowering into my eyes, urging me to believe that what he just said isn't fiction.

"I don't *want* you to lie to me," I say. "I need to know the truth."

"I've bloody well told you. I am *not* lying."

I break down.

Little sniffs at first, but they quickly give way to deeper, heaving sobs. Soon, I'm wailing like the congregation at an African funeral. Intense pain radiates from the scar in my chest, but the pain doesn't stop me from crying.

Mal gets out of his chair and hugs me, gripping the back of my head, pulling me tightly into his chest. His reek of booze and fags wraps around me like a comfort blanket. He smells like a glorious pub, pre-smoking ban. He smells like the good old days.

"It never went in," he repeats. "I promise you, my lad."

"Then why did you ask me about my arse? Why *does* my arse hurt so much?"

After a long pause, during which Mal sniffs several times, he eventually says:

"The haemorrhoids, of course."

The beach: I must have drifted off. With the dosage I'm on, it doesn't take much for me to hit the snooze button. I've no idea how long I was out, but it was long enough for my dried tears to form a salty crust, fusing my eyelids shut. I hear low voices and decide to keep my eyes closed.

Mal is still here. His inability to whisper means his words are mumbled in a bass-heavy croak.

The other voice is female. It's too quiet for me to make out what it's saying but, as pumped full of boner-killing drugs as I am, it's a voice that still elicits a twitch from my shrunken nubbin.

She finally came back.

Why has it taken her so long?

It doesn't matter.

She's here now.

And yet.

My eyes remain closed.

Why haven't I opened them?

This is something I used to do when I was a little boy.

My mum would come home after a late shift and sneak into my bedroom to kiss me goodnight. Sometimes I'd be awake, and I'd hear her as she tiptoed over to my bunk.

And I'd keep my eyes closed.

I knew how happy it'd make her if her little man woke up, just for a few seconds, to give her a cuddle. I knew how happy it'd make me too.

But something always stopped me.

I'd lie still, pretending, breathing deeply to replicate the sounds of sleep.

Why?

I've never understood it.

Was it laziness?

Was I avoiding the miniscule effort required for that simple interaction, even though it would bring me joy?

Was it more profound – some sort of subconscious anxiety linked to waking up? To facing reality?

Now, the same deep-rooted behaviour emerges.

And still my eyes are closed.

I hear Mal rise from his chair, slip on his coat and pick up his whisky bottle.

"I'll leave you two to it," he says.

The door to my private room squeaks open, then clunks shut.

It's just me and her.

She takes Mal's seat, and I imagine her fixing her skirt as it rides up her smooth legs. Her scent fills the room, coconut oil and ocean spray replacing cigarettes and alcohol. I hear her breathing, picture her chest rising and falling with each breath. I could see it for real if only I'd open my eyes.

But I don't.

She sits for a while. She doesn't tap her fingers or jig her knees. She doesn't leaf through the magazine that Mal left behind. She just sits there silently projecting that gorgeous aroma.

I don't know how long she stays – how long I keep my eyes closed. It could be half an hour. It could be three. But eventually she stands and walks slowly over to my bed.

She squeezes my hand and I smell the beach.

Her soft lips touch my cheek.

And still my eyes are closed.

end.

Why did I write this book?

It's a fair question. After all, we just covered some pretty unpleasant ground together.

I had a few sources of inspiration, starting when I was a teenager. As with a lot of people of my generation, *Eurotrash* was my first introduction to the sex industry. It might not have been a serious TV programme, but it did open my eyes to the idea that there are people who live their day-to-day lives making money from sex. The *Porn* episode of *Louis Theroux's Weird Weekends* was obviously another influence, although the LA porn industry has a very different culture to its European counterparts.

Sometime in the late 90s or early 00s, I read an interview with American film director Barry Sonnenfeld (*The Addams Family, Get Shorty, Men in Black*) in *Empire* magazine. Seeing a successful filmmaker talk so candidly about his early work in porn showed me it was possible for people to use it as a platform for some sort of career progression.

At the grimmer end of the pornographic spectrum, the Channel 4 documentary *Dark Side of Porn: Diary of a Porn Virgin* was released around the same time. It is a depressing exploration of the British porn industry, particularly the sleaziness of the men working behind the scenes and the awful coercion of some of the women in front of the camera.

Then there's my pal, J, whose name I'm omitting because I know how much they hate being associated with porn. Nevertheless, their stories about the job that they once did (and the extent to which they despised doing it), sparked off an idea that would become this book. A small number of people find filming a cum shot to be as ordinary as the rest of us find opening a tab on an Excel spreadsheet – and that is fascinating.

Please, some small applause

Niamh – thank you for reading my edits and pushing me to get this finished, even though I know it's not the sort of book you'd usually pick up in a bookshop for yourself. Now it's your turn.

Thank you to my Substack readers for their support and feedback – especially Nathan Feddo, Tom Gibbon, Katherine Khorey, Lauren Gold, Agnes Fisk, Dan Lawrence, Matilda Murphy, Tom Hardy, Ben Osmond, Emilie Lemons, Wes Lawrence and Gill Burton.

The members of Kunstwo had a significant influence early on, as did my Creative Writing tutors Ian McGuire, MJ Hyland, Martin Amis and, most of all, Geoff Ryman, who made sure this thing had a plot (even if I would go on to make that plot utterly ridiculous).

A conversation with Beth Billing gave me the idea for the title a very long time ago – so long, she probably doesn't remember it. Danny Solomon once performed *The Golden Hole* as a one man show at the Contact Theatre in Manchester. Seeing such a talented actor bring my words to life is an experience I'll never forget. And then there's Simon Magill (AKA Typegraft), who did a cracking job designing the cover.

Lastly, thanks to Ajda Vucicevic, who was the first agent to give my manuscript serious attention. It was important to me that I was represented by a woman, given the nature of the story. Ajda gave me the belief that I had written something others would actually want to read, and the confidence that I could call myself a writer. For that, I will always be grateful.

Did you like That Black Pig? Did you hate it?

Either way, please leave a review. All feedback is welcome.

Want to get in touch? Send an email to **convenientcomedy@gmail.com** and I'll do my best to answer any questions.

Printed in Great Britain
by Amazon